A BITTER PILL TO SWALLOW

ALSO BY CORNELL GRAHAM

Prophet Priest & King

Cornell
Graham

A BITTER PILL TO SWALLOW

A Self-Published Novel

A Bitter Pill To Swallow is a work of fiction. The characters, incidents and dialogue are the results of the author's imagination and are not to be construed as actual. Any references to real products, events and/or locales are intended only to give the fiction a sense of authenticity.

A Bitter Pill To Swallow is a self-published title by Cornell Graham

Book & Cover Design: Cornell Graham
Front Cover Photographs: © Cornell Graham
Author Photograph: © Cornell Graham

First Printing: April 2003
ISBN: 0-9715949-1-0
Library of Congress Control Number: 2003090888

Please address questions, feedback as well as requests for additional copies to:

CORNELL GRAHAM
P.O. Box 2124
Alpharetta, GA 30023
Email: scrg400@att.net

Printed in the United States by Morris Publishing, Kearney, NE 68847

Dedicated to

Shirley McCoy

My mom

acknowledgements

As always, thanks to my Father above for truly making all things possible for those who believe. Without a doubt, I *am* because You *are*.

Thanks to all my family members, both immediate as well as extended, who express support of my efforts in one way or another, and especially to Debra, Zachary and Kristyna.

Thanks to dear friends Tracy Bronaugh and Ylorie Anderson for your incredible enthusiasm and continued support. I certainly appreciate your willingness to promote my efforts at every opportunity.

Thanks to Maya Lawrence for all your help as my assistant during the early stages of my first novel.

Thanks to Terri Miller of *INK* newspaper in Ft. Wayne, Indiana and to Richard Linnett of *Advertising Age* magazine for your reviews written on my first novel.

Thanks to *Amazon.com* and *Barnes & Noble.com* for being the firsts to provide a retail source for readers to purchase this book as well as my debut novel.

Thanks to all the guests who attended my private book signing for my debut novel. Thanks to *Borders Books* in Ft. Wayne, Indiana for hosting my first public book signing.

Last but not least, thanks to all the readers of my debut novel and thanks in advance to the many readers of this book. I welcome your feedback and comments at any time. Your support is greatly appreciated. May God bless you all!

A BITTER PILL TO SWALLOW

chapter 1

A hastily arranged Friday afternoon meeting was about to get underway. Some two hundred-plus employees all had somehow managed to pile onto the narrow first floor lobby inside the midtown Atlanta office building known as 33 TOWER PLAZA. The fifteen-story concrete and glass-framed structure comprised a mix of law firms, financial services firms, various business consultants, a couple of international companies and one advertising agency.

The predominant gender among the employees was female, which was obvious to the ears as the click-clack of low and high heels against the limestone floor resonated like amateur tap dancers in desperate need of choreography lessons. Maximum capacity for the posh two-story atrium lobby was around one hundred and fifty. It wouldn't be the first time that this group had exceeded the limitations imposed by others.

They were standing shoulder-to-shoulder. Some of the height-challenged stood atop the startling light blue lacquer receptionist center, while others simply stood on their toes and attempted to peer over broad shoulders or peek around wide middles that just happened to be obstructing their view.

Of course everyone was being patient and noticeably polite. They were, after all, one big happy family. And similar to little children who were anxiously awaiting the return of their parents on the first day of kindergarten, their anticipation was building.

Chatter and laughter saturated the air. Was this the day that the *good news* would finally come? The past couple of months had been quite tense, to say the least. But they had an unbelievable amount of faith within their leaders–their mentors.

Suddenly, the thump thump thump of a hand tapping against the head of a microphone echoed from within the center of the lobby.

"May I have your attention?" the female's soft voice piped through the intercom system.

And like students standing around socializing after an impromptu fire drill had sent them scurrying from classrooms, from pop quizzes, or from frog dissecting, these employees seemed to be enjoying a break from their routine tasks.

Therefore, the polite request to stop conversing and

listen up went largely ignored. Although, unintentional.

"Let me have your attention, *please*?" the request was quickly repeated, a little louder and more authoritative.

Within seconds a veiling hush pervaded the room, bound and secured by an impenetrable solidarity. The silence was like the tranquility one often found on an early Sunday morning, in which few cars could be seen, less people going to and fro.

Hundreds of eyes, eyes belonging to the old, the middle-aged and the young, eyes that were uniquely attached to the various faces of such a diverse group of employees, became transfixed on the individuals who were now standing within their midst. And what an impressive standing it was.

They stood ever so tall, graciously confident, and genuinely united. Like pillars of strength, rays of hope and deliverers of empowerment, they were truly a dynamic trio.

All three of them.

All black.

All women.

The image was picture-perfect. Indeed, a *Kodak* moment for the founders of Atlanta's up-and-coming advertising agency, ADDISON JAMES & SHEPHERD.

Rivals and adversaries alike had doubted their ability to survive within an industry so dominated by white males. At best, critics said that they would rise to being nothing more than a *boutique* shop handling only the *minority* portion of traditional larger *general market* accounts. But now, few could deny their remarkable achievements.

Their path to unquestionable success had been short and sweet. In just six years they were billing $360 *million* a year, positioning ADDISON JAMES & SHEPHERD as the country's largest African-American-owned *and* largest female-owned advertising agency.

Gently tapping on the microphone to quiet the room was the agency's president, *Blu Addison*. She was thirty-eight years old and a former JET magazine's BEAUTY OF THE WEEK. One look at her and it became palpable that such an honor had been deserved. Her five-foot-six physique was fashionably adorned in a BURBERRY suit. She had brown skin and a symmetrical face that accommodated a captivating pair of raisin-colored eyes. And her jet-black hair consisted of curls in abundance that cascaded just slightly beyond her diminutive shoulders.

Standing to Blu's right was forty-seven year-old agency partner and media director, *Flavia James*. At six-foot-two she was the tallest of the three women. Her fair-skinned frame was fashionably outfitted in an ADRIENNE VITTADINI ensemble, which consisted of navy pinstripe pants, a matching vest and a white cotton blouse. Flavia's hair was a caramel-colored bob that was cut to hug the nape, with a complimenting front drape.

And standing to Blu's left was the youngest of the three partners, twenty-nine year-old *Kiwi Shepherd*, head of client services. Her fashion taste was quite eclectic. On this particular day her petite figure was wearing a head-turning black leather skirt and a cropped tweed jacket by CHANEL. Kiwi always seemed to opt for the glamorous, ultra femme fatale look. A heavy swept bang accentuated her long, silky straight, cranberry hair. Her swarthy face displayed high cheekbones and her colored contacts made her celestial eyes a beautiful jade.

Blu Addison beamed her infectious smile as she surveyed the anxious faces of their staff. "Thank you all for gathering here," her eloquent, yet authoritative voice continued. There was definitely a nervous excitement in the air. The employees knew that they were about to share in some incredible news. The long awaited news had actually been delivered earlier that morning.

What a great day it was for receiving good news. The September weather was absolutely inviting. It seemed as if all the sparrows in the south had summoned one another and then gathered at the entrance to their office building to begin a well-rehearsed, melodious chorus of song and praise for ADDISON JAMES & SHEPHERD. And stretched for miles over the southern city was an azure sky, augmented by the brilliance of the late summer's sun, which displayed itself unashamedly, like the clear-skin radiance of a *Miss Teen Georgia* contestant.

Blu continued, "As you guys are aware, our agency has been involved in the review to handle the *MerLex Motors Corporation* account."

A plethora of heads began to nod up and down from amongst the employees.

"Well, as of this morning, I am very happy to report to you all that we have been officially notified that we are one of only two agencies making the final cut!"

An enormous and thunderous applause erupted immediately. So many high-fives were being smacked that the noise in the room sounded like firecrackers exploding. And there were others who embraced for spontaneous hugs and kisses.

MerLex Motors was a multibillion-dollar German automotive company that had recently moved its U.S. headquarters from the west coast to the Atlanta area. The company manufactured and marketed luxury automobiles that competed with the likes of BMW, INFINITI and JAGUAR. Their overall advertising account was handled in New York. However, with the recent completion of a manufacturing plant south of Atlanta, in Savannah, the company sought a local ad agency to help launch their new SUV, the MERLEX MANIFESTO.

The sport utility vehicle was being readied for a *Spring 2004* debut – only eighteen months away.

ADDISON JAMES & SHEPHERD was among ten other Atlanta ad agencies that had received the initial invitation to pitch the $140 million account. And although they had an impressive client list and numerous awards for their creative talents, the three women believed that their chances of actually winning the account would be a long shot.

There had been a total of three rounds of grueling presentations to MerLex's corporate management, which included practically everyone from the CEO, Chief Marketing Officer, VP of Product Design, and a Senior Brand Manager, to what seemed like a slew of lesser corporate peons. But ADDISON JAMES & SHEPHERD had made the final cut. And now they would be going head-to-head with Atlanta's largest ad agency and one of the South's most prominent – a $2.2 billion in annual billings powerhouse named MARTIN/McFINLEY. Undoubtedly, it was going to be a *David vs. Goliath* match-up.

The principals of ADDISON JAMES & SHEPHERD were keenly aware that it would be no easy task to defeat the venerable MARTIN/McFINLEY. Its agency head, sixty-nine year-old *Leland Martin* spearheaded the overwhelmingly successful creative conglomerate. His long-time business partner, Chester McFinley, had died suddenly this past New Year's Day, leaving Leland Martin to steer their high sailing ship alone. He was more than equal to the arduous task.

MARTIN/McFINLEY lost very few account pitches. And it was a sure bet that they had no desire to lose to three young cohorts, whom Leland Martin always believed were flying by the hem of their skirts.

But these three women believed otherwise. They recognized and understood MARTIN/McFINLEY to be a formidable competitor. However, this tough threesome had no intentions of just rolling over to die. They were ready to compete. Eager to win.

Blu Addison was reluctant to interrupt the joyous moment being shared by the employees, but being the *strictly business* type that she was, she couldn't help but feel the urge to bring all the cheering, whistling and even dancing to a screeching halt so that she could speed the afternoon along.

"Don't even think about it, girlfriend!" chided the feisty Kiwi Shepherd. "I know what you're thinking!"

"Yeah, it's written all over her face, too!" echoed the appeasing Flavia James. "But we're going to let them have a little fun!"

Blu simply shook her head, accepting apparent defeat as Flavia and Kiwi grabbed hold of her hands and began to engage her in a little dancing routine of their own.

After ten more minutes of cheerful celebration, though it seemed much longer to Blu, the lobby was once again quiet and everyone was giving their undivided attention to their leadership team.

"Now, while today's news is certainly a cause for celebration, we must recognize that our mission isn't complete," Blu spoke solemnly. "Making it to the final round of presentations is just a stepping stone toward our ultimate destination, which is to become the new home for the MERLEX MANIFESTO!"

More claps, cheers and whistles erupt.

"And let me add this . . . " she quickly interjected. "The success of this ad agency, unmistakably, has always been due in large part to the individual efforts made by each and every one of you!" Blu stretched forth her hand and began to point randomly at employees around the room. "And *when* we win this account, it will not be by the effort of any one person, but rather, by the sheer determination, dedication and concerted effort of us all!"

Another eruption. Much louder this time, more intense.

ADDISON JAMES & SHEPHERD was renowned for its talented group of employees. And while Blu had started in the advertising industry right out of college, she was careful to surround herself with a wealth of creative and management experience that she found within others.

As the small agency grew from a base of one client to three by the end of its first year, they also began to attract personnel from other ad agencies who wanted to become an integral part of what the women seemed to be on the verge of building. By the end of its third year in business, the agency had already blossomed into billings of $135 million a year.

"Is anyone hungry for lunch?" Blu's voice resounded throughout the room again.

A chorus of *yeses* eagerly responded.

She instructed the agency's receptionist to phone PIZZA HUT and order as many pizzas as necessary to feed everyone. "We might as well add some nourishment to this afternoon's celebration!" she shouted into the microphone.

Then without warning, three bulky guys from the creative department pushed their way forward and each one took one of the three partners into his arm and lifted her toward the crowd while chanting *Addison-James-and-Shepherd!* Before long the entire staff had joined in the chanting.

Flavia and Kiwi shot a mute look of appeal towards Blu, who in turn simply shrugged her shoulders and shot a piercing glance back to them that said, '*hey, it was you guys who wanted to keep this thing going*'.

The excitement and enthusiasm permeated from the lobby and throughout their first floor offices. Blu, Flavia and Kiwi each realized during that precise moment that they had created something very special. Not just a special place in which to work, but an incredible special group of people with whom to work. Six years ago they dared to even dream of building a *billion-dollar* advertising agency. Yet with the potential win of the $140 million MerLex Motors account, they knew that they could be halfway to that once elusive reverie.

chapter 2

Blu Addison was preparing to leave the agency's offices just after six o'clock. It was no big surprise that the Friday evening mid-town traffic was still intense. Sometimes she regretted not having chosen office space that was a little closer to her north suburban home.

Commuting to and from work was often times more of an adventure than anything else. Would she make it all the way down *Georgia Highway 400* and into the city without some impatient driver attempting to teach her *sign language*? Could she avoid getting sandwiched between the *minivan* sect? Blu believed wholeheartedly that those wide-bodied vehicles were out to take over the world. And don't even get her started on the *dream weavers*. These were the *skillful* drivers of the mid-life crisis camp who were found weaving in and out of traffic in their sports cars trying to fulfill a lost dream of having never qualified for the *Indianapolis 500*.

Flavia and Kiwi had departed the office hours earlier. How fortunate for them. Their drive home to the North Fulton County suburbs must have been smooth sailing. Meaning that they had to have left the office by three o'clock in order to avoid this gridlock.

As she strapped herself into the comforts of her midnight blue MERCEDES E500 sedan, Blu removed her small flip-top cellular phone from her PRADA bag and dialed Flavia's home telephone number. When Flavia answered she asked her to hold on the line while she called Kiwi for a three-way.

"You still there, Flavia?" she confirmed after Kiwi had answered.

"I'm here," Flavia replied.

The ever-impatient Kiwi piped in, "What's up, Blu?"

"Just a minute," Blu told her. She wanted to make sure that she had exited the office building's parking garage and that she was safely merged into the on-coming traffic rendezvous. "Okay," she breathed a sigh of relief. "You guys know that I do not like talking on the phone while driving," she reminded them.

"Excuse me, but didn't this little heifer call *us*?" Kiwi asked rhetorically.

Both Blu and Flavia laughed. Then Blu explained the reason for her call. "Guys, I just wanted to remind you both that we have a seven-thirty tee-time tomorrow morning, so let's plan on meeting at the golf course no later than seven-fifteen."

"I thought we were going to practice *next* weekend?" Flavia asked, taking a quick peek at her calendar.

The women were preparing for the sixth annual *AAACC* golf tournament, which was the *Atlanta Ad Agencies Charity Classic.* It was a two-day event consisting of all female teams with four members each. One of the requirements was that each participating golfer must also work for an Atlanta advertising agency. The proceeds derived from the popular fund-raiser went to support neglected children throughout the metropolitan area. This year would be the fifth event that Blu, Flavia and Kiwi participated. Their best finish was a tie for second place last year.

"I know that's what we talked about," Blu explained. "But there's a tournament next Saturday at the course, so I had to move our practice up a week."

"Why so damn early?" protested Kiwi.

"Because I don't particularly care to spend my Saturday afternoon searching for lost golf balls or navigating my way through trees, sand, and water," said Blu.

"Speak for yourself, girlfriend!" Kiwi countered. She spoke so boldly because she currently carried a *nine-handicap* index.

A handicap index is the number of artificial strokes a

golfer receives to adjust his or her scoring ability to the level of *scratch* or *zero-handicap* golf. It involves a complex calculation that basically reflects a golfer's *potential* ability. The person with a *one* handicap would typically be considered the better golfer of someone with a *ten* handicap.

Blu's handicap hovered around fifteen. And even though Flavia has been playing golf longer than the other two women, her handicap was a whopping twenty-eight.

"I'm with Blu," Flavia told Kiwi. "My boys have a soccer game tomorrow afternoon, so I'd like to be finished with the practice as early as possible."

"Fine," Kiwi said tersely, realizing that she was outnumbered anyway.

"We'll be playing as a threesome," Blu told them. Their fourth member, Blu's former executive assistant, twenty-seven year-old *Gail Adams*, had been on maternity leave since June. She was a pretty good golfer, nonetheless, boasting a handicap that was just a notch higher than Kiwi's.

"When is this year's tournament?" asked Kiwi.

Flavia was the person responsible for signing up the women, so she answered. "Saturday and Sunday, November ninth and tenth at *Sugarloaf Country Club*."

"The TPC course?" Kiwi asked excitedly.

Blu piped in, "You go it. The same course that the PGA uses for the *Bellsouth Classic*."

Kiwi was definitely considered the golf fanatic among the three women. She tried to play a full round of golf at least twice a week, often times sneaking away from the office early in order to accomplish her goal of one day carding a zero handicap.

"By the way, when is Gail coming back to work?" asked Flavia, changing the subject.

Blu breathed a heavy sigh. "Well, unfortunately she won't be coming back. Apparently, she's become accustomed to being a stay-at-home mom."

"How can she afford to do that?" Flavia was curious. They were all aware that Gail Adams was a single parent.

"Hey, I'm not trying to get all up in the woman's personal business," Blu retorted.

"Well, did she ever tell you who the father is of her bouncing baby boy?" asked Kiwi.

"No, she did not. And frankly, it's none of my business."

"Humph," mumbled Kiwi. "I mean, we threw Gail a baby shower, and bought all kinds of baby stuff for her behind. You'd think she'd at least share some juicy tidbits with us!"

"You need *Jesus*, Kiwi," Flavia told her.

"No, Flavia. What *you* need is to stop trying to bring Jesus into every damn conversation we have, okayyy? Hell, if

I wanted to hear all that, there are churches all over Atlanta for me to go to."

"Well, Miss Thing, you should consider joining one."

"Whatever, Flavia!"

"Guys, we have nothing but love for one another, all right? And while Gail may not be working with us any longer, we still should respect her privacy."

"Blu's right," remarked Flavia. "It's wrong for us to even be discussing her like this."

"Well, I'll bet that the baby's daddy is a *brotha*!" Kiwi said, unwilling to end the chitchat just yet.

"And what makes you say that?" Blu asked her.

"I mean, why else would she be so secretive about it. As a white woman she probably feels a little uncomfortable revealing him to us."

"Kiwi, that's absolutely ridiculous!" Flavia told her. "Gail may be white, but I'm sure that if she had hooked up with a black man she'd have no qualms about telling us. She's been around the three of us long enough to know that we wouldn't have a problem with it."

"I ain't so sure about that," was Kiwi's response. "I mean the brothas are in short supply as it is." Kiwi had encountered her fair share of failed relationships lately.

Blu decided to put an end to the gossiping. "Guys, I didn't bring Gail's name up for a round of tittle-tattle. I just wanted you both to know that we will have to find ourselves a fourth player if we're going to compete in the tournament this year."

"Well, I've already submitted the tournament entry form with Gail's name listed," Flavia stated. "But we do have until mid October to make a change."

"Yeah, I know," Blu said, almost to herself. She wasn't sure whom they'd get to replace Gail. "Maybe we can ask around the office. A lot of women are playing golf these days."

A name popped into Flavia's head. "Hey, what about that woman in accounting? I think I remember her mentioning something about playing golf."

Kiwi was quick with a response. "Oh, hell no! Not *Marilyn Waters*!"

"Yeah, that's her name – Marilyn. What's wrong with her?" asked Flavia.

"Well, for one thing she plays like crap! I just happened to meet up with her earlier in the summer at that new *Creek Pines* course and we played together. Girl, I'm telling you, the woman was all over the freakin' place with her shots. After nine holes I had to fake an illness just so I could quit, otherwise those eighteen holes would have taken us over six hours to play!"

"Oh Kiwi, she can't be that bad," Flavia remarked.

"No offense, Flavia, but her handicap is probably *twice* that of yours!"

"Ouch!" said Blu.

Flavia took the remark in stride. "Well, I guess that just goes to show that there's hope for her after all."

"Humph. You can keep hope alive all you want. I know that Marilyn Waters will not be playing golf with me anytime soon," Kiwi firmly stated.

"Of course not, because no one can play on *your* level." Flavia did not try to hide her sarcasm.

"I don't play golf to waste my time or anyone else's. If that woman wants to take six hours to play eighteen holes then she's obviously on a level that I choose not to be on."

"Well, Kiwi, I'm sure that you're bound to meet your match one day."

Kiwi restrained her tongue.

Blu could sense hostility brewing and decided that it was time to wrap up the call. "Guys, we don't have to decide on a replacement now. I'm sure we'll find someone to replace Gail," she told them. Then she reminded her cohorts of the tee-time again before finally terminating the call.

A few minutes later Blu had successfully navigated her way through rush-hour traffic and was now waving a *hello* to the security guard as she drove through the gated entrance to *WindFair Estates Country Club.*

She was quite hopeful that they'd eventually find a fourth person for their team because she really wanted to beat the smirks off the tournament's three-time consecutive winners – the boastful, arrogant and snooty women from MARTIN/McFINLEY.

chapter 3

Each of the three women of ADDISON JAMES & SHEPHERD owned exquisite homes within the prestigious and exclusive country club community of Alpharetta's *WindFair Estates*. Alpharetta was one of Atlanta's most sought after suburbs. Many of Atlanta's top corporate executives, music industry celebrities and professional athletes maintained their domiciles behind the iron gates of WindFair Estates. Homes, currently numbering over five hundred and building, were appropriately priced from $700,000 to well over $2 million. There were only three homes priced over the two million dollar mark within WindFair Estates, and one of them belonged to none other than ADDISON JAMES & SHEPHERD's archrival, Leland Martin.

Blu had to wait for a couple of joggers to pass by in front of her car before she made the turn onto *Galloping Horse Circle*. Her home was a 6,400 sq. ft. red brick and stone country estate that she shared with her husband of fourteen years, Damien.

As she carefully positioned the MERCEDES into the first slot within their three-car garage, she became disappointed when she noticed that her husband's black JAGUAR was not already parked in the adjacent space. She'd hoped that he would be home by now. They really needed to talk about last night's heated argument.

Lately, it seemed that most of the conversations with her husband had ended with the two of them choosing new, and less than flattering, nicknames for one another.

Blu met Damien while pursuing her *Master of Fine Arts* degree from Ohio State University. He was obtaining an MBA in Finance as he prepared to become a *Certified Public Accountant*. Both had grown up in small towns – Blu in Muncie, Indiana where her father and mother worked as professors at Ball State University, and Damien in Bloomington, Illinois where his father worked as a vice president of finance for *State Farm Insurance Company.*

The two of them graduated the same year. Six months later they were married in Blu's hometown. They would reside one year in Columbus, Ohio before relocating to Atlanta.

Blu initially resisted the move to the south. Not only was it far from her parents, but also the city of Atlanta held a painful past for her. She'd spent a large part of her life trying to forget and even erase such a past, but to no avail. Besides, the job offer that Damien had received from a major accounting firm was too generous to pass up.

She would later come to love the city, however, along with its endless road construction, growing traffic jams and six months of summer weather.

After moving to Atlanta, Blu eventually obtained a position as an *assistant copywriter* with an Atlanta ad agency where she later rose to the position of *senior copywriter.*

Their young marriage had started off very smoothly. But their fourteen years together had seen more than its share of planks missing from the fence. Weeds growing inside the garden. Petals constantly falling from the rose.

If it weren't for Damien's incessant desire to have children, their marriage would otherwise be quite blissful. Blu wanted children too – eventually. It was just that their careers took so much of their time that she didn't think it was fair to bring a child into a situation where both parents worked a lot of hours. At least that had been her rationalization throughout the course of their marriage. And until recently, it had proven effective.

She'd been trying her best to hold Damien at bay. She once told him that they could start trying to have a baby when she turned thirty. But by the time she was thirty-two she'd already made the decision to start her own ad agency, which of course, required an immense amount of time and energy. And now that she was thirty-eight, she felt that she'd waited too long. However, her husband had been determined to make her believe that it wasn't too late.

As Blu exited the car, she set her attaché case and purse on the hood of the car's trunk while she walked over to the mailbox and retrieved the stack of mail that had begun to protrude from the custom-made mailbox. She hadn't picked up the mail over the last three days. And she knew that if she didn't get it, she certainly couldn't depend on Damien to do so.

She dropped the stack of envelopes, handful of magazines, sale flyers, and a surplus of other junk mail onto a small table that stood in the corner of the marbled foyer. The inexpensive piece of furniture had been put there for such uses.

The Addison home contained five bedrooms. Tall chimneys lent elegance and support to five fireplaces that graced the beautiful home. One fireplace stood in the grand room, one occupied a corner in the gathering room, one resided in the study, another one accented the kitchen and the last one warmed the master suite on an occasional chilly fall evening.

The master bedroom suite was on the main floor of the house. It was an enormous bedroom with huge his and her walk-in closets and French doors that opened to a veranda. A bonus room over the garage maintained a fully equipped exercise gym and lounge. And the finished basement housed an elaborate home theater.

Upon entering the master bedroom, Blu kicked off her black stiletto heels and headed toward her walk-in closet. After disrobing, she contemplated what to put on.

Exhausted from a long day at the office, she knew that she was in for the evening. Her favorite attire to meander around the house in was her black NIKE sweats. But, since the loose-fitting and extremely comfortable clothes were currently resting upstairs, inside a white basket holding other dirty laundry, she decided to simply put on one of Damien's casual button-down shirts. He loved it whenever she wore one of his large shirts, which resembled a dress on her. Maybe seeing her in it when he got home this evening would spark some much-needed romance between them.

When Blu arrived at Damien's closet, what she found was an unexpected surprise. She stood in the doorway to his closet with her hand clasped over her mouth. She was in absolute shock as she stared at the rows of empty hangers that were dangling from the rod. She suspected, just like her, they too were left wondering why they had been stripped bare.

Just this morning her husband's closet was full of

ARMANI and HUGO BOSS suits, shoes that included DOLCE & GABBANA and SERGIO ROSSI, numerous silk ties and an assortment of leather belts. And being the meticulous man that he is, everything was kept neatly arranged. Suits were sorted by style and color, his shirts had their own space within a corner of closet, and the soles of his shoes never touched the floor until he wore them. They were maintained on a special shoe rack that he installed himself.

But now, his entire closet was vacant. Empty. Deserted. Free. No more *his and hers* to speak of. Just hers.

Blu couldn't help feeling as though a part of her had also been left with a deep void.

For a while she just stood there. Her arms wrapped, crisscrossed, over her chest as she shivered from the coolness of the air conditioning system breathing quietly throughout the room.

Her figure, one that could easily rival that of *Tyra Banks*, was clad only in her red VICTORIA SECRETS underwear. Her earlier hopes of donning one of her husband's shirts suddenly dashed. Her mind began racing. How long had he been planning this? He must have taken the day off from work in order to move everything out so quickly.

She walked hurriedly into the bathroom. The second vanity that once held all his cologne, shaving gel, and other toiletries was bare as well.

Blu wanted to cry, but couldn't. The moment certainly called for it. She could actually hear it beckoning to her. *Cry. Cry. Cry. Don't be ashamed. Everyone did it sooner or later. Simply let your body drop to the floor, pull your knees to your chest and sob uncontrollably.*

But the tears didn't come. Couldn't come. Absolutely refused to come.

She also wanted to scream her lungs out. And rightfully so. Her husband of fourteen years had walked out on her. Would it be so unusual if she chose to pretend she was *Marion Jones?* Because right now she wanted to sprint through the house – trying to burn off her ensuing anger. Maybe along the way she'd even find herslef throwing a few things. Anything. *Breakable* things.

Blu found herself filled with hostility, resentment and betrayal. Yet at the same time she was also feeling lonely, abandoned and incredibly *guilty.*

Was it all a way of simply telling her that she needed to face the truth of the matter? That it was now time to pay the piper? *Naïveté* was not one of her closest friends. But she did have her share of frequent visits.

Hadn't it been said that *everybody* plays the fool? *Sometimes?* But Blu wasn't a fool. And she was no simpleton. She was fully aware of the risks associated with her actions, or perhaps *inaction.* By virtue of her fear and silence over the years she knew that this day might come. Now it had finally happened. She never dreamed that it actually would, but often feared that it most certainly could.

Damien Addison had bailed on his wife.

. . . .

After failing to reach her husband on his cell phone, Blu spent the next hour or so on the telephone with her mother, *Audrey Knight*. She was reluctant to call her mother, but at the moment she needed to vent. And Flavia and Kiwi were not an option because she just couldn't bear the thought of them knowing that her private life was in shambles. They both had always assumed that she had the perfect marriage – free from turbulence, absent of discord, and not lacking in trust. If only they knew.

After Blu revealed to her mother that Damien had apparently moved out, her mother's response was about what she would've expected.

"Listen to me, honey. You and I both know what this whole mess is about. It's been going on far too long."

Blu remained silent.

"Just how long were you planning to wait, Blu? Were you going to keep him in the dark forever?"

"Mom, I was waiting for the right time, okay?"

"Honey, the *right time* passed fourteen years ago. Had you been open with your husband from the very beginning, maybe you could've saved yourself a lot of headaches."

"To be honest, my head feels just fine," Blu replied, unable to resist the opportunity for sarcasm.

"Well, I'm glad to see that you're able to treat the situation so lightly. Or, maybe you're just too stubborn to allow yourself to realize how much you're hurting."

"Mom, you and dad raised me to be a strong independent woman – don't hold it against me now."

"Yes, we did. But honey, we also raised you to *think*! Your decision to keep something so important from Damien all these years has been nothing short of irrational!"

"Mom, please don't lecture me right now, okay?"

"Honey, I'm not trying to lecture you. But Damien has a right to know."

"He just wouldn't understand, mom. I know he wouldn't."

"Blu, honey. At least give the man some credit. There is nothing wrong with wanting a family. I knew things would eventually get to this point if you kept this all to yourself." Her mother's own frustration was beginning to settle in.

"It sounds as if you're blaming everything on me?"

"*Blu Marie Addison*!" her mother shouted into the phone. The outburst startled Blu because her mother rarely raised her voice to anyone. "Stop focusing on who's to blame. It's not about placing blame or pointing fingers. It's about doing what's right. Now, your husband needs to know what has been causing you so much anxiety over whether or not to have children. And the sooner you share it with him, the sooner the both of you can close this widening gap within your marriage."

Blu stood from the over-stuffed wing back chair where she'd been sitting and paced around the den, occasionally drying her eyes with the sleeve of the white terry cloth robe she was now wearing. Her eyes were welling up, but she still refused to cry. How could she? She was not a little girl anymore. No one else could be expected to pick up the broken pieces of her marriage. And even though a good cry would probably do her a world of good, she fought back the urge. The head of a multimillion-dollar advertising agency would not succumb to tears just because her husband had walked away. She was certain that she wasn't the first woman to come home to an empty closet. And she was reasonably certain that she wouldn't be the last.

"How can I share anything with him when he's gone," she replied solemnly.

"Blu, it's not as though the man has left the country. You will see him again. And when you do, you need to be prepared to lay everything out on the table." Audrey Knight emitting a heavy sigh. "Honey, that's really the *only* option that you have."

Blu realized that her mother was undoubtedly right. She should have told Damien years ago, even before they got married. But she kept hoping that she would be able to put everything behind her. After all it was the *past.* And everybody had a past that they weren't exactly proud of. She was certain that even Damien hadn't told her everything about his past. So why was it necessary for her to spill her entire guts to him?

Maybe because it's a burden that you can't bear alone, she silently answered to herself.

"Mom, you're absolutely right."

Her mother said, "Honey, I take no pleasure in being right in this matter. I care about you and I hate to see you going through this turmoil. I only want what's best."

"I know you do," said Blu. "I know you do."

Audrey added, "And despite how you may feel now, I am not blaming you. I am proud that you've become a strong and independent woman. But honey, even the strong *and* the independent need someone to lean on once in a while."

Deciding to change the subject, Blu inquired how her mother was doing. She often worried about her being alone since the death of Blu's father seven years ago at the age of sixty-six. He was only three years older than Blu's mother, who, at the age of seventy, was now a retired college professor. She still lived in the split-level home in Muncie, Indiana where Blu and her older brother, Lance, grew up.

"When was the last time you spoke with your brother?" Audrey wanted to know, after saying that she was doing fine.

Blu thought for a moment. She mostly only heard from Lance when he wanted her to invest in another one of his crazy business ideas. "I don't know. I guess it's been over a month since we talked last."

"Well, I suspect he'll be calling you very soon," her mother warned.

"What's he up to now, mom?"

"Honey, I spoke to him last weekend and he told me that he's been laid off from work."

Blu frowned. "That's unfortunate . . . wait a minute! Mom, Lance is *self-employed*!"

"Honey, I know that. But he said that that's just how tough things are right now. He had to go and lay himself off."

"Mom, that's crazy! How is he going to lay himself off from being self-employed?"

"Well, that's what he did. He said he didn't even see it coming."

Blu couldn't keep herself from laughing. Her brother was ten years older than she was. He lived less than an hour from their mother, in Indianapolis. He divorced after only two years of marriage. But fortunately, there were never any kids.

And his life since has been marred by a string of failed businesses, which were mostly a result of his insatiable appetite for get-rich-quick schemes.

"Well, he can call me any time he chooses," began Blu, "but I have no intentions of investing money in any of his planned ventures. I've been burned already."

"Yeah, you and me both," her mother remarked.

They chatted a while longer and before the call ended Blu told her mother about the agency making the final cut for the MerLex Motors account. Her mother congratulated her and wished her luck in winning the account. Ironically, that particular piece of news had turned out to be the one bright spot in her entire week. She wasn't sure how she was going to cope with Damien moving out. His actions couldn't have come at a worst time. *Long term* she needed to focus on winning a $140 million account. *Short term* she needed to try and improve her golf game in an effort to win the *AAACC* golf tournament. And now on the immediate front she needed to win her husband back. That is, if she even *wanted* him back.

She quickly reprimanded herself for such a hideous thought. Then again, perhaps the *need* for a husband was just highly overrated.

Blu realized that she needed a drink to calm herself. She walked into the kitchen and retrieved a wine glass from the cupboard. A bottle of BERINGER GAMAY BEAUJOLAIS was chilling in their SUB-ZERO refrigerator. The red wine was a flavorful, yet subtle drink – a much needed and often called upon respite. She'd placed it there before she left for the office this morning, anticipating the good news from MerLex Motors. It was supposed to have been used for a celebration toast with Damien, and to help make up for their argument last night.

Blu stared at the bottle in her hand. Toast or not, she had no intentions of allowing the inviting spirit to resume its place within the wine rack. Not this evening.

After filling her glass, she retreated back to the den and began looking through her enormous CD collection. Music for her had always been a much-needed catharsis. Her favorite was *seventies* pop songs. Muncie, Indiana did not have a black radio station when she was growing up, so she became acquainted with pop songs from listening to radio station WLBB FM – B105.

Losing herself in music was one of her great escapes as a teenager. Whether it was *James Taylor*, *Phoebe Snow*, *Elton John* or *Carole King*, certain songs from the seventies still left her yearning at times for her youthful days. Those days of seemingly innocence.

Days of self-discovery.

Days wrapped in cool summer breezes.

Days silenced only by a whispering wind.

Days that brought opportunities full of optimism.

Days that would sneak up on you without so much as a warning.

Days that would abandon you as quickly as the eye could blink.

Days that brought experiences that should have been captured.

Days that brought never-ending disappointments and inevitable heartaches that always seemed to linger.

Days that would live inside her forever.

Along with the seventies sound, Blu also enjoyed the music of current artists such as *India Arie*, *Norah Jones*, *Natalie Merchant*, *Jewel*, and *Sade*.

But one of her absolute favorites was *Alanis Morissette*. Many of her songs touched her heart. The lyrics are telling. And her voice is incredibly spellbinding.

She set down her glass of wine on a nearby table.

It was Alanis' MTV UNPLUGGED album that Blu popped into the CD player. She liked every single one of the twelve tracks. But tonight track *number one* couldn't have been more relevant to her life.

The volume on the CD player was turned up. She hit the REPEAT button before pressing PLAY. She needed to hear these lyrics more than once.

As the music and Alanis' vocals began to serenade

from the speakers, Blu picked up her drink and retreated to her sofa.

As she lay on the sofa she allowed her legs to curl and her eyes to close. She drank a long sip from her wine and then she permitted her brain to absorb the lyrics.

The song was simply titled, YOU LEARN.

chapter 4

There are times when *second* is better than *first.* And the second time around had proven to be much better for Flavia James. Her first marriage had ended about as quickly as it had started. One week after returning from her honeymoon in the Virgin Islands she had the misfortune of coming home from work early one day and finding her husband in a disreputable position, to say the least. Less than three months later she found herself angry, heartbroken, and divorced all at the mere age of twenty-three.

Four years later she would remarry. And now, after twenty years, she sometimes still find it hard to believe that God had smiled upon her so graciously when he brought *Parker James* into her life.

Parker, a six-foot-four tower of charisma, had turned out to be everything that Flavia dreamed. He was strikingly handsome. And even though he sported a full facial beard, he he looked quite younger than his fifty years.

Parker and Flavia shared their 5,000 sq. ft., four-bedroom home with their six year-old twin boys – *Corey* and *Corbin*.

Their home, which was just around the corner from Blu, was perched on a hill and located on *Rolling Waves Drive*. The style was *Old World Plantation* that was supported by six classic white columns. The extra wide front porch provided ample space for two large white rocking chairs. And a loss of breath was to be expected upon entering their palatial two-story foyer, which was flanked by a stately dining room on the left, and a meticulously decorated living room on the right.

Flavia's partnership in the ad agency along with Parker's role as a senior partner with one of Atlanta's most prestigious law firms, allowed the James' to enjoy an enviable and comfortable lifestyle.

But success had its price. And for Flavia it was the time spent away from her boys and a lost personal connection with them that she was forced to ante up.

Corey and Corbin were born six years ago – not long after she'd entered into a partnership with Blu and Kiwi to form ADDISON JAMES & SHEPHERD. She realized then that starting the agency was going to require personal sacrifices. But she had no idea that she would feel so much guilt for allowing an *Au Pair* to provide much of the love and care for her boys. Her decision to place a high importance on her career was rationalized by convincing herself that what she was doing would ultimately allow for a more financially secured future for the twins. Having grown up under the auspices of government assistance, she knew all too well what it was like to live without.

Two years ago Flavia James committed her life to Christ. It was just the perfect balance that she'd been searching for. Having a meaningful spiritual life has benefited her beyond comparison to anything she could imagine. She wasn't raised in a religious home. And even as an adult the depth and degree of her religion consisted mainly of giving thanks for the food at dinnertime. Yet she always tried to do the right thing.

She chuckled as she remembered her mother's admonition that was taught to her and her three siblings as children back in St. Louis. Flavia's mother would tell them that it was okay if you didn't go to church. She instructed them that if they stayed away from *cussing*, *lying*, *stealing* and *killing*, God would be pleased. Flavia had dubbed the *sins*, the *core four*. And as a child, she found herself wondering why her mother left out *smoking* and *drinking*. Especially since the public schools had made it clear that no such antics would be tolerated. However, she would later learn that moms had a certain weakness for old *Jack Daniels* and an addicting fascination with the *Marlboro* man.

Six months after her commitment to the Lord, Parker did likewise. Now, they worshiped as a family every Sunday and attended bible classes on Wednesday nights. Flavia recommitted herself to her family. She adjusted her hours at the ad agency so that she was home when the boys arrived from school, eliminating the need for the Au Pair.

On Fridays she only worked half days. And at least twice a month she volunteered at the twins' private elementary school. Still, she often wondered if she'd waited too late. The boys would sometimes ask for the Au Pair – they'd become accustomed to her greeting them at the bus stop, preparing their after-school snacks, helping with homework and even, and unfortunately at times, tucking them into bed at night. But Flavia was determined to connect with them. She had to. She was their mother.

It was just after nine-thirty. The twins had been put to bed already, even though it was a Friday night. They had a big soccer game tomorrow afternoon and Flavia wanted them well rested.

"So, are you excited about the prospect of landing your agency's largest client to date?" Parker asked his wife. They were sitting at the kitchen table enjoying the remains of a strawberry cheesecake that she'd made earlier in the week.

Flavia smiled. "Of course. I just hope we can pull it off."

"Sure you can!" Parker's booming voice resonated. He was so incredibly supportive.

"Thanks, baby," she acknowledged sheepishly. "It's just that . . . I mean, I know we're capable of handling this account, it's just that sometimes I can't help but wonder if we're moving too fast."

"Sweetheart, in a business like yours, I believe you have to take advantage of the opportunities whenever they present themselves."

"I realize that. But if we win this account, we've got to move to larger office space, recruit new personnel, and – "

He interrupted her. "Sweetheart, where is all this apprehension coming from?" Flavia allowed her eyes to fall towards her saucer. She began to use her spoon to dabble with the cheesecake. Parker reached across the table and rested one of his hands atop hers. "Sweetheart, something is bothering you, what is it? I didn't think anything of it before, but I've noticed that you haven't been looking too well, are you feeling okay?"

"Other than a little fatigue, I'm fine."

Parker eyed her guardedly. He could read her like a book. The man didn't make law partner by being a dumb attorney. "Talk to me, sweetheart," he coaxed her gently.

"Baby, I'm fine!" she said, serving him a spoonful of cheesecake, which he readily accepted. "I mean, yes I've had some nausea here and there, and maybe a little more bloating than I care to deal with, but really, I'm feeling fine."

"When was your last doctor visit?"

"Parker! You're overreacting!"

"Sweetheart, I'm serious. You've been working awfully hard these past few months. A little check-up might be in order."

She smiled demurely. "You know what?" Then she lost her train of thought. "Actually it's nothing at all, baby. I'm just a little overwhelmed, I guess."

"Then you won't mind indulging me by calling your doctor first thing Monday morning, okay?"

"Baby, that's not necessary," she protested.

When he flashed that diplomatic smile of his, Flavia knew she was dead in the water. What did she expect? She was married to the sexiest fifty year-old man alive. She easily surrendered. "You know you don't play fair," she teased him. "I'll phone Dr. Levinson for an appointment on Monday."

"That's my girl! And I'm sure it's nothing to be concerned about, but it's better to error on the side of caution."

"Right as always," she told him, taking another bite of the scrumptious dessert. "But I know it's just stress from everything that's going on at the agency. I'm just probably nervous about this MerLex review."

"Well, you have every right to be. But don't worry. I trust that you guys will give one heck of a presentation in January. And of course, it goes without saying that you have my full support."

"Thanks, baby."

The two of them devoured their remaining cheesecake before retiring upstairs to their splendidly adorned master suite.

. . . .

The one-level, four-bedroom, European stucco home nestled on a cul de sac on *Falling Leaves Court*, belonged to Kiwi Shepherd. She'd fallen in love with the house, which measured just over 4,000 sq. ft. overlooking the golf course, when the realtor first showed it to her. The master bedroom was a luxurious retreat. It included two fireplaces and a large sitting area. And she simply adored the secluded den, which was opposite her gourmet kitchen.

Kiwi was single. But she hoped it wouldn't be for long. She hadn't fared too well within the relationship department. Until a couple of months ago she only had her three cats to keep her company at night. But now there was a new man in her life. And while the relationship was going to have to overcome some obstacles to be successful, she was certain that the two of them were meant to be together.

Her last three encounters with men had been absolutely horrendous. In fact, it was after each failed relationship that she went out and bought a cat and named it for the loser boyfriend. The first cat she had to purchase was appropriately given the name *Crazy*. While her relationship with this particular guy had lasted three years, the brotha had absolutely no sense whatsoever. He would eat his cereal with a fork. He preferred to shower with his pajamas on, mumbling something about protecting his sensitive skin. During their last year together he insisted that she start calling him *The One Chosen To Be*. And since he would give no reasonable explanation for the eccentric request, Kiwi *chose* to tell him that he was a damn fool and then she *chose* to send him packing.

Her second cat was named *Lyin'*. This doomed relationship only lasted six months. The brotha lied about every possible thing that he could. He told her that he drove an SUV. She would later find out that it was a *stolen used van*. He told her that he was a pharmaceutical sales representative. Liar. He sold drugs all right – the illegal ones. And he had the audacity to tell her that he was a YALE student. Apparently they had different interpretations of *Yale*; she assumed the Ivy League university, but it turned out that he was just a *Young Addict Lacking Employment*.

Unfortunately Kiwi found herself buying a third cat last spring. His name was *Cheatin'*. No details warranted. The name itself was self-explanatory.

So until last month, her beautiful home could only be shared with Crazy, Lyin' and Cheatin'. They were precious little cats, however. And she wouldn't part with them for the world. Although there seemed to be a slight problem with the new man in her life – he wasn't too fond of cats. She's hoping that he'll grow to love them as she does. If not, then who knows – maybe she *could* part with the little bastards after all.

Kiwi's new man had run out to pick them up something to eat on this late Friday night. He'd just moved in with her, so she didn't have time to stock the refrigerator and cabinets. Besides, she ate out most of the time.

She was reclining on the sofa with Crazy snuggled beside her. She wasn't sure where Lyin' and Cheatin' were. She sometimes thought that they had a little attitude problem. Whenever she came home from the office Crazy would always run to her and begin rubbing against her leg. The other two would only stare, giving her the once over before they scampered away. She had warned the ungrateful felines not to test her love for them. They were not indispensable. It wasn't as if she'd actually given birth to the furry creatures.

Kiwi diverted her thoughts to her new man. It was funny how things tended to work out sometimes. She had never felt this sure about a relationship before.

The two of them didn't have a whole lot in common, but she considered that to be a *good* thing. Whether opposites attracted or not, she believed that he was definitely the man she'd been searching for.

She was going to do whatever was necessary to make certain that this relationship evolved into a permanent one. Somehow she knew that he was her last hope at love. True love.

The two of them had to make it work. She realized that she wasn't getting any younger.

Besides, they had a motivating reason to make it work. But Kiwi was convinced that, even without the reason, they were going to solidify their relationship. Lay a firm foundation of love and trust. Build on it from there. One day at a time.

Just then the other two cats scampered into the room and sprang up on the sofa beside her. She gathered all three of them into her arms. They'd been pretty good company. Giving her someone to talk to whenever she was home alone. But she realized that the line had been drawn at *three*.

The thought of having to buy another cat made her shudder.

chapter 5

The private *Golf Club at WindFair Estates* was a beautifully landscaped and designed, par seventy-two eighteen-hole golf course. An army of trees guarded the lush Bermuda fairways like loyal soldiers. And the soft, undulating bentgrass greens proved challenging even for the most seasoned golfer.

Although somewhat sleepy-eyed, Blu, Flavia and Kiwi were each doing some quick stretches to loosen themselves as they prepared to tee off from the number one tee box.

The early fall morning was perfect for a round of golf. The skies were smiling with sunshine. The warm breeze was gingerly in its attack. The air incredibly fresh. And the temperature, never one to be stingy in the south, handed out digits of seventy-two.

The first hole was a *par four* measuring three hundred and ninety-seven yards from the white tee markers. From the red markers it only measured three hundred yards, which is where the three women were going to play.

"We're just out here today to hone our skills, guys," Blu admonished. "So let's not get all competitive," she added, directing her gaze toward Kiwi.

"Hey, I just play my own game," Kiwi remarked, taking offense.

Flavia was up first to hit. She chose a five-wood club because she never seemed to have much success with her three-wood or her driver. She was dressed in pink-flowered Capri pants and a white sleeveless top. A pink sun visor graced her head. She did one practice swing before she took full assault on the ball. She made solid contact. The ball took off straight down the middle of the fairway before it quickly detoured right and came to rest just inside some trees. It was about a one hundred and eighty yard drive.

"I think you'll be able to find it in there," Kiwi told her. She was never shy about offering advice to the other two women. After all, she did have a *nine* handicap.

Blu was next on the tee box. She was wearing white shorts with a lavender blouse. A white TITLEIST golf cap donned her head. Although she could swing her driver relatively well, she chose a three-wood club instead. She rarely took practice swings. Her routine was to stand directly behind her ball, select her target and then take her stance. Her back swing was slow and methodical.

She made great contact and the ball sailed high into the air and landed in the center of the fairway. However, it was not a long drive, only about one hundred and sixty-five yards.

"Nice shot!" Flavia commended her.

"That'll work, Blu," Kiwi chimed in.

"Thanks," Blu acknowledged as she bent over and retrieved her tee from the ground. She stepped aside as Kiwi prepared to hit next.

Being the risk taker that she was, Kiwi didn't have to think twice about pulling out her *driver* from the bag.

She was dressed fashionably as usual. Sporting flared-leg tan trousers and a cream-colored pinstriped polo shirt, Kiwi looked like she was preparing to walk the runway as opposed to the fairway. Holding her long cranberry hair in place was a tan COACH bucket hat. A pair of black OAKLEY sunglasses were protecting her eyes.

Kiwi was simply being true to form. She said that if she dressed nicely she played well. And considering her low handicap it was difficult to argue against the woman's theory.

"Are you sure you want to hit a driver?" Blu questioned Kiwi's decision. "You realize that it's two hundred and twenty yards to carry the water?" she tried again after Kiwi ignored her first question.

Kiwi didn't bat an eye. "Of course. I've played here

enough to realize that," she answered, taking a couple of huge practice swings. "That's why I have the *big stick*," she said, holding up her driver in front of Blu.

Blu shrugged her shoulders. "Go for it, girl." Even though she'd never seen Kiwi carry the water from the tee box. For each of them it had always been a lay-up shot somewhere short of the lake. Especially since you gained no significant advantage by hitting over the water.

Kiwi took her stance and then she ripped the ball with everything she had. It accelerated off the tee mightily, traveling left initially and then veering towards the center of the fairway. She held her breath as the ball remained airborne when it reached the water. "Get over! Get over!" she began yelling. But the screams would prove futile as she watched an almost perfect tee shot nose dive into the lake with a gentle splash, only a couple of yards shy of dry land. "Dammit!" she shouted, banging her club against the ground.

There was no mistaking how seriously Kiwi took her golf game. After calming herself, she quickly teed up another ball. The rules required that she hit from the same spot and take a one-stroke penalty. It now would be her *third* shot. Reluctantly, she slammed the driver back into her bag and retrieved a five-iron. She hit a nice recovery shot that flew for a hundred and seventy yards and landed in the middle of the fairway – just barely ahead of Blu's ball.

That's what you should have done the first time Miss Thing, Blu thought to herself as they walked toward their golf carts. Kiwi would have to start playing smarter golf if they were going to try and win the tournament this year.

Flavia and Kiwi were riding in a cart together. Blu was in a cart alone since she was without her former executive assistant, Gail Adams. As they prepared to pull away from the tee box, one of the course Marshals pulled up beside them. He was an older gentleman, a retiree who worked at the golf course, not so much for the minimum pay but for the free rounds of golf that came with the job.

"Excuse me, ladies," he said as he drove his cart (which was easily identifiable as a Marshal's cart because it had a long flagstick connected to the back with a red flag on top) alongside them. "Would y'all mind if this young lady joined your group?" he asked, referring to the youthful female sitting in the cart next to him. "Her playing partner had to cancel, and I'd hate for her to have to play all by herself."

Blu looked at Flavia and Kiwi for their thoughts. Flavia indicated her acceptance with a nod of her head. Kiwi seemed nonchalant about the request, choosing to avert her gaze when Blu looked her way.

"Of course," Blu gave the Marshal the okay. "She can ride with me."

"Fantastic!" the Marshal responded. "I promise y'all

that she won't hold you up none either."

"Oh, we're not worried about that," Flavia remarked. "We just hope that *we* don't hold *her* up!"

The young woman smiled as she strapped her LOUIS VUITTON golf bag onto the back of the cart next to Blu's bag.

"Thanks. I really appreciate you guys allowing me to play along with you," she said.

After the Marshal had driven away, the young woman introduced herself as *Yelsi Nitram.*

"What a unique name," Blu told her.

"It is different," added Flavia.

The three women introduced themselves. Although Kiwi regarded the young woman with a hint of suspicion, she improvised a polite 'hello'.

Yelsi was baby doll gorgeous. Her dimpled cheeks were easily discernable when she exhibited a breath-taking smile. Her glistening white teeth were nothing short of an arrangement of pearls. Her plum-colored lips defied adequate description. And her dark brown hair was very long and soft. It was styled straight, allowing her tresses to flow well below the slender shoulders of her five-foot-four frame. Adding to her beauty even more were her hazel eyes set against her olive skin.

Her ethnicity was unbeknownst to any of them. Although Blu said that the young woman reminded her of someone whom she knew in high school.

"We've already hit our tee shots, so you can go right ahead and swing away," Blu told Yelsi.

"Have you played here before?" Flavia asked.

"Yes," was Yelsi's answer. She chose her three-wood club from the bag and took her position on the tee box. Her attire was simple – white Capri pants and a light blue IZOD shirt. Her golf cap was white with CALLAWAY printed across the top in black lettering. Before swinging she quickly tied her hair into a ponytail. She stuck the tail through the opening in the back of her cap. Then she made what looked like an effortless swing at the golf ball. The swing was about as beautiful as she was. The other three women looked on in awe as Yelsi's ball rocketed two hundred and thirty yards straight down the fairway and landed on the *other side* of the lake – only seventy yards away from the green.

"Great shot!" Blu and Flavia nearly shouted. Kiwi was speechless.

"Thanks," replied Yelsi as she picked up her tee and trotted back to the cart.

Show off, Kiwi thought to herself.

"The Marshal could have warned us that we would be playing with a pro," Blu joked, as their golf cart bounced down the cart path.

"I wish," Yelsi replied. "But I did play on my college

team," she added quite modestly.

. . . .

During the next few hours Blu learned a lot about Yelsi. The young woman was twenty-five years old. She'd been playing golf since the age of seven. Both her parents were avid golfers. Unfortunately, however, she lost her mother to breast cancer three years ago. She had no brothers or sisters. Yelsi graduated near the top of her class from *Wellesley College* in Wellesley, Massachusetts with a degree in philosophy. She had been a member of the college's golf team all four years.

It was her flawless play during many of the school's tournaments that helped the team win the Massachusetts State Championship during her junior year and then the Northeast Championships during her senior year.

Many of her college teammates, including her coach, thought that she would pursue golf on a professional level. Her handicap was zero. But Yelsi didn't think that she was mentally ready to take that step. Although, she hadn't ruled out the possibility for the future.

She also told Blu that she'd always had an interest in advertising. She considered herself to be very creative. Poetry was often penned in her spare time. And she enjoyed perusing magazines just to look at the ads as well as watching commercials on television.

Blu couldn't believe how fortunate they were to have met her. Surely, a blessing in disguise. She would eventually discuss with Yelsi, between holes, the possibility of coming to work for her as her executive assistant. Yelsi said that she would love to.

Her enthusiasm at the prospect of having Yelsi work for her *and* having her join their golf team as their much-needed fourth player, did help to ease her mind about Damien.

Eighteen holes later the four women were pulling into the *Cart Return* area of the golf course. Flavia had recorded a final score of *115*. She typically shot between a hundred and ten and a hundred and twenty. Blu managed to break one hundred, squeezing out a final score of *94*. Her best on this course was an eighty-seven. Kiwi's entire game fell apart. She seemed so rattled by Yelsi's superb playing that she was all over the place with her golf shots. Blu had never seen Kiwi rifle through so many golf balls in one round before. She ended up shooting a *105* – her absolute worst finish on this course. Kiwi typically shot in the low eighties and she's even broken eighty a couple of times as well. But today simply wasn't her day. And the gold star for the round went, hands down, to Yelsi Nitram. The young woman shot an impressive *two under par* with a final score of *70*.

Blu was thrilled. Her mind had already begun racing

with possibilities.

As the women unstrapped their bags from the carts, Blu asked Yelsi, "So, would you consider playing in a charity golf tournament with the three of us?"

Before Yelsi could respond, Kiwi blurted out, "*All* participants have to be employed by the advertising agency in which they're playing for!"

"I'm aware of that Kiwi," Blu shot back. "Yelsi mentioned to me that she just graduated from college this past spring and that she is looking for a job within the advertising industry."

"Oh, really?" said Kiwi. "What a coincidence."

Yelsi could sense this woman's apparent hostility toward her, yet she had no idea what was causing it.

"Well, I think that it works out perfectly," continued Blu. "I mean, we need a fourth member for the team and I need to find a replacement for Gail at the agency. I've already discussed the executive assistant's position with Yelsi while we were out on the course, and she's willing to give it a try."

Un-freakin' believable! Kiwi thought to herself. Blu had only known this girl for about five hours and she'd already hired her to work at the agency. "It's your decision," she muttered.

"I think it would be great to have Yelsi on our team," said Flavia. She also knew that Kiwi's *resistance* probably had more to do with jealousy than anything else. Kiwi never had any serious competition when she played with her and Blu. And now someone comes along and blows her game out of the water. It's something that Kiwi simply wasn't used to.

"Well, I gotta run," Kiwi told them as she headed for her guards red PORSCHE 911 CARRERA CABRIOLET. "Have a nice weekend!" she waved to them. "And it was nice meeting you, Yelsi." She had to literally force the words from her mouth.

They all waved good-bye.

Blu gave Yelsi one of her business cards and set an appointment for Monday morning at ten o'clock. "Be prepared to start," Blu told her. "This is not an interview – we've already completed that on the course."

Yelsi smiled. "Thank you so much." She then told Blu and Flavia that she was going to go and hit a few more balls on the golf range. They were amazed at her dedication, though not totally surprised. How else does one card a *zero* handicap?

After saying good-bye to Yelsi, Blu and Flavia headed for the parking lot as well. Their cars were parked beside one another. When they reached the vehicles Blu said, "I hope you don't mind me saying this, Flavia, but you look like you've lost some weight."

Flavia blew it off. "Girl, it'll all be back before you

know it," she said as she placed her golf bag into her SUV.

"Well, anyway you look great!"

"Thanks, Blu. I guess I have to try and keep pace with you young guns," she said, referring to Blu and Kiwi.

"Yeah, right! You're only nine years older than me."

"True. But trust me, girlfriend – a lot of changes take place within those nine years!"

They laughed out loud.

Blu watched as Flavia drove off in her black CADILLAC ESCALADE. She had a gnawing feeling that something wasn't altogether right with Flavia. Not only had she noticed the loss in her weight, but also Flavia's demeanor seemed different lately. Around the office, she no longer walked with that extra pep in her step. Saying that she was tired, she had chosen not to join her and Kiwi for weekend shopping excursions the last couple of times that they invited her.

Blu made a quick mental note to schedule lunch with her one day next week. They were all good friends as well as business partners. And if something was bothering Flavia, then she certainly wanted to try her best to help in any way that she could.

As she steered her car toward home, which was only two blocks away, Blu reminded herself that she had her own problems to contend with right now as well.

chapter 6

Like a *jealous girlfriend* who'd just found out that she'd been cozying up to her boyfriend, the blaring buzzer from the digital alarm clock went off on Blu. And the best defense that her languid body could offer was to pull a pillow on top of her head. It was six o'clock.

Minutes later, with the alarm still blaring in her ears, attacking her with such a vengeance, like it had some kind of a score to settle, Blu rolled out of bed, hitting the floor with a thud. As she slowly reached her hand toward the nightstand to silence the *intruder*, it occurred to her that she should have gone to bed last night when her tired body was beckoning her to do so, instead of staying up to watch *The Practice*, the eleven o'clock news *and* some late night music videos on *BET*.

She suddenly remembered how she could always count on Damien to make sure that she went to bed on time.

Although, it was often for his own selfish reasons.

Barely getting her body to move, Blu began the process of placing one foot in front of the other in an attempt to somehow make it to the bathroom. The hot shower would invigorate her. She knew this to be true. But the power of her bed, with those soft silky sheets, and warm covers, kept tempting her to return. *Lie down for just five more minutes.*

She stopped in her tracks and weighed the offer. Five more minutes of sleep would feel good. Probably clear her brain of the cobwebs and make her that much more effective when she arrived at the office. Besides, she was *the* president of ADDISON JAMES & SHEPHERD; she didn't have some hard-driving supervisor that she had to answer to. Why not go in late today?

The answer quickly thumped her upside the head. *Because you have a ten o'clock appointment with your new executive assistant this morning. And you need to be prepared. Because you also need to try and reach your husband at his office and see what the devil is going on with him. And since Mondays were generally crazy anyway, the earlier you got started, the better handle on the day you'll be able to get.*

"All right!" she said aloud.

She resumed her steps and eventually found herself setting one foot into the shower stall. She turned the nozzle so that the water came out hot and at full blast.

The water's attack against her smooth, delicate brown skin was vicious. She was being pelted nonstop. The rising of the steam all around her giving some indication of the water's velocity. The *jealous girlfriend* had returned.

Beat me all you want, she thought to herself. This was one beat down that she was going to simply savor. Enjoy. Relish.

. . . .

"What's going on, Damien?" Blu demanded as soon as her husband answered his direct line at his office on Monday morning. She'd made it to her own office just before eight o'clock. She didn't reach Damien, however, until after nine.

"Why don't you tell me?" he threw the ball back into her court.

"Damien, I'm not the one who moved out! And, without so much as a phone call!"

"As if you didn't see this coming?"

"No Damien, as a matter of fact I didn't *see this coming*. Forgive me, but I guess I didn't expect my husband of fourteen years to wake up one day and decide to walk away from his marriage without a single word to his wife!"

Damien began to massage his temples. "Listen, Blu. I just can't continue on like this . . . "

She interrupted him. "Like what?"

"Come off it, Blu!" His patience was wearing thin. "Stop acting like you're a victim here. You and I both know that the marriage is over and it has been for some time."

Blu began to feel flush. Her heart was racing. "Why Damien? Is the marriage over simply because *you* say so?"

"Don't try and pin this whole break-up on me, Blu. If anyone is to blame then you might want to take a good look in the mirror!"

"How's it my fault?"

Damien banged his fist against his desk. "I cannot believe you! You really have the audacity to try and convince me that you're innocent in all this?"

Blu was silent.

"For the last several years all you've cared about is building your career, Blu. You haven't cared one bit about my feelings. You haven't cared one bit about my interest in starting a family and – "

She interrupted him again. "So is that what this is about? You're walking away from your marriage because I don't want to have children right now?"

"*Right now?*" he repeated. "Blu, I don't believe that you want children ever! And rather than be straight with me about it, you chose to lead me on, just lying every step of the way!"

"That is not true!"

"The hell it isn't! Have you so quickly forgotten your promise to begin a family when you turned thirty, huh?"

She knew all to well the promise that she'd made. To some extent her husband was right. She had been lying to him all these years. She was even hoping that he'd become so wrapped up in his own career that he wouldn't want children right now either. "Damien, I had every intention of trying to start a family when I turned thirty," she attempted to explain. "But you know that having a baby and trying to start this ad agency would not have been feasible or smart."

Damien let out a heavy sigh. "Blu, do you take me for a fool?"

"Of course not."

"Then allow me to refresh your memory . . . "

She remained silent.

"You didn't start your ad agency until you were thirty-two, that was two years later, okay? So don't try and use your business as the reason for putting off having a child."

Right again.

"True, but that doesn't mean I wasn't thinking about it, Damien. I mean, I have always wanted to start my own ad agency. The idea didn't just pop into my head when I turned thirty-two."

"You know what? This conversation is getting us

absolutely nowhere. I apologize for moving out without letting you know ahead of time, but to be honest, it wouldn't have made a difference. I just wanted to do it quickly and without a lot of drama."

"Damien, let's talk things through, okay?"

"I'm done talking, Blu."

"Please don't say that."

"Blu, it's not going to work! Think about it – you're not slowing down in your career. I mean, you are about to commit a helluva lot of time and energy trying to win MerLex Motors, I know you're not about to begin thinking about having kids."

"How did you know about MerLex?"

Damien hesitated. "I know you guys made it to the final presentation stage, didn't you?"

"Yes, but I was planning on telling you that last Friday when I came home. How did you find out about it?"

"It doesn't matter. The fact remains."

Blu decided not to press him. "Damien, we have to try and work this out. There's a reason for my apprehension over having kids, and I know that I should have shared it with you years ago, but I thought I could work through it."

"Is it medical related, Blu?"

"No, nothing like that."

"Then I don't want to hear your reason. If it was really

important you would have shared it with me long before now, Blu."

She couldn't understand why he was being so harsh. "Damien, don't do this, okay?"

"Blu, for the last time, it's over."

"Where are you staying? At least tell me where I can find you?"

"I'm taken care of."

"What does that mean?"

"It means I have a place to stay for now. It's not your concern."

"Of course its my concern – you're my husband!"

"Blu, I'm late for a meeting. We can't continue this discussion right now."

"Damien, where can I call you then?"

"You have my cell number and you know how to reach me at the office. I need to sort through some things, Blu. The best thing for you to do right now is to allow me time to do that."

"How much time?"

"I don't know. I'll be in touch." Damien quickly hung up the phone without saying good-bye.

Blu sat at her desk for a moment with her telephone receiver still in her hand. She couldn't believe that this was all happening. Then it dawned on her just how patient her husband had actually been over the years.

Her mother was so right about all this. Why didn't she just tell Damien everything when they started getting serious back in college? And certainly she should have been open with him *before* they got married. Fourteen years was a very long time to carry around a secret. Now she wondered if her decision to keep things from him had become a devastating burden? Or simply a *necessary* evil?

A knock at the door interrupted her thoughts.

"Come in," she called out.

It was Yelsi Nitram arriving for her ten o'clock appointment.

"Hi Yelsi," Blu greeted her while trying to compose herself at the same time.

"Good morning, Mrs. Addison."

"Yelsi, as I told you on the golf course last weekend, no formalities here. Just call me *Blu*."

Yelsi displayed a nervous smile. "Okay."

"So, are you ready to get to work?"

"I'm ready."

"Great. Let's go into the small conference room. I have some paperwork for you to fill out and then we can talk. As my executive assistant I want to make sure you understand fully my expectations."

Yelsi nodded as Blu led her from her office and into an

adjacent conference room.

. . . .

As Flavia James lay on a gurney inside the emergency room of the *NorthView General Hospital*, she allowed her eyes to focus on the round, white-faced clock that hung against the wall above the room's metal double doors. It was almost ten-thirty.

Just after the twins had been put on the school bus, Flavia was in the kitchen pouring herself a cup of coffee when she suddenly doubled over in pain. It was the crashing of the glass coffee pot onto the kitchen's tile floor and Flavia's shrill screams that sent her husband rushing down the stairs. When he arrived into the kitchen he found his wife on the floor in the fetal position clutching her stomach. After realizing that she was in too much pain to try and move her, he dialed 911. Less than an hour later she was being wheeled down a long corridor into the hospital's emergency room.

Dr. Laura Levinson had been Flavia's personal physician since her pregnancy with the twins. She was BOARD CERTIFIED in obstetrics and gynecology, and she had three children of her own. Dr. Levinson just happened to be completing rounds at the hospital when Flavia arrived.

"How are you feeling?" she asked upon entering the room. She stood beside the gurney. Parker was sitting in a chair on the opposite side.

"Well, the stomach pains have stopped."

"I'm sure that's a relief," the doctor remarked, scanning Flavia's medical chart. "It appears that you've been losing some weight over the past few months. Has this been intentional?"

"Not really. I mean, I have been working a lot, but not enough to cause a loss of twenty pounds. I'm sitting at a desk a good part of my work day." Her weight had dropped to one fifty-five over the past couple of months. And other than golf, Flavia did not have a regular exercise regime.

The doctor joked, "if only we could all be so lucky as to shed twenty pounds from simply sitting at our desks." She then scribbled some notes on the chart. "I'm going to recommend that you see a specialist, Flavia," Dr. Levinson stated firmly.

"A specialist?" Flavia repeated. "What kind of a specialist?"

"Well, based on the fact that you've been experiencing abdominal pain for a while, some nausea and the unexplained weight loss, I want to refer you to a *Gastroenterologist*."

Parker and Flavia exchanged concerned glances.

"Now, there's nothing to be alarmed about. However, I am recommending that you see him right away." Dr. Levinson reached down and took hold of Flavia's hand. "He's a personal friend of mine so you'll be in excellent hands," she told her, giving her hand a gentle squeeze. "His name is *Dr. Jerry Jacobs* and he does have an office right here in Alpharetta. I've already taken the liberty of speaking with him and he can fit you in tomorrow afternoon."

"Is it that urgent?" Parker asked.

"Well, I would prefer that your wife see him right away, Mr. James."

"Laura," Flavia began, "I need for you to be totally honest with me. What's going on?"

Dr. Levinson averted her gaze from the chart and directed it to her patient and friend. "Right now, nothing is definitive. Your blood tests did not reveal anything out of the ordinary. However, with the symptoms that you've been experiencing, I believe that it would be in your best interest to see Dr. Jacobs. He's a specialist in diagnosing and treating diseases of the digestive system.

"*Diseases?*" Flavia became alarmed. Parker stood from his chair and took hold of her hand.

"Flavia, I'm not suggesting that you have any kind of disease. I'm simply trying to explain what a Gastroenterologist does."

"I understand that, but why are you referring me to one if you don't think I have a problem?"

"Flavia, my specialty is O-B-G-Y-N. I'm not qualified to delve into matters dealing with the digestive system. Now,

Dr. Jacobs will be very frank with you. If there is nothing to be concerned about he will tell you. And likewise, if there is anything abnormal, he will provide the best advice. And as your friend as well as your physician, I have no intentions of simply handing you off to another doctor. I will keep close communications with Dr. Jacobs on your condition."

Flavia realized that Dr. Levinson was being about as open with her as she could. She just didn't like the idea of seeing another doctor and probably having to go through a bunch of tests. But she also knew that something was wrong with her and it would be foolish for her to ignore the doctor's advice.

"Okay. I'll go and see the specialist tomorrow," Flavia agreed reluctantly.

Dr. Levinson tried to reassure her that everything was going to be fine. She signed Flavia's discharge papers and told her to stop by the nurse's station to pick up the referral information after she got herself dressed. Then she gave Flavia a hug and shook Parker's hand before exiting the room.

chapter 7

Yelsi Nitram had adjusted quite well to her new role at ADDISON JAMES & SHEPHERD by Monday afternoon. Her desk was located just outside of Blu's enormous office. An office that was huge enough to fit at least three additional offices inside. Large double doors to the entrance of Blu's suite were the first sign of authority and success. Yelsi was amazed at how grand everything looked. Blu had a magnificent custom made desk that stood catty-cornered in the office, adjacent to a wall of windows that were fitted with custom silk drapes. And a Chenille-covered cream sofa with matching chairs graced another area of Blu's working quarters. The abundance of dark colors in the suite gave the office a very cozy feel.

Earlier she had been introduced to some of the agency's key personnel. Blu explained some of her expectations, including her request to have all her calls screened. Yelsi only answered calls for Blu. The receptionist transferred all calls for Blu directly to Yelsi who would then screen them before announcing the calls to her boss. And because of her knowledge of the advertising agency business already, Blu informed Yelsi that she would serve as her mentor in helping her to learn all that she could about ADDISON JAMES & SHEPHERD.

Yelsi's true interest was account management. Of course, account management within the agency was considered *client services*, and that area came under the direction of Kiwi Shepherd.

"Did you have a nice lunch?" Blu asked Yelsi, as she returned to the office from her own lunch break.

"I wasn't really hungry. I just grabbed a soda and some chips from the vending machine in the break room," Yelsi answered.

"Well, just keep in mind that I allow you to take an hour and a half for lunch," Blu reminded her of her liberal lunch policy. "So you have plenty of time to get away from the office if you choose to."

"Thank you. I'm sure I will."

Blu smiled at her. "Hey, you haven't seen Flavia today have you?"

Yelsi thought for a moment. She knew which one was Flavia, because not only was she the tallest of the three women, but she was also much nicer than Kiwi. "Um, no I haven't seen her today. Not yet anyway."

"All right. Well, I'll check with Kiwi. We have a meeting at two o'clock this afternoon and I just wanted to make sure that she was aware of it."

Blu was about to close her office door before she stopped. "By the way, Yelsi," she called back to her. "I would like for you to sit in on the meeting as well."

Yelsi quickly made a note of the meeting on a *Post-It* note. "Where will we be meeting?"

"It will be in the main conference room behind the receptionist station. You can walk over with me," Blu told her.

Yelsi nodded.

Blu closed her door and sat down at her desk. She liked this young woman a lot. Even though she was only twenty-five, she seemed to have such a good head on her shoulders. Yelsi was focused. And she learned very quickly. Blu was so taken with her that she didn't even bother to have her human resources director conduct the usual background check and employment reference verification.

Unlike a lot of young people these days, Yelsi seemed to show little concern about how much money she was going to be paid. She was totally absorbed with the details of the job and learning more about the agency. And although Blu had enjoyed having Gail Adams work for her, there seemed to be an immediate bond with Yelsi.

All things work together for good, she recalled one of Flavia's often recited Scripture quotations. She only hoped that this would ring true between her and Damien as well.

. . . .

The main conference room within the offices of ADDISON JAMES & SHEPHERD was located just behind the receptionist station. The room was very private. It had been designed with privacy in mind, a way to minimize external distractions. There were no windows. No opportunity for occupants within the room to view the outside, despite how bored with their speaker or how mundane a topic they may find themselves. A quick glimpse of the sun, a lingering gaze at the trees, or any other daydreaming was stifled. And acoustics were as such as to keep any noise from the lobby out and all conversations spoken, inside.

Just sitting, as an employee or other visitor, around the black, marble-top, 25-foot-long conference table, gave anyone the feeling of presiding over or participating in something of importance. Something with substance.

As the room's centerpiece, the table was surrounded by fourteen tan leather low-back swivel chairs. And enclosed behind the walls was a sophisticated communications and audio-visual system, which served a variety of purposes including the ability to review television ads and radio spots.

Present at their two o'clock meeting were the three agency partners, the chief financial officer, and the human resources director. The purpose of the meeting was to begin putting into place a plan, in the likelihood that the agency won the Merlex Motors account, which would affect the overall operations of the agency.

The meeting had been going on for no more than fifteen minutes already. Blu was speaking to the agency's chief financial officer, "Are you saying that there is no space within this entire building in which we can expand?"

The chief financial officer was a short, stocky African-American. His caramel baby face belied his fifty-three years by at least ten. And despite the generous salary the agency paid him, he seemed quite content wearing thick black eyeglasses. "Not *contiguous* space," he answered. "I'm told that what's available is some limited office space up on the fourteenth floor."

"That won't work," Kiwi immediately interjected. "How much sense does it make for us to be on the *first* floor and then have people fourteen floors above us?"

"I agree," said Flavia. "It doesn't sound practical."

"Which is why I believe that our only option is to look outside the building," the CFO stated.

Blu placed her head within her hands momentarily. The day seemed to be getting longer by the hour. She began a slow methodical massage of her temples with both her middle fingers. "I really hate to have to go through a situation which requires us to move our entire offices."

"I agree," he told her. "But if we win MerLex, it's going to be inevitable."

Blu leaned back in her chair, momentarily locking her hands behind her head. "Okay. Go ahead and meet with some real estate brokers. And remember, we've already stipulated that if we have to move from this building we want the new location to be within the same proximity. And make sure that you let these brokers know that everything right now is strictly preliminary, so the strictest of confidence is required."

"Yeah, we don't want to be inundated with calls from everybody-and-his-brother asking if they can show us a new building," remarked Kiwi.

The CFO jotted down some notes on the yellow legal pad that lay in front of him. "That won't be a problem," he assured them. "I plan to use the previous brokers. They're very professional and they're discreet in situations like this."

"Good," Blu said. "Okay, let's move on. I know that you have to leave at three o'clock Flavia before your boys arrive home from school, so the final matter that needs to be addressed is *personnel*." Blu directed her attention to her human resources director. "I know you've been working on some numbers with regards to MerLex's impact on personnel, what have you come up with so far?"

The human resources director, a middle-aged Asian woman who'd been with the agency for the past three years, retrieved some papers from a manila file. "I've taken the liberty of outlining my thoughts and recommendations into a report format," she answered, as she handed each of them a copy of her report. She was meticulous in that way. She was about to also hand a copy to Yelsi when Kiwi quickly interrupted.

"Excuse me, but is it really necessary that *she* see this?" Kiwi asked Blu.

"She's my assistant, Kiwi. I want her to know what's going on."

"I don't have a problem with her knowing what's going on, Blu. My problem is that this is her first day on the job."

"And your point is?"

"Wouldn't it be better if we allowed her to get to know the job first, and maybe we get to know her, before entrusting sensitive information to her?"

Yelsi, feeling about as uncomfortable as *Saddam Hussein* at a banquet honoring *President George Bush*, spoke up. "It's okay, Blu. Miss Shepherd's right, I don't have to see this *now*."

"No, I want you to be involved, Yelsi," Blu said to her. She then directed her words to Kiwi, "if you have a problem other than your *personal* feelings on this matter, then you and I can discuss this further after the meeting – *in private*, all right?"

Kiwi deliberately rolled her eyes. She couldn't believe that this girl had already gotten her hooks into Blu. It was so unlike Blu. Especially since she was usually the one who was always making sure that every "i" was dotted and every "t" was crossed.

"She's your assistant," Kiwi finally said. "You do what you want."

"Thank you," Blu replied, as she handed a copy of the report to Yelsi. She instructed the human resources director to continue.

Yelsi couldn't believe what had just transpired. What was Kiwi's problem? What had she possibly done to this person to cause her to get her panties tied in a big ol' knot? The woman was obviously knitting with just *one* needle.

Twenty-five minutes later the meeting wrapped up. Kiwi made a quick exit from the conference room without saying anything further to anyone.

"I'm going back to my desk, Blu. Is there something specific that I should work on?" Yelsi asked.

"Not at the moment, Yelsi. You can start on those files

that I gave you earlier."

Yelsi nodded and then made a beeline back to her desk.

Flavia was still in the conference room. Blu walked over to her as she was gathering up her files. "I didn't see you this morning, is everything all right?"

"Of course. Everything's just fine," Flavia answered, stuffing papers into her attaché case without even looking up at Blu. "I just had some errands to take care of this morning, that's all."

"Well, I was just concerned. I'm not trying to pry or anything."

"Oh, of course not, Blu. We all look out for each other. I appreciate your concern." Flavia snapped her attaché case shut. "What about you? Are things going well with you?"

The question caught Blu by surprise. "What do you mean?"

"Oh, nothing in particular. I know you're putting in a lot of hours these days, as we all are, and I just want to make sure that you're keeping it balanced."

Blu smiled. "Well, I've had my moments of frustration. But it's all been good."

"Anything you care to share?"

Blu gave her a dismissive gesture with her hand. "Oh, please. It's nothing that serious."

Flavia changed the subject. "So, you're happy with your new assistant?"

"Most definitely. For her first day, she's adapted quite well."

"I'm glad to hear that. She seems like a very smart young lady. I think that you two will complement each other well."

The two women chatted some more briefly. "By the way, Blu," Flavia spoke as they exited the conference room. "Do you want me to go ahead and replace Gail's name with Yelsi's on the tournament entry form?"

"She's onboard with us, so sure!" Blu answered. "I think we may have just found our ace in the hole!"

chapter 8

Kiwi's office was located on the opposite end of the floor from Blu's office. It wasn't as large but it was spacious enough for her and any guests to feel comfortable. And her love for decorating allowed her to add various pieces of furniture and art that reflected her own sense of style and taste.

She had chosen a tangerine shade as the color for her walls, which contrasted quite nicely with the burgundy leather sofa that was positioned adjacent from her desk. And, being on the backside of the building, her office windows provided an enthralling view of dense trees that towered like armed guards over the office complex.

Kiwi was alone in her office. It was after five o'clock. Her male executive assistant had already gone home. The other two women had given her a lot of flack for hiring the male executive assistant, but *Nathan Nichols* could hold his own. Not too many thirty-two year-old black men could boast a typing speed that was over *one hundred* words per minute. The brotha was very efficient. Not to mention handsome.

Besides, Kiwi originally had a *female* executive assistant but after only three months on the job, she had to let that trifling heifer go. The sista had a serious attitude problem.

Kiwi didn't understand why some women chose to sista-hate. If she had her choice the entire agency would be employed with all *males.* It was a good thing that everything was copacetic with Blu and Flavia, otherwise she'd have to consider flying solo in this whole ad agency business. Attitudes were something that she just didn't have time to fool around with. Especially when they came from another sista.

The telephone rang. After hours, the receptionist would program the telephone system so that all calls could ring directly into each office.

"Kiwi Shepherd," she answered.

"Hello there."

Her heart warmed immediately. It was *him.* "Hi," she greeted, a wide grin forming across her face. "You must be missing me?"

"No doubt about it. Say, I was on my way to the house and I wondered if you wanted me to pick up anything for dinner?"

"That is so thoughtful of you! But I'm really not sure

what time I'm going to be done here."

"So are you saying that I gotta eat all alone?" he teased.

Kiwi began to twirl a strand of her hair as she leaned back in her chair. "Well, you can always *wait* for me."

He thought for a moment. "But what if your man is starving?"

"Well, then I guess I'll just have to make it *worth* my man's wait," she said, giggling.

He let out a lascivious laugh. "You drive a hard bargain, Miss Shepherd."

"Does that mean we have a deal?"

"How can I refuse? I guess I'll see you at home, where you can expect me to be waiting patiently for my *worth*."

The two of them burst into laughter. "You need to quit!" she told him.

"What can I say? You bring out the best in me!"

They continued the impromptu interlude a while longer. Kiwi had become so engrossed in her phone conversation that she failed to notice that Blu had since arrived at her opened door until Blu tapped lightly against the door.

Kiwi quickly brought the call to an end.

"Am I interrupting something?" Blu asked.

"No, girl. Come on in," Kiwi answered.

Blu stood in front of Kiwi's desk with her arms folded across her chest. "*Miss Thing*, your eyes are shining with pleasure! I assume that wasn't a client's call?"

Kiwi blushed. "Oh, I was just having a little fun."

"Well, Flavia told me that she thought you were seeing someone new. When do we get the pleasure of meeting this *Prince Charming*?"

Kiwi ran her fingers through her hair nervously. "In due time. I want to get this one right."

"Well, more power to you, *Miss Thing*. Anyway, I thought I'd drop by to discuss this issue with Yelsi."

Kiwi stood from her desk and walked over and closed her office door. She invited Blu to have a seat in one of the chairs that sat across from her desk. She took the chair opposite Blu and crossed one leg over the other. Blu couldn't help but notice Kiwi's fashionable shoes.

"Kiwi, those shoes are absolutely gorgeous! Where did you get them?"

Kiwi beamed with pride. "I snatched these up last month when I was at that conference in New York."

"Designer shoes?"

As if you have to ask, she wanted to say. "Of course. They're MANOLO BLAHNIK."

Blu stared at the shoes again. "Five hundred dollars I bet?"

"Six fifty, girlfriend." Kiwi corrected her.

"Well, I'm scared of you."

"Just keeping it real, Blu."

"Well, that's a little *too real* for me."

Kiwi fanned the air with her hand. "Yeah, right. Like I don't see *you* prancing around here in BURBERRY and PRADA!"

"Well, I suppose I do have my weaknesses. But *you!* Kiwi, sometimes I think you missed your true calling!"

"Like what?"

"A runway fashion model!"

"Oh no, honey. I don't think so! At least not at five feet, anyway."

Blu just shook her head. "Well, back to the issue at hand. What is your problem with Yelsi? I mean, has she done something to you? Or have you guys crossed paths before?"

Kiwi uncrossed her legs and sat up straighter in her chair. "Listen, Blu. It has nothing to do with whether or not *I* like her. I mean *we* barely know the girl, which is why I can't believe that you're moving so fast with her."

"What do mean by *fast*?"

"Blu, the girl just started working here today and already you're sharing sensitive company information."

"I hear what you're saying, Kiwi. But my instincts tell me that she's fine. You see how well she's adapted after just one day on the job. And she's perfectly qualified."

"Humph. I don't see how you can honestly say that when human resources tells me that you told them that it wasn't even necessary to do a background or reference check. Now Blu, what's up with that?"

Blu gave a sigh. "Kiwi, you know that every time we use that background agency it costs us a fee. I was simply trying to save a little money. Especially since I'd already made the decision to hire her. And I do have good instincts. After all, they were good when it came to *you*."

Blu was referring to when she first met Kiwi at an advertising seminar along with Flavia. All three women had an immediate camaraderie. They had talked about their desire to go into business for themselves. And while Kiwi had the least amount of experience within the ad agency business and practically no funds at all to invest, Blu was able to see her strengths as well as her potential. Blu even loaned Kiwi the majority of the money necessary for her to acquire her share of the agency.

Kiwi rolled her eyes. "Please do not compare me to Yelsi Nitram, okayyy?"

"I'm not comparing you. I was simply trying to get you to see the similarities in your situations."

"Blu, why can't you just follow the same procedures that we've followed for all the other employees and do the background and reference checks?"

Blu was growing exasperated. "Why are you so hung up on this, Kiwi? It's not as though she reports to you – she works for *me*!"

"No, she works for this ad agency! And therefore it concerns me."

Blu stood from the chair and began pacing around Kiwi's office, occasionally stopping to admire a piece of art as she tried to keep her emotions in check. "Did I hassle you when I didn't necessarily agree with you hiring Nathan Nichols?" Blu asked.

Kiwi got up from the side chair and took a seat behind her desk, plopping down with extra force. "As a matter of fact, Blu, you and Flavia certainly did hassle me," she responded.

"I did not! I simply expressed my opinions and then I left it alone. Now, maybe Flavia hassled you but I certainly didn't. And be that as it may, you *still* hired him. Why? Because it was *your* decision, not ours."

Kiwi allowed her eyes to close for a moment. Then she surrendered. What else could she do? Blu was the majority owner in the agency. "Fine, Blu. Just as long as you understand that I totally disagree with how you're handling this."

Blu was relieved that she didn't have to declare *mea culpa*. She trotted over and gave Kiwi a hug. "Stop worrying so much," she whispered into her ear. "We've got MerLex Motors to give us enough to worry about without expending time and energy on these petty matters, all right?"

Kiwi resented her use of the word *petty*, but she decided to ignore it. "Yeah, yeah. I guess you're right."

Long after Blu had departed from her office, Kiwi remained at her desk. She pulled her leather-bound address book from her desk drawer. There was no way in hell that she was going to allow some unknown twenty-five year-old to come into their business without so much as a reference check. Blu could choose to be blind as a bat if she wanted, but Kiwi was going to satisfy her curiosity. There was something strange about this Yelsi girl. Oh, she had a captivating smile, but she wasn't *all that*. And Kiwi wondered if behind that smile there was some sort of a hidden agenda.

She thumbed through the pages of her address book until she found her uncle's telephone number. She quickly dialed it. Denver was two hours behind Atlanta's time so she figured that he should still be in his office.

"Good afternoon, FLETCHER INVESTIGATIONS," answered his secretary in a surly voice.

"Hello. I'd like to speak with Benjamin Fletcher, please."

"Who's calling?"

"It's personal. I'm his niece."

"Wait a minute." The secretary placed her on hold before she could even utter a thank you.

What's with these attitudinal women?, she thought to herself. Less than a minute later her uncle's jubilant voice answered on the other end.

"Uncle Benny! How are you?" Kiwi greeted him.

"Well now, if it ain't my *Special K*!" He replied, referring to the nickname that he'd given Kiwi when she was just a little girl. She'd always been his favorite niece. Actually, she was his only niece. He had several nephews but only one niece. "I ain't talked to you in a good while! What you been up to?"

"Oh, I'm just trying to stay busy. Nothing new."

"Uh-huh. Well, from what I *heard* you damn-near own Atlanta!"

"Sorry unc, that's not me! But hey, I'm doing all right."

"Well now, that's good Special K. I always knew you would be livin' large one day. You always had that certain somethin' about you – that's the reason I started callin' you *Special K*!"

Kiwi allowed him to reminisce for a little bit longer before she addressed the reason for her call. "Uncle Benny, I need to hire you to check someone out," she told him, matter-of-factly.

"Uh-oh. You gettin' ready to get married or somethin'?"

Kiwi laughed. "No. Not yet anyway. It's someone that

our business is considering hiring and – "

He interrupted. "Special K, you ain't never hired me to check anyone out before, and from what I *heard* you got hundreds of people down there workin' for you."

Who in the hell was his source for information? "We don't employ *hundreds* of people, Uncle Benny. Around two hundred and twenty is all."

"Well, I ain't never checked any of 'em out."

"That's because we use a local firm that handles all our employment screenings. But this is a *special* situation, which is why I'm calling you. Now, I will pay your standard fee plus throw in a bonus if you can do it pretty quick."

Uncle Benny's eyebrows arched. "How quick we talkin'?"

"I'd prefer *yesterday*. But I can live with one or two weeks."

He scratched his head. "I think I can handle that. I mean, it's a simple background check, ain't it?"

"That's all it is," Kiwi assured him.

"Then your uncle is ready to go to work!"

Kiwi told him that she would fax all the necessary information to him first thing in the morning. She also told him that he was to communicate only with her about this request. He understood.

The call ended and Kiwi dialed the human resources

director's extension to make sure that she had left for the day.

When there was no answer she quickly made her way over to her office. She needed to get her hands on a copy of Yelsi Nitram's employee file. She hoped that Blu had *at least* made a file for the girl.

chapter 9

She noticed the red light on her answering machine flashing wildly as she walked into her two-bedroom condo. After leaving ADDISON JAMES & SHEPHERD, Yelsi decided to stop by the driving range and hit a few golf balls. She didn't live too far from the Golf Club at WindFair Estates, only a mile or two.

Trying to ignore the flashing red light that was obviously beckoning her to come over to the little machine and retrieve its messages, she kicked off her JEAN PAUL GAULTIER boots and allowed her trim body to sink into the comforting cushions of the sofa.

She'd had a busy first day at the office. But the job at ADDISON JAMES & SHEPHERD had been her goal since she first read about the ad agency in an issue of ADVERTISING AGE magazine three years ago. She held great admiration for what the three women were accomplishing.

Starting any type of business had to be difficult. And she realized that being a female probably didn't make things a whole lot easier – especially for African-American females. Yet Blu, Flavia and Kiwi seemed to be charting their own course. A very successful course at that. And it was doing her junior year at Wellesley College that she'd decided that she wanted to become a part of their pursuit.

Meeting the three women at the golf course last weekend had been purely coincidental. Yelsi had initially planned on putting together some type of a portfolio showcasing her skills and then arranging for a meeting with Blu Addison. But fate intervened and rendered her plan unnecessary.

Blu seemed so happy to meet her, like she was meeting a long lost sister for the first time. Of course, Yelsi also felt an immediate bond with Blu, which is why she had no qualms about taking the position of an *executive assistant*, even though her intentions had been for a much higher role at the agency.

Yelsi was also impressed by the diversity of employees at ADDISON JAMES & SHEPHERD. While the women outnumbered the men, it was still an eclectic group of young and old. And not just African-Americans, but there were also Asians, Hispanics and Caucasians. She was more than thrilled to be included. Everyone welcomed her with open arms. Kiwi Shepherd, however, seemed to be reserving her welcome for another time, for whatever reason.

Yelsi did a quick review of her mail, which consisted of a handful of envelopes containing a couple of utility bills, her COSMOPOLITAN magazine subscription bill, and three different credit card offers.

Yelsi was debt free and she wasn't interested in taking on any credit card debt any time soon. Although she did have a VISA which was used only for airline tickets, hotel reservations or car rentals. Her car had been bought and paid for in cash. There were no college loans since she had received a full scholarship to attend Wellesley. The monthly bills that she did receive were simply for utilities and the *small* mortgage payment on her condo.

Yelsi tossed the credit card offers into the trash without opening them. Then she made her way over to the answering machine, which was setting beside the telephone on a glass end table in her living room. She pressed the *message playback* button. Her father's insipid voice began to emanate from the recorder.

"Hello, darling. I just wanted to see how you were doing. I do hope all is well."

The speaking paused momentarily before resuming. *"Listen, darling. I know you're perhaps still upset with me, but we need to talk. I hope that you're not planning on avoiding my calls forever. I know that I've hurt you with my actions, and for that, I'm deeply sorry. I did not realize how inconsiderate I was behaving."*

Another pause.

"Darling, I really miss you. It's been several months since I've seen you. We cannot allow this rift to continue. We only have each other now. I need you, darling. And I hope that you need me. Please call me at home or at the office. I love you."

It was the only message on her machine. Yelsi rewound the tape and played it again. As she listened to the message a second time, she was powerless to stop the tears from forming.

Her vision began to blur from the uninvited fluid that invaded the sockets of her eyes. And what beautiful eyes they were. But not so because of what a person could look upon, but more so because of that which was unseen.

Behind those mesmerizing eyes of Yelsi Nitram lay an inner beauty that was incomparable and amazingly genuine. To see her shed a tear, regardless of the quantity, was nearly unbearable. It was a rare occasion for anyone to witness hurt or pain from this young woman.

Nevertheless, her father *had* hurt her. How dare he?

Less than one year after her mother's death three years ago, Yelsi's father began seeing another woman. A much younger woman. Somehow, he failed to realize just how much she needed him during her mother's absence. And yet, with his all-consuming business and new fling, she was left to handle her grief alone. She wasn't sure if the other woman was his way of dealing with his own pain, or if he simply didn't care. It was still no excuse for his behavior. She pleaded with him to be there for her. Especially since he'd always been the caring and supportive father to her growing up. She had always been able to depend on him for anything. She couldn't remember any particular instance where he'd let her down.

Now, the two of them hadn't seen or spoken to each other at all for the past ten months.

It was just before Thanksgiving Day last year when she learned that the woman her father was seeing would be moving in with him. He was sixty-nine years old! What was he thinking? It was that disturbing revelation that pushed Yelsi over the edge, in terms of her feelings towards her father. She could not believe that he would be so quick to disgrace her mother's memory. His behavior was nothing short of salacious and disrespectful.

Yelsi's mom had been unable to conceive children of her own. Her parents were in their forties when they decided to adopt her. Yelsi knew how much it pained her mother not being able to give her father a child of his own flesh and blood. But because they had such a strong marriage, they were able to work through it. They had always shown immense love toward one another.

When she learned that her father was seeing someone else so soon after her mother's passing, Yelsi was unable to shield her displeasure and resentment. Especially since she'd overheard him tell her mother during her last days that he would never be involved with another woman. That he wanted their memories together to remain in his heart forever.

Yelsi believed now that maybe her father had been seeing this other woman even *before* her mother died. It was an appalling thought, but it was her strong belief.

Her father even had the audacity to invite the woman to spend Thanksgiving with the two of them. In her anger Yelsi told her father that she wanted nothing more to do with him. And she'd made a point not to invite him to her graduation this past spring. He didn't attend.

Yelsi gave in to the mounting tears. She buried her head in one of the sofa pillows and sobbed almost uncontrollably. She missed her mother so very much. It was the loss of her mother that had caused her to begin thinking about her birth parents. It wasn't an area that she wanted to venture into because to do so would mean coming to terms with all the unanswered *why* questions. *Why did her parents give her up? Why did they choose not to even see her at birth? Why didn't they love her? Why didn't they care?* The questions burned so closely within her heart. And she wondered if the answers would forever remain aloof.

Perhaps the reason she spent so much of her time either on the golf course or on the driving range was to escape the emptiness she sometimes felt. Maybe the reason she was so giving to others was because she had such a deeper lacking. Golf forced her to concentrate on matters other than who she really was or where she'd come from.

She thoroughly enjoyed the peacefulness and the mesmerizing surroundings that could be found on so many of Atlanta's public and private golf courses. And while the Golf Club at WindFair Estates was considered her home course, she played many others in the area whenever she could. She also participated as a volunteer during the LPGA's *Chick-Fil-A Charity Championship* golf tournament that was held south of Atlanta each spring.

Yelsi walked into her powder room and yanked a KLEENEX tissue from the box and dried her eyes.

Her father was right about one thing. She couldn't avoid him forever. He was getting older in years, and God forbid, if something happened to him before she had an opportunity to make matters right she'd never forgive herself.

But *now* simply wasn't the time.

Especially with her new job. She didn't know how he would react if he found out that she'd taken a job somewhere else. He'd always wanted her to work with him. Standing beside him. Being groomed by him to one day take over the business.

But Yelsi was certain that that was the one career move she did not want to make. Just because she loved him and cared about him didn't mean that she wanted to stand in his shadows.

In the business world she didn't want to be looked upon as her father's daughter. Trying to succeed in *his* footsteps. Basking in *his* glory.

Yelsi was determined to make her own mark, not just in business but also in society. And she was hoping that her role at ADDISON JAMES & SHEPHERD would help her do just that.

Someway.

Somehow.

chapter 10

Trying to maintain focus on her boys' soccer match was like trying to stare directly into the sun without blinking. Yet, as Flavia sat on the aluminum bleachers at the local soccer field, she was doing her best to keep her head in the game.

Parker was supposed to be there as well but his flight from New York had been delayed. He phoned her earlier that day and told her that it was unlikely that he'd be back in time for the boys' game.

The difficulty in giving her full attention to her twins was due to her anxiety over her test results. The jury was still out. She'd given Dr. Jacobs her cell phone number and asked him to call her as soon as he knew something.

If she never took another medical exam in her life again it would be too soon. She didn't mind the CAT-scan as much as she did the *Upper GI*. Dr. Jacobs had explained that G-I stood for *gastrointestinal*. The procedure was basically a series of x-rays of the upper digestive system. The one particular thing that Flavia found disgusting was when she had to drink the *Barium*, which was a white, thick, milkshake-like liquid that, through its coating process, allowed for an enhanced view of the digestive system. Hours after the procedure she found herself constipated like crazy. Which, of course, the doctor had told her beforehand the Barium was likely to cause such a side effect.

If Dr. Jerry Jacobs knew precisely what it was he was looking for, he certainly was being tight lipped about it with her. Although, he did attempt to assure her that he should have all the results in by Friday. Monday at the latest. She was hoping he'd call her *today*. She did not want to have to go through the entire weekend waiting. Her nerves were already getting frazzled with each passing hour.

"Run Corey! Run!" Flavia yelled, as Corey attempted to chase down the soccer ball. Corbin was also in the game. Flavia thought the boys looked so handsome in their gold and black team uniforms.

Just as Corey caught up to the ball and prepared to give it a swift kick, in the direction of his team's scoring goal, two opposing team members also arrived and were attempting to steal the ball away from Corey. All three boys missed the ball completely, colliding with each other instead. The ball veered out of bounds and the referee blew the whistle as time had run out. The boys' team recorded their third straight loss. Although this game had been close. They only lost by one point. As all the soccer players headed toward the bleachers, the parents stood and clapped excitedly.

"Where's daddy?" Corbin asked, as he ran up to his mom.

"Can't you see he couldn't make it, mush brains!" said Corbin's twin brother, Corey.

And before Flavia could reprimand Corey, Corbin shouted, "mom! He called me mush brains!"

"Don't call your brother names, Corbin," she told him, giving him *the eye*. "You know better than that."

"But he called me a name during the game!" Corey whined.

"I did not!"

"You did too!"

Flavia quickly intervened. "Boys, that's enough! I suggest you both settle it now or there will be no video games when we get home."

The threat of 'no video games' never failed to be effective. The twins uttered a quick *'I'm sorry'* to each other as Flavia ushered them into the SUV. And surprisingly, they remained cordial the remainder of the way home.

As she drove the SUV into their garage, the boys

began to jump for joy in their seats when they saw their father's ACURA parked inside. "Daddy's home!" they shouted, hurrying to unbuckle their safety belts.

"Wait until I *stop* the car before removing your seatbelts!" Flavia had to remind them. Two clicks were heard as the boys snapped their safety belts into place again. "Thank you," Flavia said. Then she put the car in park and turned off the ignition. "*Now* you may unbuckle them."

Two hours later everyone had finished their dinner and Flavia was clearing the table when the telephone rang. The call was from Dr. Jacobs' office. His assistant was calling to set a time for her to meet with him on Monday. This was unacceptable to her. If he had the results pertaining to her medical tests then she wanted to know right away. Flavia told the assistant that she wanted to speak with the doctor. And while the assistant initially refused, citing that the doctor was seeing another patient, she acquiesced. But she told Flavia that she would have to hold on the line a few minutes. Flavia told her that she didn't mind.

Minutes later the doctor was on the phone.

"This is Dr. Jacobs," he answered.

Flavia repeated what she'd told his assistant.

"I can certainly appreciate your concern, Mrs. James. However, Monday would be the earliest that we could meet. I just received the final results back late this afternoon and I would like to have time to review them more closely over the weekend."

Flavia could detect some concern in his voice. "Well, can you at least give me an idea of what the tests found?"

He gave a heavy sigh. "I really do not like to handle a patient's medical matters over the telephone, Mrs. James. It's just so impersonal. Nevertheless, I can assure you that everything will be disclosed and discussed to your satisfaction on Monday."

Flavia had a bad feeling about all this. But what else could she do? "Okay. I guess I don't have a choice but to wait until Monday," she told the doctor.

"Good. Let me give you back to my assistant and she will schedule the time, okay?"

"Fine."

Seconds later the assistant was back on the phone. A time was scheduled for eleven o'clock on Monday.

She realized that she would have to cancel her *last Monday of the month* meeting with Blu and Kiwi. She hoped that they would understand because she wasn't going to be able to go into any details.

. . . .

Blu kept glancing at the FENDI watch that was strapped around her wrist. This was not how she planned on spending her Friday evening.

She was on the phone with her brother, Lance Knight. More than an hour had passed and he didn't seem to want to take 'no' for an answer.

"Lance, please listen to me for the umpteenth time!" she found herself begging him. "It's not that *I* don't have faith in you, but it's my *money* that doesn't have faith in your business ventures."

"Don't be that way, little sis," Lance said. "So I've had a few failures over the years . . ."

"A *few*?" Blu interjected. "Lance, when was the last time you had a job?"

"Sis, I've been trying to tell you that I just got laid off from my job, otherwise I'd still be working."

"No, Lance. I'm not talking about how you laid yourself off because that's just pure craziness. I'm talking about a real-life J-O-B."

"That's just plain cold, sis."

"I'm serious. Mom and dad did not raise any fools or bums, so why are you dead set on becoming one?"

"Why you being so hard on your brother, sis? I know you probably can't relate and all, but times are hard right now. The republicans control *Washington* and they control the economy."

Oh, don't even go there!" she scolded him. "It's not going to help you to score any points with me by blaming somebody else for your problems."

Lance was silent for a moment. "Well, all I know is that every time I take *one* step forward I end up having to take *three* steps back. Sometimes more."

"Maybe the problem isn't in the steps you're taking, Lance. Maybe the problem has to do with the paths that you keep taking those steps on."

"Sis, I know I've made my share of mistakes. But that don't mean that I should just quit! Give up. If momma and daddy taught us anything, it was to always keep trying."

So he did retain something their parents had taught him. "Lance, I'm not telling you to give up. But you might want to reassess your situation. Maybe it's not meant for you to be self-employed. If you were to take all your energy from these failed business ventures and put it into . . . I don't know, maybe working for someone else you'd probably find a little more success."

Lance grew agitated. "Hey! I'm not going to become a slave for *the man*! Ain't no way! I'm not punching somebody's damn clock every day! That ain't me!"

One of her long curly strands fell across her eye. She blew it aside. "I'm sorry you feel that way, Lance. But I simply can't invest in any more of your businesses."

"You *can't* or you *won't*?"

"Both."

"I don't believe you! You own a multimillion dollar advertising agency and you won't even lend your brother, your flesh and blood, a lousy five thousand dollars!"

"Lance, I have given you over *twenty* thousand dollars over the last three years! Now, you tell me what do I have to show for that investment? Huh?"

Lance remained silent.

"Better yet, tell me what do *you* have to show for it?"

His anger began to swell. "I tell you what, sis. Why don't you do us both a favor and just go to hell!"

She heard the phone click on the other end.

He had a lot of nerve, she thought. It was time that he stopped using her and their mother as a safety net. The man was forty-eight years old! Time for him to grow up and take some personal responsibility for his actions, or lack thereof. He was not going to make her feel guilty for the successes that she had achieved. They both grew up in the same house with the same parents, and they both had the same educational opportunities. Lance had graduated from college with a degree in management. The man was not dumb by any stretch of the imagination. It was his misguided efforts to latch onto the next get-rich-quick scheme that had become his nemesis.

Blu decided that she wasn't going to allow her brother's attitude to get to her. She had enough drama in her life right now with her husband. She certainly didn't need Lance Knight throwing his asinine theatrics at her.

A few minutes later, she attempted to reach Damien on his cell phone. He wasn't answering it. His attitude was also beginning to get on her last nerve. She didn't know how much more of this she could take. She thought about phoning Flavia. She needed to talk to *somebody*. And Flavia seemed to have her head on straight these days, now that she'd become a Christian. Maybe Flavia could spread some much-needed encouragement to her.

Blu didn't go to church or read her Bible with any regularity, but she always considered herself to be a *good* person. She *believed* in God. She was aware that He created the entire world. In a very short period of time, too. The exact number of days was escaping her memory at the moment, but she knew it took him no time at all to do it. Less than a month probably.

In fact, she realized that she couldn't even take all the credit for her successes in life. Nobody was *that good*. There definitely had been some divine intervention. His blessings were evident throughout her life. And she was grateful.

Maybe one day she'd find the time to attend church. Flavia certainly had extended numerous invitations to both her and Kiwi to come and visit her congregation. But since the last time that she could remember going to church was when she was a little girl, she felt a little uncomfortable walking into any church building after such a long absence. It was crazy thinking, but Blu wondered if God would give her some kind of a detention. Or, simply stop her at the door and told her that her presence wasn't necessary. That she could go back to sleeping in on Sunday mornings. Catch up on all those novels that were piling up near her bed.

God wasn't like that, she thought to herself. God forgave people. Plenty of people. People that got angry. People that lied. People that hated other people. People that killed. People that made mistakes when they were too young to understand the mistakes. People like her.

Perhaps it was her distance from God that had made it nearly impossible for her to deal with her past. A past that just might have cost her a future with her husband.

chapter 11

Most of the leaves on the trees around Atlanta were still as green as the grass that blanketed the yards within WindFair Estates. The month of September was coming to a close. The temperatures over the past month had been mild during the day and comfortable at night. However, not quite cool enough to set flames aglow in the fireplace.

Kiwi had just gotten off the telephone with Flavia on this lazy Sunday morning. Flavia informed her that she would be out of the office tomorrow and would not be able to make their end of the month luncheon. She told Kiwi that she had some personal business to attend to at home. And Flavia was glad that Kiwi didn't press her for more information. Earlier she had called Blu, who did not answer, so Flavia left a message on her voice mail.

Kiwi was lying on the floor in the den with the ATLANTA JOURNAL-CONSTITUTION sprawled before her. "I sure hope that the *Falcon's* mediocre start is not an indication of how their entire football season is gonna turn out," she commented to her *man* as she perused the sports section of the newspaper.

Her man was sitting at the kitchen table sipping a glass of orange juice while he worked his way through some files that lay scattered across the table. He didn't usually bring work home from the office, but he was working on a special project and the hours that he was putting in this weekend couldn't be helped.

"I don't think *Vick* has had time to settle in yet," he responded, without lifting his eyes from the files. "But once he does, the *NFC South* division better look out!"

"Yeah, the boy is bad!" said Kiwi. "What he needs, though, is some help from that offensive line. I mean, in last week's game their blocking was whacked-out!"

"Uh-huh," her man said. Then he glanced up from the files and noticed Kiwi lying on the floor. "Hey, sweetie. Is it all right for you to be down on the floor like that?"

She looked up at him and smiled. "Yeah. Lying on the floor won't hurt the *baby*."

The day after *Labor Day* Kiwi had found out that she was four weeks pregnant. At first she was hesitant about revealing it to her man. After all, they'd only been seeing each other for a couple of months at that point. Then she realized that she didn't want to start the relationship off with secrets. So she told him that same day.

His response to the news surprised her. She could not believe how excited he was. The way he screamed into the phone you would've thought that he'd just won the *Mega Millions* lottery. His unexpected response put her at total ease. She couldn't have loved him more at that moment.

Blu and Flavia knew nothing about the pregnancy. She would tell them in due time. Her relationship with her new man was a delicate one.

He left the kitchen and strolled into the den and kneeled beside her. "I just want to make sure you stay healthy," he said.

Kiwi sat up and gave him a kiss on the lips. "I wouldn't do anything to jeopardize the baby or myself," she assured him.

"Good. Because even though we haven't been together that long, I don't know how I would be able to handle it if anything happened to you or our baby."

"Nothing is gonna happen to us."

He returned a kiss to her on the cheek. "Hey, what about you playing golf? Did the doctor give you the okay on that?"

"Yep. Sure did. Said that it was good exercise. And besides, you should've seen *Pat Hurst* out there on tour playing while she was pregnant!"

"Pat who?"

"She plays on the *LPGA* tour – something I'm sure you never watch."

"Nope. I only watch my man *Tiger Woods*!"

"Well, the ladies are just as good."

"Oh, I have no doubt that they are! But, they can't roar like the Tiger!"

"Well, if you're trying to say that a woman golfer can't compete with a man, then I will gladly challenge your sorry butt to a round, *Mr. Big Mouth*?"

He chuckled at her challenge.

"What's so funny? I'm serious."

"What's your handicap?" he asked.

"What's yours?" she countered.

"Right now, I'll say it's about a *three* – give or take a point."

"Yeah, right! When we played together just before the Fourth of July you couldn't even break a hundred!"

"Hey, I just didn't want to show off. I mean, it was our first time playing together and I didn't want you to feel intimidated."

"You are such a liar! I kicked your butt and you know it!"

He still refused to admit defeat. "I guess we'll just have

to let our clubs do all the talking," he said.

"Fine. Name the date, time and place."

"Well, uh, as you know, we're getting ready to enter into the fourth quarter, and well, you know – work at the office might keep a brotha chained to his desk."

"Oh, don't even try it!"

He then wrapped his arms around her waist and attempted to nibble on her ear as their two bodies fell gently to the carpeted floor.

. . . .

Blu had invited Yelsi over to her house for Sunday brunch. She was enjoying her assistant's company as they sat on the patio discussing everything from advertising to their love for seventies pop songs.

"You were probably not born until the late seventies," Blu said to her. "How did you come to love the music so much?

"Nineteen seventy-seven to be exact," said Yelsi, referring to the year in which she was born. "But the music is still popular today," she continued. "I don't know. There's just something special about the *sound* and the *lyrics*. And for me, the lyrics are always important in any song that I like."

"Is that because you told me you enjoy writing?"

Yelsi smiled. "Yes. But I mostly write poems, though."

"Have you ever thought about copywriting?"

"Yes, I have. But you see, from an advertising standpoint, I want to be involved in the entire creative process, not just one aspect of it."

"I see. So, tell me what are some of your favorite tunes from the seventies?"

Yelsi thought for a moment. "Well, my mom liked *Carly Simon* a lot, so I grew up listening to *'Haven't Got Time For The Pain'* over and over."

"Carly Simon is good."

Yelsi thought some more.

Blu interrupted her thinking. "Tell you what, I'm going to give you a lyric from a *seventies* song and you see if you can guess either the song title, artist or both, all right?"

"You're giving me a test?"

"Not a test – just a little game. For fun!"

"Oh boy. Now I'm nervous."

"Well, it's not that serious. In fact, after I give you one you can give me one as well."

Yelsi allowed herself to relax. "Okay, I'm ready."

Blu closed her eyes as she tried to think of a seventies song. "All right, guess the song to this lyric – *I'd rather live in his world than live without him in mine*?"

"Oh, that's so easy!" Yelsi screamed. "That's from Gladys Knight and the Pips' *Midnight Train To Georgia*!"

"That's correct. Well, now here's a harder one. Guess

the song to this lyric – *Let me drown in your laughter, let me die in your arms*?"

Without hesitating Yelsi answered, "John Denver's *Annie's Song*!"

Blu was surprised. "Well, I'm scared of you!"

Yelsi chuckled. "Okay, I have one for you."

"Bring it on, missy!"

"Guess the song to this lyric – *I can't remember if I cried, when I read about his widowed bride*?"

Blu began to think hard. "It *is* a *seventies* song, right?"

"Yes, it is."

Yelsi began to sing the lyric to the tune of the song to try and help Blu out.

"It sounds so familiar! But my mind is going blank!"

"Give up?"

"Oh, all right. I give!"

"It was from Don McLean's *American Pie*!"

"Hey, that song was from the *sixties*!" protested Blu.

"Noooo, I don't think so!"

"Yes it was! You cheated!"

Yelsi broke into a huge laughter. "I did not! That *was* a seventies song! I swear!"

"All right, young lady. I'll accept defeat for now, but I'm going to check this out," Blu said as she fanned the air in a peremptory gesture.

"Check it out then! It's a song from the seventies!"

"Mm-mm. Hey, I'm going to get something else to drink, can I get you anything besides more water?" she asked Yelsi.

"Um, do you have any ginger ale?"

"I do. But it's raspberry ginger ale."

"I'll take it."

Blu disappeared into the house and returned moments later with another mimosa for herself and a raspberry ginger ale for Yelsi.

"By the way, I also like Hip-Hop," Yelsi remarked as she popped the top on the ginger ale's can. "But you know, one of my absolute favorite song has always been Janis Ian's hit, *'At Seventeen'*. There's so much truth in those lyrics."

Her remark caught Blu by surprise. She remembered this song quite well. Although she was more like fifteen or sixteen when the song first held significance for her.

Yelsi continued. "When I was in high school, I met a seventeen year-old girl who had just transferred to our high school her senior year. She didn't seem to fit in that well. I mean a lot of the other girls picked on her. And just like in the song, this girl wore hand-me-downs, and she never had a boyfriend. I guess she was considered an outcast."

Blu could feel the lump rising in her throat. "Were you friends with her?"

"Sort of. I mean I wasn't rude to her or anything like that. And I would speak to her. I guess I felt sorry for her. She seemed like a really nice girl. But she kept to herself a lot."

"Whatever happened to her?"

Yelsi hesitated a moment. "Well, one month before our high school graduation she committed suicide. It hit me so hard. If only I had gotten to know her . . ." Yelsi's voice trailed off.

Little did she know the song had been a very poignant one for Blu as well. The memories surfaced so quickly for Blu that she felt a sudden rush of emotions. "Excuse me for a moment," she told Yelsi as she made a hurried disappearance into the house. She ran into the downstairs powder room and shut the door. The mere mention of that song caused Blu to recall her own teenage angst.

Back in the late seventies, growing up in Muncie, Indiana, Blu had very few friends. Most of the black students at the public high school that she attended had been bussed there from their predominantly black neighborhoods. And practically every one of the black girls thought that she was stuck up simply because she lived in a mostly white neighborhood. And she never really felt that she fit in with the handful of white girls that she did associate with.

But Blu did have one true friend. It was a boy named *Schuyler Conklin*. His parents had moved to Muncie from

Toronto, Canada during the middle of Blu's freshman year in high school. Schuyler kept to himself most of the time. He wasn't into athletics, and he was a bit scrawny. But Blu considered him to be the nicest boy that she'd ever met.

Before long they'd become good friends. She learned that Schuyler was half Dutch and half Chinese. Blu thought he was quite handsome. His hair was dark brown and it covered his ears.

She remembered Schuyler to be the first person to ever write her a poem. Not just any poem. A *love* poem. No one else has ever done so since.

By the time they had entered their sophomore year they'd decided to become a couple. Of course, they kept the decision between themselves. Her parents had already told her that she couldn't date boys until she was seventeen. She was fifteen at the time and he was sixteen.

Blu dried her eyes as she recalled those years. She didn't' think that she'd ever loved anyone more than she loved Schuyler Conklin. Not Damien Addison, not anyone.

A knock at the bathroom's door ended her thoughts.

"Are you okay, Blu?" came Yelsi's voice from the other side of the door.

Blu quickly grabbed some tissue and dabbed her eyes dry. "Yes, I'm fine. I'll be right out," she answered.

A couple of minutes later she rejoined Yelsi on the

patio. "Sorry," she apologized as she sat back down at the table. "Something must have gotten into my eye," she lied. She didn't want her newly hired assistant to see her crying.

"Were you able to get it out?"

"Yes. A piece of dust is all it was."

The two women chatted some more. Although Blu attempted to steer the conversation toward subjects that were a little less reminiscing and less emotional.

"By the way," Yelsi said as she suddenly remembered something. "I have a card for you in my car."

"Really?"

"Yes. It's just a sort of *thank you* for all that you've done. I'll go get it." Yelsi scampered around the house to the driveway where her urban green BMW Z4 ROADSTER was parked. She pointed her key ring at the sports car. The lights flashed quickly and the horn emitted two beeps, signaling that the doors to the car had been unlocked. She reached inside and retrieved the red envelope containing the card. She returned to the patio.

"Here," she said, handing the envelope to Blu. "I hope you don't mind, but I wrote a little poem for you."

Blu accepted the card with gratitude. "That's very sweet of you, Yelsi. But you didn't have to."

"I know. I wanted to, though."

Blu pulled the card from the envelope and opened it.

Yelsi had written, with a calligraphy pen, a poem simply entitled *A Poem For Blu*. She began to read it.

A chance meeting
  Or was it divine fate
That allowed our paths to cross
  And a new friendship to mate

My years are young
  And my knowledge is growing
Everyday I'm understanding the
  Difference between reaping and sowing

I've seen many smiles
  That usually ends only as grins
But yours I know to be genuine
  Because now we are friends

Thanks for opening your heart
  To someone unknown as me
I am forever grateful for
  All your kindness and sincerity

Blu fought back her tears. They seemed to be attacking her with a vengeance lately. "This is a beautiful poem. Thank you so much." She stood from the table and gave Yelsi a heartfelt hug.

"You're welcome."

Blu thought about how wonderful it might have been growing up as a teen together with Yelsi. The young woman was exactly the sort of person that she would have loved to have had as a friend. She'd never met anyone before whom she felt so comfortable being around.

Yelsi's father had to be very proud of his daughter.

Blu found her to be an absolute joy to have around. Aside from the superb job that she was doing as her executive assistant, she was also providing her with some much-needed company. Something that she didn't think she'd ever enjoy again with her husband.

chapter 12

Within the space of one hour their agency had lost two clients, representing a total of $30 million in annual billings. The larger of the two losses materializing in the form of a national bookstore chain which billed $20 million per year; and the lesser being $10 million from a local financial institution. It was not how ADDISON JAMES & SHEPHERD would have preferred to start the week.

Blu was impatiently awaiting Kiwi and her account management team to assemble in her office for an emergency meeting on the matter. She'd also tried calling Flavia at home and on her cell phone, but to no avail. She'd gotten Flavia's message over the weekend indicating that she would not be in the office today. But Blu needed her here. Personal errands would simply have to wait.

Ten minutes later Yelsi was announcing to Blu the arrival of Kiwi, two female *management supervisors* for both accounts, and their respective *account executives* – one male, one female.

"Good morning, everyone," Blu greeted them as they entered her office. "Please have a sit anywhere you like."

Once the team had made themselves comfortable, Blu began with Kiwi. "All right, what's going on?"

"Well, first let me say that I am just as surprised as you are. We had no indication whatsoever that these two clients were planning to jump ship."

One of the management supervisors spoke, "As a matter of fact, I just had a conference call with *BooksAmerica* last week."

"And what was the nature of the call?" Blu asked her.

"We were discussing the final plans for their Christmas campaign. They were actually expected to sign off on the plans over the weekend and have everything back to us by tomorrow."

"Well, they *signed off* all right," remarked Kiwi.

"Apparently there appears to have been some *behind the scenes* shenanigans going on," stated Blu firmly.

Everyone nodded in agreement.

"Kiwi, you said that no review is going to be held for either account?" Blu inquired.

Kiwi shook her head 'no'. "Both clients say that they have made their decision. Basically, we have ninety days to wrap-up any works in progress before turning over the accounts."

"Which agencies are the accounts moving to?" Blu was curious.

The same female management supervisor, who had commented earlier, spoke again. "Actually, it's more like *'agency'* – singular."

"Excuse me?"

"Both accounts were awarded to MARTIN/McFINLEY," she continued.

Blu was shocked at this bit of news. "You've got to be kidding!"

Kiwi nodded in agreement. "Looks like old man Leland has drawn the battle lines."

"Is this how he plans on winning MerLex Motors? By stealing our other accounts?"

Kiwi answered her. "Maybe he thinks that these losses will be enough for us to lose focus on the bigger picture."

The second female of the two management supervisors spoke. "Check this out – from my conversation this morning with *BooksAmerica*, I'm told that the campaign strategy that MARTIN/McFINLEY proposed to them is in line with what they were looking for."

"And what campaign strategy was that?" asked Blu.

"Advertising that could be integrated with a tie-in

promotion that would include a different best-selling author each month."

Blu absorbed the reply. "Wait a minute! Isn't that's what we were going to propose during next month's meeting?"

"You got it!" replied Kiwi.

"So they beat us to the punch, huh?"

Kiwi snickered. "Humph. That's not how I see it."

"Meaning what, Kiwi?" Blu asked.

"Well, from what we've learned so far, MARTIN/McFINLEY's proposal was practically *word for word* what we'd come up with. Now, that's a little too much for coincidence. And as far as *CapTrust* is concerned, MARTIN/McFINLEY has been wooing them ever since we won the account two years ago. I wouldn't be surprise if they got a little *inside* help on these losses."

"Inside help? What are you insinuating, Kiwi?"

She rolled her eyes. "We can discuss it later."

"No! If there is something pertaining to this agency's clients that you feel you need to share, then now is the time."

"Fine." She took a deep breath before venturing into the uncharted waters. "*Who* is it that you have given total access to files as well as other agency information recently?"

Blu realized where she was heading and quickly decided to cut her off at the pass. "Oh, give it a rest, Kiwi!"

"I'm serious, Blu. I don't believe that these sudden client losses are a coincidence."

Blu made it a point to excuse the other members from the meeting. She wanted to hash this out with Kiwi in private. Once the others had left her office she ripped into Kiwi. "How dare you sit your behind here in my office and insult not only my intelligence, but my assistant – whom I consider to be a very good friend!"

"*Friend*?" Kiwi repeated, astonished that the two of them had become so chummy so soon. "Blu, you just met the girl a little over a week ago! And yet it seems that you've given her the keys to *Fort Knox*!"

"Just listen at how ridiculous your accusation sounds!"

She paused for effect.

"You expect me to believe that in *one week*, Yelsi Nitram has been able to land herself a job at this agency, befriend me, steal client information from us, which by the way she doesn't have access to, and then sell that so-called information to MARTIN/McFINLEY? And within that *same* week, MARTIN/McFINLEY has had *enough time* to put together a proposal and *then convince* our clients to allow them time to present such proposal, thereby affording them the opportunity to yank the account from us and give it to them?"

Kiwi didn't respond, choosing instead to stare at the floor, twirling a strand of her cranberry hair.

"It's not only ridiculous, Kiwi, but it's also totally absurd!"

"Well, I guess we're looking at it from two different sides."

Blu glared at her. "Kiwi, I'm going to say this in the most polite way possible, so try not to get offended – but if you do, then so be it."

Kiwi's eyes began their trademark roll again.

Blu continued. "If you even as so much breathe another negative word about Yelsi to me, then I assure you that you and I are going to have some serious problems."

Kiwi was stunned. "Are you threatening me, Blu?"

"Call it whatever you like! But I know this; your apparent hostility where Yelsi is concerned isn't going to be tolerated any longer. So I highly suggest that you find a way to either *deal* with the attitude or *lose* it altogether."

Kiwi attempted to shield her hurt feelings. She couldn't recall a moment where Blu had spoken to her in this way. Like she was nothing. Nobody. "You and I have always been close, Blu. But I guess since your new friend has come along, it seems like you're all-too-willing to kick me to the curb now. I mean, you're sitting here talking to me like I'm a child or something."

Blu hesitated slightly before responding. "It's not my intention to treat you like a child, Kiwi. But apparently you're not aware of how you're behaving."

"I'm fully aware that you're allowing this girl to come between us!"

"Kiwi, Yelsi is not coming between us. Tell me, is that what all this is really about?"

"What?"

"Jealousy."

"I am not at all jealous of that girl!" Kiwi shot back. "Puh-leeze!"

"I wish you would stop referring to her as a *'girl'*. She's *twenty-five* years old. That's a *woman* in my book."

"Whatever."

Blu folded her hands in her lap and allowed her head to drop for a moment as she contemplated the situation. "Listen, Kiwi. If this does have anything to do with jealousy, then I understand how you might feel that way. I mean, now that I think about it, I recall that not so long ago you were a young twenty-something woman whom I'd taken under my wings. You didn't have a lot of experience in this business, but I saw your potential. And yes, we became more than business partners but best friends as a result."

Kiwi kept her gaze away from Blu. She realized that there was some truth in what Blu was saying. But she was not *jealous* of Yelsi.

"I treasure our friendship. I enjoy hanging out with you.

Although *lately* you've been a little *preoccupied*," Blu teased, referring to the new man in her life.

Kiwi couldn't contain a grin. "Well, what can I say?"

"Just say that you'll give Yelsi a break, okay? Cut her some slack and give her the benefit of doubt."

She'd give her the benefit of doubt when she got her uncle's investigative report back, Kiwi thought. "I guess I've got a lot of things going on right now. Maybe it's all making me a little cranky."

"Anything you care to discuss? With a *friend*?"

"Thanks, Blu. But I can't get into it right now."

"Well, you know that I'm always here if you need me."

"Yeah, I know."

The two of them embraced. "All right. I guess there's nothing more we can do about the account losses," Blu said.

"No. But I'm going to begin shoring things up with all the other clients. Who knows where Leland Martin is snooping around. We can't afford any more surprises," said Kiwi.

"Ain't that the truth," replied Blu. Although, she was thinking more about her personal life than the business. Damien had sprung on her a surprise that could last a lifetime. She certainly didn't need any more.

chapter 13

Despite a mountain of case files on his desk, a maxed-out voice mailbox, and enough email messages to possibly fill the GEORGIA DOME, Parker James took the day off from work. Senior law partner or not, he was committed to accompanying his wife to her meeting with Dr. Jerry Jacobs.

The Gastroenterologist's office was located within a recently constructed, three-story medical office building. And since the office was very close to their subdivision, they both were relieved that they did not have to travel on *Georgia Highway 400* this morning.

Upon their arrival, Flavia checked in at the front desk, showing her HMO identification card, and signing her name to the clipboard that lay on the counter. Within minutes they were being escorted by one of Dr. Jacobs' assistants to a small conference area. It was a windowless room. Inside, a round, shiny conference table, made of mahogany wood, with six burgundy chairs positioned around it, stood in the center.

As Parker and Flavia entered, they noticed three people already seated around the table. Dr. Jacobs, Flavia's personal physician, Dr. Laura Levinson, and another individual who was unbeknownst to them. He was an older man with a head full of wispy gray hair.

"Good morning," Dr. Jacobs said as he invited Parker and Flavia to have a seat.

Everyone exchanged greetings.

"First, allow me to introduce you to another specialist," he began, pointing at the unfamiliar gentleman sitting to his right. "This is *Doctor Tyler Matthews.*"

Dr. Matthews stood from his chair and reached across the table to shake the hands of Parker and Flavia.

"Dr. Matthews is an *Oncologist*," Dr. Jacobs added.

Immediately, Flavia felt her body stiffened. She'd been holding Parker's hand beneath the table. Her grip tightened considerably.

"Are you familiar with the work of an Oncologist?" Dr. Jacobs asked them.

Of course they both knew that such a doctor specialized in the treatment of cancer. They nodded their heads 'yes'.

"Well, along with your personal physician, Dr. Levinson, I've asked Dr. Matthews to join us."

Flavia's heart was pounding so rapidly that she thought she would pass out at any given moment. The entire room seemed to be spinning around her. She would have preferred to be any place other than here, right now. *Lord please, don't let the news be as bad as it appears it's going to be.*

"Mrs. James, I don't quite know of any other way to say this . . . " Dr. Jacobs seemed to be having as difficult of a time saying the words as she was preparing herself to hear them. "Your test results indicate that you have a tumor in the pancreas."

Flavia couldn't move. She couldn't speak. Her gaze was fixed directly onto Dr. Jacobs. The words from his mouth kept penetrating her ears over and over, seeming to get louder each time – *you have a tumor. You Have A Tumor. YOU HAVE A TUMOR*!

Parker was the first to speak after the cutting words had been delivered. "Is it cancerous?"

Dr. Matthews spoke. "Unfortunately, we believe that it is. However, the only sure way to know is by doing a *biopsy*."

"How certain are you that it's a tumor?" Parker asked.

Dr. Jacobs and Dr. Matthews glanced at one another. "We're fairly certain," answered Dr. Matthews. "In fact, it appears that the growth of it is quite advanced."

Flavia finally broke down in tears. She buried her face

within her husband's embrace. Dr. Levinson stood from her chair and walked over to Flavia and Parker and attempted to console them both.

The conference room was quiet for several minutes. Only the soft sobs from Flavia were audible. Although Parker had quite a task trying to control his own emotions.

The doctors were being very patient while they allowed the terrible news to settle in. This wasn't the first time that they've had to make such an unsettling revelation to a patient. In fact, approximately *thirty thousand* Americans developed pancreatic cancer each year. And unfortunately, more than *ninety-eight* percent died from it.

Dr. Matthews spoke, "if it is agreeable with the two of you, what I'd like to do is take a moment and explain the pancreas, and then proceed from there."

Parker and Flavia nodded. Dr. Levinson was now seated next to Flavia on the opposite side from Parker.

Dr. Matthews pulled a small colored laminated chart from a file. The chart displayed a full internal view of the human body. Using his silver CROSS pen, he pointed to the pancreas. "This is the pancreas. It is a six-inch long, pear-shaped gland that lies behind the stomach. It has two main functions within the body. One, to produce juices that facilitate the digesting, or break down, of food. And secondly, to produce hormones, such as *insulin* and *glucagon*, which helps to control blood sugar levels. Now, the digestive juices are produced by something referred to as *exocrine* pancreas cells, while the *endocrine* pancreas cells produce the hormones. Approximately ninety-five percent of pancreatic cancers begin in the *exocrine* cells."

He paused, as he watched Parker and Flavia study the chart. "Mrs. James, it is within the exocrine cells that your tumor appears to have begun."

Flavia retrieved a tissue from her purse and gently wiped her eyes. "You said earlier, Dr. Matthews, that the only way to know for sure if the tumor is cancerous is by doing a biopsy?"

"That's correct, Mrs. James."

"Yet you are already referring to it as *pancreatic cancer*?"

"Let me explain. Right now, as a result of your *Upper GI* exam and the *CT-scan*, we are reasonably certain that we're dealing with pancreatic cancer. Of course, the biopsy will allow us to be definitive. Thus, for all intents and purposes, at least until we get the biopsy completed, I'm approaching this from the standpoint that cancer is what we're facing. And believe me, Mrs. James, there's nothing I'd prefer more than to be proven wrong in this particular case. However, I must say that it is more *likely* than *not* that the tumor is cancerous."

"I would have to agree with Dr. Matthews," Dr. Jacobs added.

"Well, if it is pancreatic cancer, is it curable?" Parker asked.

Dr. Matthews gave a sigh. "That all depends on which particular stage the cancer is in." He went on to explain the four stages of the disease. "In *stage one*, the cancer is found in the pancreas only. In *stage two*, the cancer has spread to nearby tissue and organs, such as bile ducts or the small intestine. In *stage three*, the cancer has spread to lymph nodes near the pancreas and might possibly have spread to nearby tissue and organs. And in *stage four*, the cancer has spread to other parts of the body. Now, stage four is separated into two parts – *stage four A* and *stage four B*, depending on where the cançer has spread. Do you both follow me so far?"

They nodded in agreement.

"If we're dealing with *stage four A*, it means that the cancer has spread to organs and tissues that are near the pancreas, such as the stomach, spleen or colon, but it has not yet spread to distant organs, such as the lungs. If it is *stage four B* we're facing, then the cancer has spread to distant organs, and it may also have spread to organs and tissues near the pancreas or even to lymph nodes."

"Then I guess maybe we shouldn't speculate about

options until we know exactly what stage, if any stage at all, we're actually in," remarked Flavia.

"That's a very good point, Mrs. James," replied Dr. Matthews. "Are you available for a biopsy tomorrow?"

"Well, what does a biopsy involve?"

"In this situation we would perform what we refer to as an *F-N-A* biopsy. Now, FNA simply means *fine need aspiration*. That is, we would insert a thin needle through the skin, and utilizing a CT-scan, the needle would be guided into the tumor, which would allow us to remove a small sample of tissue. We would then be able to examine this tissue under a microscope. An FNA is the most commonly used biopsy in this type of situation."

Flavia thought for a moment. "What about getting a second opinion?" she asked.

Dr. Matthews answered. "You are certainly welcome to do that, Mrs. James. And, I would even recommend that you do so. However, time is of the essence."

"This is just so much to take in," she commented, to no one in particular.

"I totally understand," said Dr. Matthews. "However, based on your test results, I must say that we are perhaps dealing with a mid to late stage diagnosis."

Flavia took a deep breath. She felt like her entire world had come crashing down around her. "Where do I go for the biopsy?"

"It would be handled at NorthView General."

"How long will it take?"

"The procedure itself generally takes no more than ten to fifteen minutes."

"How long before I know the results?"

"Generally, around thirty-six hours. Maybe sooner."

Flavia glanced at her husband. "We have to know, sweetheart," he said to her.

"Fine. Let's schedule it for tomorrow."

Dr. Matthews took a moment to complete the necessary paperwork. He also went ahead and scheduled another meeting with Flavia and Parker for Friday morning at his office, which was located next door to the hospital.

Dr. Levinson informed Flavia that her schedule would not permit her to be there on Friday, but she assured her friend that she'd follow-up with a phone call. Dr. Jacobs said that he would be in attendance.

When Parker and Flavia returned to their house, she collapsed into his arms and cried like she'd never cried before. "It's all going to work out fine, sweetheart," he tried to console her. But inside, Parker himself was devastated. Although he knew that Flavia was a strong woman, he realized that something like this would ultimately test the resolve of even the strongest of beings.

chapter 14

Blu had just finished a phone call with Flavia. Flavia informed her that she was going be away from the office for the remainder of the week. Although she said that she would try and handle some responsibilities from home.

It was Flavia's quavering voice that caused Blu some concern. And when asked if she was feeling okay, Flavia assured Blu that she was fine. She told Blu that she was just having some flu-like symptoms and that her doctor had advised her to get some much needed rest for a few days. Blu wasn't quite satisfied with her explanation, but decided not to press the issue. She did have her own personal matters to contend with.

When the lunch hour arrived Blu told Yelsi that she might be a little late coming back from lunch, and that if anything urgent came up to call her on her cell phone.

After failing several times to reach her husband on

either his cell phone or at the office, Blu had made the decision to pay him an impromptu visit. She'd grown weary of all this nonsense. He was going to have to *make* the time to sit down and talk things over with her or else. And while she didn't quite know what the *'or else'* meant, she knew that something would have to give. Or, *someone*.

The accounting firm where Damien worked as a CPA was located in the Perimeter Mall area – just north of ADDISON JAMES & SHEPHERD's offices. As Blu rode the glass elevator to the tenth floor she tried to gather her thoughts. She'd never barged into his offices before. And she wasn't sure if his secretary or any of the others at his firm knew about their separation.

Well, it didn't matter. She was his wife. And if he'd answered her phone calls then she wouldn't have to take this drastic course of action.

"Hello, Mrs. Addison!" the ever-grinning receptionist greeted her as soon as she stepped from the elevator.

"Hi," Blu returned a cursory greeting. "I need to see Damien."

The receptionist took a quick glance at the calendar on her desk. "Um, is he expecting you?"

"I don't have an appointment if that's what you're asking."

"Um, well. He is on another call at the moment."

"Not a problem. Just let him know that his *wife* is here," Blu stated emphatically. "In the mean time I'll have a seat over there," she said, pointing to the sitting area of the lobby.

The mild-mannered receptionist was taken aback by Blu's tone. "Sure, of course. I'll let Mr. Addison know that you're waiting to see him."

"Yes, you tell him that."

Twenty minutes later, and trying very hard not to lose her composure, Blu was becoming edgy as she sat, still waiting for her husband, in the lobby.

Finally, unable to stand it any longer, she marched back over to the receptionist desk. "You know what, I'm going to go on back. I know where his office is."

"Wait, Mrs. Addison!" the receptionist called, but Blu had already turned the corner and was headed down the corridor toward her husband's corner office. When she arrived at the large door, with a brass handle as its knob, she didn't bother to knock. She quickly thrust the door open. Damien was seated behind his marble-top desk, fully engaged in conversation with someone on the telephone.

"So how long were you planning to make me wait?" she demanded to know, ignoring the fact that the man was in the middle of a business call.

Damien, embarrassed and growing angrier by the

second, politely told the client on the other end of the phone that he'd have to call him back later. He quickly hung up the phone and then stared at her with such a menacing scowl on his face.

"What in the hell is your problem!" he attempted to shout quietly, although failing miserably.

"What is *your* problem? Keeping me waiting out *there* like I'm some copier salesman!"

"Well, unless you're going blind, I'm sure you could see that I was on the telephone!" he retorted. "With a very important client!" he added.

"How was I supposed to know that it was an important client?"

Damien stood from his desk, slamming his MONT BLANC pen onto the desk. He then shoved his hands into the front pockets of his trousers. At the moment he wanted them *restrained* as he approached his wife, fearing that he might use them to shake some sense into her head. "What exactly are you doing here?" he asked, now standing next to her.

"What I am doing is trying to communicate with my husband, who has apparently been avoiding me!"

"I haven't been avoid . . . " he stopped his words and quickly trotted over and closed the door to his office. She hadn't closed it all the way when she entered so abruptly. "I have not been avoiding you," he continued.

"Oh, really? So I guess all those messages I've left for you just somehow disappeared?"

"Listen. Blu. I told you that I would contact you when I was ready to talk. You have no right to barge into my office raving like some lunatic!"

"What would you have me do, Damien? You move out of our home without any sensible explanation, you won't tell me where you're staying, you refuse to sit down with me and talk through this, and I can't even get you to return my phone calls!"

Damien loosened his silk tie. He returned to sit in the black leather chair behind his desk. "It just drives you crazy, doesn't it?"

"What are you talking about?" She sat down in one of the chairs across from his desk.

"That you're not in control."

"Control of what?"

He began shaking his head, stifling a laugh. "You're pathetic Blu. When it's something that *you* want, you want it now! I told you, plain and simple, that I needed to sort through some things and that *I* would *contact* you at the proper time, but noooo! That's not good enough for you, is it? You want to control *when* I sit down with you. And you probably want to control *what* I say as well, don't you?"

"You know that's not true, Damien."

"Oh, give me a break! You know something, Blu – the biggest mistake that you can make where I'm concerned is to underestimate me."

"I've never done that."

"I beg to differ. Not only do you underestimate me, but you also *assume* too much. Now, you can take what I'm saying for what it's worth, or you can let it go through one ear and out the other."

Blu remained silent.

"You *assume* that just because we've been married for fourteen years that all is great. You *assume* that just because we both have good jobs, a nice home, and fine cars, that I'm happy or content. You *assume* that just because I'm not roaming the streets late at night, or hanging with the guys on the weekends, that all is right between us. And you *assume* that just because our bodies occasionally share an intimacy of sorts that it's love. Well, Blu, my one piece of advice to you is that you cease with all the damn assumptions! No one gets through life successfully by *assuming* every damn thing."

Blu tried not to flinch, but his words cut through her like a sword – a two-edged sword.

Damien continued. "Consider for a moment, a solider in battle; he cannot afford to assume that just because he shoots his gun that the enemy will lay down his and surrender.

He can't even assume that his comrade, fighting alongside him, is also watching his back. For a soldier in battle to erroneously rely on such assumptions as these might very well cost him his life."

"Is there a specific and relative point that you're trying to make, Damien?"

"We've come to end of the road, Blu. The end of our road."

"Well, I don't believe that to be true."

"You would if you didn't *assume* otherwise."

"So, do I not get a say in the matter? Is it totally up to you to decide when we've reached the end of the road?"

"Trust me, Blu. The decision has been a mutual one."

"How can that be true when I've sat here and said practically nothing at all!"

He shook his head again. "Come on, Blu. You don't really believe that my coming to this conclusion was just reached *today*?"

She chose not to answer.

"And you may not have done a lot of communicating to me with your *mouth* over the years, but believe me when I say that your *actions* have been unmistakably clear."

Frustrated, Blu threw her hands up into the air. "So what is it you want, Damien! A divorce? Is that what you want? Because I can't take any more of this!"

"Oh, I bet you can't. I'm sure that it's very difficult for you listening to me whine and gripe about wanting to spend more time with you. And I'm sure you just can't stand to have me bugging the hell out of you about having a child, can you?"

"That's not what I mean! I was talking about us being separated, not communicating! That's what I'm tired of."

Damien stood from his chair again. He turned from her and walked over to his window and peered out below. The day was shaping up to be a beautiful one. Sunny skies ruled over the city like an emperor. A rule so strong and mighty that the clouds and the rain dared to defy such an emperorship.

"You know, it was never my intention for things to turn out this way, Blu," he spoke solemnly.

"What *way*, Damien?"

"I'm not ready to get into it, Blu."

She joined him at the window. "Damien, look at me," she told him. Reluctantly his eyes met hers. "Is there someone else?"

He averted his eyes from hers.

She had her answer. "Who is she, Damien?"

He retreated back to his desk. "Aren't you even listening to me, Blu? I said *now* is not the time!"

Blu hung her head for a moment, and in that moment she painfully realized how much of this could have perhaps been avoided had she been open with her husband from the very beginning.

Slowly, she walked over and sat down again in one of the chairs that were positioned in front of his desk. Minutes later she found herself rambling.

Damien didn't interrupt her. She didn't know if he didn't do so out of courtesy or simply because he was willing to allow her to do or say anything if it meant quickly getting rid of her.

Before long she found herself telling Damien about her *past*. The past that she had tried so hard to erase. She told him about her best friend in high school, *Schuyler Conklin*. And how he eventually became her boyfriend. Then she told him about the most *difficult* part. The part where, in her junior year in high school, at the age of sixteen, she became pregnant with Schuyler's child. She explained that, on the one hand, she was happy because she loved Schuyler and he loved her, but on the other hand, she knew that it would devastate her parents.

She had been right. The news of her pregnancy would overwhelm both her parents as well as Schuyler's.

It was April 1981. There was only a month and a half in the school year remaining. She was glad that she finished her junior year without anyone at her high school knowing about her pregnancy. But once school let out that following

June, her parents had decided to send her to Atlanta to live with her aunt and uncle.

When the new school year began that fall, her senior year, she attended a special private school in Atlanta for girls who were pregnant.

Her parents had already decided that the baby was going to be given up for adoption immediately upon birth. And while Blu had agreed, she would later come to realize that it had been a horrible decision. One in which no sixteen year-old girl could possibly understand its ramifications.

The baby was born on *December 16, 1981*. It was a baby girl. Neither Blu nor her parents wanted to see the baby. They felt that to do so would have only made it even more difficult to go through with the adoption. Blu's mother told Schuyler's parents about the successful birth.

She would learn later that Schuyler nearly didn't finish his senior year because he'd become so depressed. He had wanted Blu to keep the baby. He cried for weeks after learning about the birth of *his* baby. A precious little girl that he would always regret not having the opportunity to ever lay eyes upon.

As for the adoptive parents, the only thing that Blu was told was that they were a middle-aged couple from Atlanta who had been unable to bear children of their own. Very little additional information was made available since it had been a *closed* adoption.

Prior to her giving birth, Blu had purchased a baby's blanket. Not just *any* blanket. This one had been a silk paisley blanket, containing dark colors – mostly green, burgundy, purple and gold. She'd taken a pair of scissors and cut the blanket down the middle into two pieces. She took one half to the hospital with her. It was given to the nurse on duty. Blu had asked her if she would mind giving the blanket to the adoptive parents. And although it was an unusual request, the nurse had been very understanding and stated that she would do so.

The other half of the blanket, Blu kept for herself. At the time, it was the only way that she could think of that would allow her some attachment to the baby. Some sense of closeness. Some motherly significance.

Yet, she was never quite certain if the adoptive parents accepted the paisley blanket or whether or not they even gave it to the baby. Her half had been placed inside a small shopping bag, and when she returned home she quietly tucked the bag away in the attic at her parent's house.

In January following the birth of the baby Blu went back to Muncie, Indiana. She re-enrolled at her high school and subsequently graduated with her senior class. There had been all kinds of nasty rumors swirling as to the reasons for her four months of absence, but Blu neither denied nor confirmed them.

Unfortunately, however, she and Schuyler remained distant during those final months of school. It was by *her* choice. She simply couldn't face him anymore. Of course, she still loved him. She would always love him.

Since the birth of the baby, Blu found it very difficult to absolve the guilt that she's felt for having to give up her only child. The little girl would now be *twenty-one* years old.

All the while she'd been speaking, Blu was staring out the window, unable to make eye contact with her husband. Perhaps *unwilling* to make eye contact with him.

"So, you see Damien, this is why the subject of having children has always been such a difficult one for me."

Damien vacated the spot behind his desk and took a seat next to his wife in one of the chairs. "Why didn't you tell me this sooner, Blu? Fourteen years of marriage and you never felt that it was important that *I* should know?"

She finally allowed her eyes to meet his. "I have always felt that you should know, Damien. The thing is, I was just so ashamed of myself. I didn't feel worthy to bring another child into this world after what I'd done to my own."

"You were only sixteen, Blu."

"I know. But it was still *my* baby. It was my little girl that I gave away." She fought back her tears.

The two of them remained silent for several minutes.

Damien would eventually break the silence. "I don't know what to say, Blu." His face had become drawn and pinched. "I really wished you would have shared this with me before now."

She took hold of his hand. "I wish I would have too. I realize that I've probably waited too late. And if that is the case, then at least now you know the truth. I didn't want you to go on thinking that I was simply being selfish for not wanting to have any children."

Damien shook his head. "You should have told me, Blu. You should have told me."

She could see his face becoming twisted with pain. A pain that she knew all too well. She didn't even know why she had been so afraid to tell him. The longer she delayed telling him over the years the more difficult it became. Her mother had been right. She should have shared something like this with Damien from day one.

She didn't really know what his response would have been had she told him from the beginning. But, she quickly realized that it wasn't going to serve her any useful purpose to dwell on *'what if'* scenarios.

The fact of the matter was that everything was all out in the open now. She'd laid her soul bare before her husband. She'd put an end to the lies and the secrets.

No more rationalizing.

She had finally told her husband the truth.

For better or for worse.

chapter 15

After leaving Damien's office, Blu did not return to ADDISON JAMES & SHEPHERD. She spent a good part of the afternoon at the Lenox Mall shopping and simply trying to clear her head. She'd phoned her mother and told her that she had told Damien everything. And while she did feel as though a heavy burden had been lifted, she told her mother that she also believed that it was too late. Audrey Knight consoled her daughter as best as she could. She told Blu that what she did was more for *her* benefit than for Damien's.

Blu also told her mother about the other half of the paisley blanket that she'd hidden in the attic. She asked her mother to retrieve it and send it to her. She never wanted it with her before because she did not want to take the chance that Damien might come across it. But since that was no longer a worry, she wanted the blanket in her possession.

. . . .

It was now almost six o'clock. Blu and Yelsi were sitting at a table for two at the CIAO BELLA restaurant on *Pharr Road* in the *Buckhead* area of Atlanta. It was one of Blu's favorite places to dine whenever she craved Italian food.

When she left Damien's office she'd called Yelsi from Lenox Mall and asked her to join her at the restaurant for dinner. Yelsi was more than eager to do so. She left the office around five-twenty and by five-forty-five she was handing her car keys over to the valet parking attendant.

The very polite waitress came to their table, armed with pen and pad, ready to jot down their order. The menu offered a fine selection of dishes from which to choose. For her salad, Blu ordered a *Cesare 6*, which was a traditional Caesar salad. And for her entrée she ordered the *Merluzzo 18*, which was served with pan seared halibut in pine nut crust with vine ripe tomatoes and orange juice.

Yelsi's salad choice was the *Mista 5*, which consisted of mixed field greens with balsamic vinaigrette dressing. Her entrée choice was the *Linguine 16*, served with shrimp, scallops and mussels in a spicy tomato sauce. And for their drinks, Blu ordered a red wine while Yelsi opted for a ginger ale.

Throughout their evening together Blu was fighting assiduously to keep from drifting deeper into the melancholy state in which she found herself.

In an effort to keep a lively conversation flowing with Yelsi, she asked her if she had a boyfriend and was genuinely surprised to learn that the beautiful young woman was not involved with anyone.

"Well, Yelsi, I would have thought that you'd have many of Atlanta's eligible bachelors trying to sweep you off your feet."

Yelsi blushed. "I can't say that they're not trying."

"Oh, I see. So, you're not allowing them to – is that it?"

"Sort of. A serious relationship is just not a part of my focus right now. Besides, there are just too many guys out there trying to play the field."

Blu nodded in agreement. "Have you ever had a serious relationship?"

"Yes. I met this guy during my junior year at Wellesley and we dated for two years."

"What happened?" Blu asked, then she quickly realized that she might be prying. "Wait! You don't have to answer that. I shouldn't even be asking such personal questions. I'm sorry, Yelsi."

"It's not a big deal, really. I don't mind talking about it," she assured Blu. "I mean, we had a good relationship and all, but he started pressuring me to move in with him and that just wasn't something that I believed in doing nor was I comfortable with it."

Blu smiled. "Good for you."

"So, the next thing I knew, he had found some other girl to move in with him. That's when I realized that he obviously wasn't the right person for me anyway."

"That decision took a lot of courage, Yelsi. I'm willing to bet that many women, young and old, face that same decision all the time. And unfortunately, many of them choose the wrong one."

"I just feel like if a guy really loves me, then one way he'll show it is by not asking me to do something that I believe is disrespectful to me."

"Well, I wish I was as focused as you are when I was twenty-five."

Yelsi displayed an animate grin.

The conversation continued well after their meals had been set before them. And Blu's heart was still aching.

Before long Yelsi's perceptivity lead her to inquire as to whether Blu was feeling all right.

"Well, I have had better days," Blu answered her with a bit of reluctance. "And, unfortunately, today isn't one those days."

"I've been there," said Yelsi.

The two friends talked about how Blu got started within the advertising agency business. Then she shared with Yelsi some good times from her college days at Ohio State

University. The conversation would eventually digress to Damien.

Yelsi said, "I guess that the bald handsome guy in the photo on your desk is Damien?"

Blu smiled as the mental image of her tall, dark and very athletic husband entered her mind. "Yes. That would be him."

"So, how long have you two been married?" Yelsi asked.

"Fourteen years this year."

"Wow! That's great," remarked Yelsi. "My parents were married for forty years before my mom died."

"That's right, you told me that your mom died from breast cancer three years ago," Blu acknowledged sympathetically.

Yelsi shook her head. "She was only sixty-three."

"I'm so sorry, Yelsi," Blu told her. "I guess it's still painful for you to talk about her?"

Again Yelsi shook her head without answering.

A few minutes elapsed before Yelsi remarked, "We were truly best friends. We told each other everything."

"Sounds like a very special relationship."

"It is . . . I mean, *was*."

Blu reached across the table and caressed Yelsi's hand.

"You know, after my mom died, I didn't think that I could ever feel close to anyone," Yelsi admitted.

"You're not close with your father?"

Yelsi looked down at her food. "Actually, my father and I are estranged."

Blu could see that it too was a painful subject. "Well, if you ever need someone to talk to, Yelsi, I am here."

"Thanks for saying that, Blu. It really means a lot to hear that. In all honesty, you are the one person who I feel that I can be open with. I mean I know we haven't known each other that long, but . . . " Yelsi didn't finish.

"But what?" Blu coaxed her.

"Well, it's just that I feel like I've known you all my life."

Her sentiments touched Blu deeply. "It's funny, but I have felt the exact same way since meeting you."

The waitress came by their table and offered them the dessert special. And with just a hint of reluctance they accepted her offer.

As the evening moved along, Blu confided in Yelsi and told her that she and Damien were now separated. She did not go into great detail. She simply told her that the two of them had some differences that were probably too great to resolve anytime soon. Although, she was still hopeful.

Yelsi felt empathy for her boss, friend and confidante. She said to Blu, "You know, *Oliver Wendell Holmes* once said, *'what lies behind us and what lies before us are tiny matters compared to what lies within us'*. And Blu, I think that within you lies a beautiful heart with a compassionate spirit."

Blu was overwhelmed by her words. This young woman had just put her entire life into perspective. For almost twenty-two years she'd been tortured by a past that she cannot undo. And since marrying Damien she'd been afraid of her future because of her guilt over the past. And yet, Yelsi had pointed out so eloquently this quote from *Oliver Wendell Holmes*. For the first time she was beginning to realize that it isn't that which was *behind*, nor that which is *ahead*, but rather, that which is *within* that matters most.

"Yelsi, what you've just shared with me means more than you'll ever know. Thank you."

Yelsi simply smiled. Her mother had shared that quotation with her years ago. And she was glad that she'd been able to share it with Blu and to have it mean something to her.

"Do you mind if I share one more with you?"

"Not at all. I can use every bit of encouragement and wisdom. No matter how small."

"Well, this is a quotation from someone named *Sydney J. Harris* and it has always meant a lot to me. It says, *'Regret for the things we did can be tempered by time; it is regret for the things we did not do that is inconsolable'*."

That one cut Blu deep within her heart. Tears were already sliding down her cheeks.

Yelsi noticed. "I didn't mean to make you cry," she offered an apology.

Blu used the white linen table napkin to dab her eyes dry. "No, no. I can be too sentimental at times."

"Same here."

"Oh, I don't think anyone cries as much as I do. Movies, songs, heart-warming articles, you name it."

"Well, you don't look like a crier."

Blu chuckled. "And how does a *crier* look?"

"I mean from a distance you appear to be a strong and authoritative woman. And that you are. But, you have a soft spot too."

"Well, lately I've been more of a softy than I usually am."

"You're like me. I tend to wear my heart on my sleeve."

Blu nodded. "The truth is, that last quote struck a chilling chord with me, Yelsi."

"Is that good or bad?"

Blu dried her eyes a second time. "It is definitely *good*. Probably as good as it will ever get."

chapter 16

If her Thursday morning start to the day was going to be any indication of how the entire day would eventually shape up, Kiwi didn't know if she would be able to survive the madness.

ADDISON JAMES & SHEPHERD had lost *another* client. This one hit her hard because it was the first account that she had personally won for the agency during their third year of operation. The account was a cosmetics and skincare manufacturer from New York. It billed *$55 million* annually.

Kiwi had spent over an hour on a conference call along with her account team trying to salvage the account. She was forced to make the call from her cell phone because she was at the PORSCHE dealership having her car serviced.

Their efforts to save the account proved futile. The client gave them some weak excuse about having to 'seek a new direction' for the upcoming year. And while the client was being reticent about naming the agency to succeed them, she was pretty damn sure it was MARTIN/McFINLEY.

A service manager from the dealership came out and informed her that it would be later that afternoon before her car would be ready. Ordinarily, they would provide her with a courtesy vehicle to drive but since Kiwi stopped in without an appointment no cars were available.

Kiwi decided to phone Flavia at the office to see if she would come by the dealership and pick her up. She already knew that Blu was out of the office attending a meeting downtown.

"*Flavia James'* office," answered Flavia's secretary.

"Hey, it's Kiwi."

"Hi Kiwi."

"Is Flavia around?"

"No she isn't. And I'm not sure if she's going to be in the office today."

What was up with Flavia? Kiwi thought to herself. She was out of the office all last week and she was yet to come in this week. "Is she sick or something?" Kiwi asked.

"Um, I'm not sure. All I know is that she's taking care of some personal business."

Kiwi emitted a heavy sigh. She couldn't have her assistant, Nathan Nichols, pick her up because she'd given him the rest of the week off since he was preparing for a trip to Los Angeles to attend a relative's wedding this coming weekend. And she realized that most everybody at the office was busy doing something that was either time-sensitive or critically important. Flavia wouldn't have mind coming to pick her up because the three of them usually did things like that for each other.

Someone needed to come and get her. She had no desire to spend the next four or five hours in the customer waiting area at this dealership. Not to mention the fact that she was up to her eyeballs in various client issues that needed to be handled back at the office.

Reluctantly, she told Flavia's secretary, "Transfer me to Yelsi." She was hoping that she wouldn't come to regret the request. But the girl was probably the least busy among all the others at the office.

Seconds later Yelsi answered on the other end.

"Yelsi, this is Miss Shepherd."

Hearing her voice came as a surprise, but Yelsi remained cool. "Hello, Miss Shepherd. How can I help you?"

You can help me by taking your trifling wannabe behind to some other ad agency. "Listen, I know Blu is downtown at a meeting, so I was wondering if you could do me a favor?"

A favor? It wasn't the sort of thing she expected to be hearing out of Kiwi's mouth. The same woman who seemed to have launched an all-out-assault on her? The same woman who rolled her eyes at her whenever their eyes met?

Yelsi tried to resist becoming paranoid, but she was definitely skeptical of Kiwi's request. "Um, what kind of favor?"

"I'm at the PORSCHE dealership over on Piedmont Road having my car serviced. And unfortunately, it won't be ready until this afternoon." Kiwi paused. She was searching for a way to propel the words from her mouth. "So, uh. Hey, I want you to come over here and pick me up!"

This sounded more like a *demand* rather than a request, Yelsi thought.

"You say you *need* me to come and pick you up?" Yelsi repeated, being careful to emphasize the word 'need'.

The emphasis didn't escape Kiwi. She hated asking this damn girl for anything. "Yeah, that's what I said. That is, if you don't mind?" *She better not mind. She's not that damn busy.*

Yelsi began to wonder. Was it possible that Miss Shepherd, in her own sneaky way, was extending an olive branch to her? There were other people in the agency. Why did she choose her?

"Yelsi, are you still there?"

"Um, Yes. I'm sorry, I got distracted for a moment," she apologized. "Sure, I can come and get you. Should I leave now?"

No, you stupid heifer – how about you leave next week sometime! I'll just camp out here! "I'm ready *now*, Yelsi. So yeah, I'd prefer you to leave *now*."

Yelsi told Kiwi that she'd be there in about ten to fifteen minutes.

While she was waiting, Kiwi got a call on her cell phone from her uncle. "Hey, Uncle Benny. What you got for me?"

There was a slight hesitation in her uncle's voice. "Well, Special K," he began. "Unless you gave me the wrong information, I got zilch!"

"Excuse me?"

"Special K, I done racked my brain on this one! I mean, I done checked out the credit bureau, the DMV and even some utility companies down there in Atlanta, and there ain't nothin' for this person."

"What do you mean, Uncle Benny? I gave you her social security number."

"Well, now . . . you gave me somebody's number, but it don't match nobody named *Yelsi Nitram*."

His response threw her for a loop. "I'm not following you, Uncle Benny."

"Special K, what I'm sayin' is that this Yelsi person don't exist."

"Well, I just got off the phone with her, Uncle Benny!"

"Naw, naw Special K. I'm talkin' 'bout on paper. In computer databases. Files. Records. Ain't nothin' on her."

"What about the college?"

"Goose egg! Them people ain't have no records for no *Yelsi Nitram* either. I don't know who you done hired, Special K, but I know one thing, she ain't who she say she is."

Kiwi was absolutely flabbergasted. What in the hell was going on? Who had Blu gotten them mixed up with? Her mind began racing. What was this girl's agenda?

Kiwi tried to quickly collect her thoughts. "Uh, okay Uncle Benny. Let me recheck some things on this end and I'll get back with you, okay?"

"No problem. You know where to find me."

As Kiwi pressed the button on her cell phone to *end* the call, she got another surprise. Pulling up in front of the dealership was Yelsi in a brand new BMW Z4.

And this heifer needed a job? As a secretary? Something just wasn't right and Kiwi Shepherd was more determined now than ever before to find out what the hell it was.

As she entered the passenger side of the sports car, Kiwi feigned a smile as well as a 'hello' to Yelsi. "Nice car," she commented as Yelsi sped from the parking lot.

"Thanks," Yelsi gave a guarded response.

As the car made a left turn on Peachtree Street Kiwi

noticed a CD case lying on the floor below her. She reached down and picked it up.Yelsi glanced over at her. "You can just stick that in the glove compartment," she told Kiwi.

Kiwi looked at the cover before she opened the glove compartment. It was an *Alanis Morissette* CD. "So, you like Alanis Morissette?"

"Yes. She's great!"

"Well, I wouldn't know. More of an R&B person myself," replied Kiwi as she stuck the CD inside the glove compartment and then snapped it shut. "But she is one of Blu's favorite artists."

"Oh, really? I didn't know that."

I bet you didn't. She wouldn't be surprised if this girl had an entire file on Blu. Apparently she chose the right person within the agency to target. "Yeah, Blu's crazy about Alanis. I'm surprised you haven't heard the woman's voice blowing from her office because she keeps a CD in her desk *and* her car."

Yelsi chuckled. "No, I haven't heard Blu playing any music from her office."

"Hey, just give her time."

They rode in silence for the remaining few minutes that it took them to arrive at the office building.

Kiwi wished that she could get her hands on this girl's car registration or her driver's license. Thanks to her uncle she was certain that her name wasn't *Yelsi Nitram.* She was also certain that their sudden loss of almost twenty-five percent in annual billings to their archrival, MARTIN/McFINLEY, has not been a coincidence either.

This *Yelsi* girl was nothing more than a freakin' mole! Some kind of a damn spy! And Kiwi was sure that the girl somehow was passing client information from their agency to MARTIN/McFINLEY. Leland Martin must have realized that he was in for some tough competition for the MerLex Motors account, so he decided to infiltrate their agency by planting this girl to pose as an employee.

Unfortunately, the snitch had succeeded at getting her hooks into Blu. Blu had been just too damn willing to share every freakin' thing with the girl! But Kiwi had not been fooled one bit. She smelled a rat from the first day the lying heifer set foot on the golf course.

Golf course. It suddenly occurred to Kiwi that she could try and find out who this girl was from the *Marshal* who had put her with their threesome over two weeks ago. She remembered the Marshal saying something about Yelsi's playing partner canceling on her, which meant that the girl had to have had a tee-time reserved. Under what *name* had she reserved the tee-time?

Kiwi decided that she'd stop by the course on her way home this evening. It was time to pay that Marshal a little visit.

chapter 17

"Baby, why don't you go on to the office," Flavia tried coaxing Parker. "You've taken a lot of time off already."

On this particular Thursday they were sitting on the sofa in their living room. It was just shy of the noon hour. The two of them had gotten the boys off to school. Parker had taken care of the breakfast dishes while Flavia sat staring out the front window, looking at nothing in particular.

"Work is the last thing on my mind right now, sweetheart," Parker assured her. He pulled her closer to him. She turned her gaze from the window and allowed her head to drop onto his shoulder.

Since yesterday's meeting at the doctor's office, Flavia had little to say. To her husband. To her boys. To anyone. She returned home and began taking care of chores around the house like it was a typical day. She phoned her secretary and told her that she wouldn't be coming in – again.

She later went shopping. When she returned from the impromptu escape to the mall that evening, she had bought the boys an assortment of video games and other cool toys.

Parker had maintained his distance. He didn't want to make matters worse. Even though his instincts told him to do *something*. Instead he tried to understand what his wife could possibly be going through. He wasn't sure how he would react if he were in her place.

According to the doctor, his wife's behavior was to be expected. Dr. Matthews had shared with him that his wife was most likely to go through a period of denial and disbelief.

Flavia's biopsy results had come back a day earlier. Her worst fears had been confirmed. She did have pancreatic cancer and it was in an advanced stage – *stage four B.*

After the dreadful news yesterday she did not shed one tear. She showed no emotions at all. Perhaps she'd been in a state of shock. There she was, caught up in a maelstrom and yet she showed no reaction.

Flavia had listened intently to everything the doctor was saying. And when it had all been said and done, she thanked Dr. Matthews, Dr. Jacobs and the Radiologist. She told them that she wanted time to consider everything. Then she put her arm around Parker's waist and said simply that she was ready to go home.

Sitting next to her husband today, feeling his warmth,

and almost hearing the rapid beats of his incredible heart, an overflow of emotions seized her at once, like an escaped prisoner recaptured. She buried her face into Parker's chest. Her body crumpled like a rag doll. Easily, she dissolved into tears. They were monstrous tears. Overwhelming. Pouring forth like *Niagara Falls*. Her husband's winter white, HUGO BOSS cashmere turtleneck sweater was drenched.

"Why! Why! Why!" Flavia shouted. She pulled slightly away from Parker's embrace. "Lord, why *me*!? Why *now*!?" she sobbed, both her fists balled tightly.

Of course, she realized that the questions would undoubtedly go unanswered. It didn't stop her from shouting even more. "What did I do wrong? Please don't let this happen to me! My family needs me, Lord! My boys are only six years old! They're only . . . Lord, my boys are just babies in this world. Don't take me away from them. Not now, Lord! Please! Please. Plea . . ." The words became strangled by her sea of emotions.

Parker didn't quite know how much more he could absorb. His wife was hurting and he was powerless to help her.

Shocked himself, and his own body nearly numb, he wrapped his arms around his wife's flaccid body. He needed to embrace not just her physical frame right now, but her spirit as well – if it was at all possible to do so. He'd never seen her experience anything like this during their entire twenty-years of marriage.

Why had God chosen them for this trial? Their faith was growing every day but it wasn't mature yet. At least not mature enough to face this.

He loved his wife dearly. She meant everything to him. He knew that he was who he is in large part because of who she is. If there was such a thing as *soul mates* then they were mates whose souls belonged to one another.

It was clearly understood that life wasn't always fair. It had always been one of those generally accepted principles. You played the hand you were dealt. Good, bad or indifferent. Those were the rules. No reshuffling the deck. No trading cards with someone else. Do the best you could with the hand that life dealt you. No questions asked.

But, Parker James had questions. Serious questions. Lots of questions.

How could something like this happen? Why would it even be *allowed* to happen? Why his wife and not *him*? Why wasn't there a cure for this disease?

Indeed, he understood that life was unfair sometimes. But right now, life was being just plain cruel.

He could feel himself weakening beneath the strain of trying to keep a check on his emotions. He kept reminding himself that he needed to be strong. Courageous. A tower for his ailing wife to run to. A shelter for her to seek during this unrelenting storm. A light for her to see that, on his face he was not giving up hope, despite the despair of darkness that had blanketed them.

Throughout his career as a corporate attorney he had handled some of the most difficult cases one could imagine, some with insurmountable obstacles. Yet he never wavered. He never quit. He never blinked.

On this cloudy October day, Parker James blinked.

Without warning, his tall muscular physique slumped to the living room floor. The reality of his wife's predicament striking at him like hammer blows. He buried his head into his hands. His chest grew heavy. He could feel his throat closing. His stomach had already contracted into a tight ball. And with his body now coiled into the fetal position, Parker's voice exploded from him. It was so thunderous that it startled Flavia as she lay back with her head against the sofa, still weeping. His unnerving wails were like those of a man whose very soul had been torn, bare handed, from his body. Flavia rushed over and threw her body alongside her husband's.

For the next two hours they would remain there – on the living room floor. Unmoving. Undisturbed. Sharing a heartache that was truly unfathomable.

. . . .

The prognosis for Flavia's pancreatic cancer held little

hope for a future of any kind. Once a patient had been diagnosed with this type of cancer, there was a ninety-five percent chance that he or she would die within five years. There was an eighty percent chance that the patient would not survive the first year after the initial diagnosis.

Both Flavia and Parker had questioned the doctor as to why the disease wasn't found sooner – before it reached a *stage four B* status. Dr. Matthews explained to them that since the pancreas is a small gland located deep within the abdominal cavity and therefore cannot be seen or felt, it is unlikely that a tumor could have been detected during a routine physical examination. He further explained that there are no *early* symptoms, and by the time any symptoms are manifested, the cancer has already spread to other organs and is in an advanced stage. Unfortunately, there were no blood tests or any other test that could detect pancreatic cancer early.

Since successful treatment of the disease was rare, Flavia told the doctor that she would have to seriously consider whether or not she even wanted to pursue the limited treatment options that he discussed with them.

The standard treatment was surgery. The most common type was the *Whipple* procedure, also known as a *pancreatoduodenectomy*. It was a procedure that was first described in 1935 by *Dr. Alan O. Whipple* of New York

Hospital. Basically, the surgical team would remove the head of the pancreas, as well as the gallbladder, part of the stomach, the lower half of the bile duct, and part of the small intestine. The entire surgery would take approximately six to eight hours to perform. However, Dr. Matthews explained that this type of surgery could be most beneficial to patients whose cancer has *not* spread. And even in those cases, the surgery was still considered *palliative* – meaning that it would only seek to lessen the severity of the disease, not cure it.

Radiation combined with chemotherapy was also discussed, but Flavia was adamant that she would not undergo either.

Part of her wished that she'd never gone to the doctor for those series of tests. Since the disease had apparently already spread, she wondered if she would have been better off not knowing. At least that way she could still go about her daily life rather than having it stopped so abruptly. So rudely. So unfairly.

. . . .

By two o'clock that afternoon, Flavia and Parker had gathered into the kitchen. She prepared turkey and ham sandwiches and served them with LAY'S potato chips for lunch.

While eating they talked about the boys' soccer team. They talked about how quickly the houses were selling in

WindFair Estates. They talked about tonight's episode of *Survivor* – one of their favorite reality TV shows. They talked about the yard work they would do for the fall season. They talked about the ad agency. They talked about an unusual case Parker was handling for a big corporation. They talked about the bombardment of political ads on television as voters prepared for next month's elections. They talked about *Ben* and *J-Lo*. They talked about last Sunday's sermon at church. They talked about their love for each other.

Then it was time to head down the street and wait on the corner for the boys' school bus. They left the house together, strolling down the sidewalk, hand in hand, like two lovebirds. Which of course, they were. And while they waited, along with a handful of other parents, they talked some more. The subject of cancer or tumors never made its way into the conversation. It had already been discoursed too much.

They wanted any discussions within the remaining hours of this Thursday to be about something that they *wanted* to talk about. And so they blabbered one another's ears off. They also laughed. Parker even broke out into a song – much to the amusement of those standing nearby.

God had given them this day. Not tomorrow, but *this* day. *Today*. It was indeed a day that the Lord had made. And the two of them decided that they would choose to rejoice and be glad in it. For *nobody* was promised anything more.

chapter 18

Gray clouds patrolled the Atlanta skies. This early October day was breezy. Although the sun had decided to sleep in for the morning, the forecast was predicting temperatures to reach a high of sixty-six.

Excellent golf weather despite the wind. But these women had more pressing concerns than their golf game. Blu had even suggested that perhaps they should withdraw from the *AAACC* tournament this year. It had been almost three weeks since they last practiced together. But Kiwi told her to hold off a while longer.

The time was five minutes before seven. It seemed like it had been such a long time since the three of them had gotten together – business or otherwise. Yet on this Friday morning they were meeting at an IHOP for breakfast.

Blu and Kiwi were already seated at the round table that accompanied four. Flavia was on her way to join them.

Kiwi was somewhat disappointed that she didn't have time to swing by the golf course yesterday before they closed. With her assistant out of the office until Monday, she was inundated with so much work that she didn't leave the building last night until well after eight o'clock.

Blu was scanning the current issue of ADVERTISING AGE magazine as she sipped her cup of decaf. "Well, it appears our trend of client losses lately has garnered us the front page," she remarked sourly, as she slid the magazine over to Kiwi.

Kiwi shook her head disapprovingly. "It amazes me how many people out there are still looking for us to fall flat on our faces."

"I cannot believe that we have lost *eighty-five million* in billings over the past two weeks!" said Blu. "Are these clients conspiring against us or what?"

"Humph. Don't be so quick to blame our clients."

Blu quickly turned a cold eye towards Kiwi, giving her a *keep-your-mouth-shut-about-Yelsi* look.

Kiwi threw her hands up in mock defeat. "Hey, I'm not going *there*. I'm just saying."

Blu was relieved to see Flavia heading their way.

"Sorry I'm late," Flavia apologized, taking a seat in the empty chair next to Blu.

Blu stood and gave her a warm hug. "How are you!?

It seems like it been forever, lady!"

Kiwi chided Flavia. "Yeah, girlfriend! Your behind has been at home handling *personal business* while our butts have been working our tails off! Fighting big-time trying to keep clients from jumping ship."

Flavia blew her off. "Whatever, Kiwi. I haven't forgot about that new man in your life. Maybe its *him* who you've been fighting off!"

"Yeah, him too!"

They all laughed.

"So, seriously. What's going on, lady?" Blu put the question out there.

"You can't be sick," Kiwi interjected. "Because girl you're looking fine as hell, okayyy!"

Flavia began to fidget in her chair, clearing her throat excessively. She realized that the questions would undoubtedly come. But she was nowhere near ready to reveal her condition to them. She told Parker last night that the best thing that she could do for herself was to simply try and continue living her life as she had before. And as impossible as that may be to pull off, it was what she wanted to do. Needed to do.

"Actually, I really haven't been feeling well over the past week," she began. "But I do feel much better now. Especially now that I'm around you two!"

"Well, it's good to have our media guru back!" Blu said.

"Yeah, 'cause girlfriend, ADDISON JAMES & SHEPHERD has got one serious crisis on our hands!" Kiwi stated bluntly.

The waitress, a middle-age blonde, came to their table and brought Flavia a cup of coffee before she wrote down their breakfast order. When she had left them, Blu and Kiwi brought Flavia up to date on what's been happening at the agency. She was astonished to learn of the client losses. She told them that she felt guilty for not having been there. But they assured her that all three clients had already made up their minds to drop them as agency-of-record. There was nothing that she could have done to prevent their actions.

While they were eating, Blu mentioned to Flavia about the possibility of canceling the golf tournament. Flavia suggested that they wait until the absolute last minute. They still had a couple of weeks before the deadline. It was an event that they'd never missed before, so they really wanted to participate. Especially since the money raised went to such a good cause.

When everyone was finished eating, Blu took care of the check with her gold AMERICAN EXPRESS card. As they exited the restaurant, the cool breeze had turned colder and much more fierce. It smacked them in the face like *Mike Tyson* delivering a sucker punch to *Evander Holyfield.*

Quickly, they hugged one another and said their good-byes, saying that they would see each other at the office in just a little while. They were only five minutes away from the office. But with it still being the morning rushhour, it would take them more like a half-hour to get there.

. . . .

Leland Martin was a man of average height with a wiry frame. He had a distinguished, aristocratic face. Not necessarily alluring, but for his sixty-nine years it was rather comely. Salt and pepper hair matted his head. Although the top of his noggin had already relinquished an abundance of strands.

What he lacked in physical attributes, however, he more than made up for in brains. Leland was highly intelligent. A fierce leader. A rugged competitor. And he could be quite charming. A smooth talker of sorts. He'd been told that he could *sell a drowning man a glass of water.*

Indeed, he was the consummate salesman. He frowned upon one's weaknesses. Marveled at one's strength.

When Leland lost his business partner, Chester McFinley, earlier this year to a rare illness, he took it quite hard. But within a *week* he had bounced back. Regained his bearings and forged ahead. Three years earlier he'd faced an even more daunting setback after losing the love of his life – his wife of forty years.

Leland had always been determined to build a multibillion-dollar advertising agency. One that would rival some of those behemoths in New York. And he was well on his way to accomplishing such a feat – one client acquisition at a time.

The corporate offices of MARTIN/McFINLEY were headquartered in a downtown Atlanta skyscraper. They also had branch offices in *Chicago*, *Boston* and *Miami*.

Leland Martin was perched behind his massive oak desk on this Friday morning, smoking one of his trademark cigars. Sitting in front of him was the person who'd been quite instrumental in helping him to steal – that was such a harsh word – *acquire* some $85 million in billings from ADDISON JAMES & SHEPHERD. He'd hoped that their mounting client losses would be enough to frighten MerLex Motors away from them. He never believed that they should even be in this final review.

It was rather flattering to him, however, that those three women even thought that they could actually compete against him and his agency. In just a matter of time they would come crawling on their pretty little hands, begging him to *buy* their little ad agency. He snickered as the image of them crawling across the floor toward his desk entered into his mind.

"I must say, that I am very pleased with your efforts

over the past few months," he said to the person, a gleeful grin forming on his wrinkly but clean-shaven face. "You have handled every *project* like a true professional."

The person smiled, beaming with pride.

Ceasing with the accolades, he continued. "Well, as promised, I am rewarding you with a nice bonus that I think you'll find to be more than generous." Leland opened his center desk drawer and retrieved a regular size white business envelope. He handed it to the person.

Staring at the amount column on the check, the person's eyes widened considerably.

"Let's complete our final task successfully and there'll be plenty more where this came from," Leland remarked haughtily.

When another visitor was announced by his secretary, he quickly dismissed the person, and eagerly awaited the presence of his newfound companion.

. . . .

"Did you get everything you needed to taken care of?" Blu asked Yelsi as she prepared to get settled at her desk.

Yelsi had asked Blu yesterday if she could be a little late arriving this morning because she had a personal errand to run.

"Sure. Everything's taken care of," she answered.

"Well, I'm glad."

Blu headed back to her office. She closed her door and took a seat behind her desk. She had a stack of phone messages staring back at her. As she began to wade through them all, Yelsi buzzed her. "Yes, Yelsi?"

"Blu, I have a call for you."

Blu waited for her to say who it was. Yelsi was waiting for Blu to give her the okay to transfer the call.

"Yelsi, who is it?"

"He says that it's personal."

The last time she received a call like that it was from some salesman trying to get her to buy refurbished computer printer cartridges. She'd had a heck of a time getting him off the phone.

"Well, tell him that if wants to speak with *Mrs. Addison*, he will have to identify himself."

"Sure."

Seconds later Yelsi was buzzing again.

"Yes?"

"It's a *Mister Schuyler Conklin*."

What! Blu wasn't certain that she heard Yelsi correctly. "Repeat that, Yelsi?"

"Mr. *Conklin*. Schuyler. He says that he's calling from Minneapolis."

Oh my god! How did he? Why was he?

"Blu, shall I transfer him?"

"Um, give me just a sec and then transfer him, please."

"Okay."

Blu quickly tried to slow her breathing. She hadn't spoken to Schuyler since their senior year in high school. And their last conversation consisted of her telling him that she couldn't see or talk to him anymore. She'd regretted those final words ever since. But she had been utterly confused at the time. It was right after she'd given birth to her daughter. *Their* daughter.

"This is Blu Addison," she answered, as professionally as possible.

"Well, well. So it's *Addison* now," Schuyler remarked.

Blu became flustered at just the sound of his voice. A rush of emotions were attacking her. None of which she knew precisely how to handle.

"Schuyler! What a pleasant surprise!"

"I'll say. I have been trying to find you, off and on, for several years now."

"Really? Why? Um, I mean, it looks like you've succeeded!"

"Well, actually I finally broke down and called your mom. She gave me your number."

"You spoke to my mother?"

"Yes I did. Just moments ago in fact. Lucky for me she

still has the *same* telephone number."

Blu emitted a nervous chuckle. "Well, that's my mother for you. Unwilling to change much. She still lives in the same house I grew up in as well."

"No kidding! That is something."

There was a moment of silence.

"So, what about your parents, Schuyler. How are they?"

He coughed and cleared his throat a couple of times before answering. "Unfortunately they were both killed in an automobile accident about ten years ago now."

"Oh, I am so sorry, Schuyler. I didn't know."

"Of course. It's okay."

Blu felt her stomach tighten. "How awful!"

"Yes, it was pretty tough losing them both at the same time like that. But you know what? Time has a way to healing even the most dire heartaches."

"I guess that's true." She never knew him to be so philosophical. Then again, there was perhaps a whole lot that she didn't know about him. A lot of years had stood between them.

"I suppose you're wondering why I called?"

She most certainly was, but she tried to keep her voice from inflecting it. "Well, whatever the reason, it's definitely a pleasure hearing from you."

"That's sweet of you to say, Blu. But of course, from what I remember you were always a sweet girl."

Her right leg began to pump up and down like a piston in a car's engine. What was he trying to do to her?

"Anyway, Blu. There's something very important that I want to speak with you about and I was hoping that you would afford me an opportunity to meet with you. Say, one day next week?"

"Um, may I ask what's it in regards to?"

"Well, I'd rather not say over the phone. Suffice it to say, however, that it's nothing bad or anything to be alarmed about. At least I don't believe that it is."

She wouldn't dare refuse an opportunity to see him again. Especially since she never thought that she ever would. Blu quickly perused her desk calendar. "Um, I can meet with you next Tuesday afternoon if that'll work for you?"

He answered without hesitation. "Next Tuesday it is! I should be able to get a flight out of Minneapolis-St. Paul either Monday night or Tuesday morning. I'll call you from the airport when I arrive to get directions to your office."

"All right. That'll be fine."

"Great. I look forward to seeing you again, Blu."

"Same here."

Long after the call had ended, Blu found herself wondering what Schuyler's request to speak to her was all about. She was a little disappointed that she let the call end too soon. There were the usual questions that she would like to have had answers to. What was he doing for a living? Was he married? Kids? How many? What were their ages? And of course, he doesn't know anything about her either.

Having heard his voice again after so many years, suddenly brought back a lot of old memories. Fond memories.

They were only teenagers when they met one another. Yet, what had developed between them was as real as the breath you take. She'd had an undying love for Schuyler. They understood each other so well back then.

She recalled the Saturday walks in the park with him. Holding hands. Gazing into one another's eyes for long periods of time.

Before she met Schuyler, she had never felt a love like that. Some might argue that it wasn't real, couldn't have been real because they were both so young. But she would counter such an argument by posing the question: *is love defined by age?* And if so, then by who's definition?

It would be terribly wrong for anyone to try and limit the scope and boundaries of love. Chronologically or otherwise.

Reaching for the phone, Blu knew that there was one person she needed to say a few things to about her sudden reflections on Schuyler Conklin. She dialed the digits hurriedly.

"Hi Mom, this is your daughter."

"Well hello there, honey. I was sitting here wondering how long it would take before you called me."

It was confirmed. Audrey Knight had been meddling.

chapter 19

Kiwi left the office on Friday at her usual three o'clock time. Not only did she want to get a jump on the impending traffic rush, but also she was planning to stop by the Golf Club at WindFair Estates to visit that Marshal.

Blu and Flavia were still at the office. She figured Flavia would be there a while. Girlfriend had messages stacked so high that she could make them into a book. But what did she expect? Missing two weeks of work running around taking care of *personal* business. Hell, their *agency* was personal business. And Flavia needed to get her behind in gear.

A car in front of Kiwi made a sudden stop, causing her to slam on the brakes. She had several magazines setting in the passenger seat of her car. There were various issues, which ranged from PARENTS, WORKING MOTHER, and CHILD to AMERICAN BABY, BABY TALK and FIT PREGNANCY. She'd planned to go through them one day next week looking for helpful articles as she prepared to become a new mom.

The magazines were now strewn about the car.

"You damn idiot!" Kiwi yelled at the driver. There had not been another car in front of the driver so she had no idea why the fool made a sudden stop in the middle of the freakin' highway.

The woman driver, clearly embarrassed by her actions, sped up so fast that her car quickly disappeared from Kiwi's view. "Crazy heifer!"

Minutes later Kiwi was exiting off Georgia Highway 400, very relieved to be navigating the more sensible two-lane road that led to WindFair Estates.

As she pulled into the parking lot at the golf course, it was packed. She was glad that she wasn't playing today. You could still play until almost seven o'clock in the evening. But when the time changes back an hour, as it was scheduled to do at the end of the month, it would start getting dark by six. That would make it impossible for her to get her usual eighteen holes in on Fridays after work.

Kiwi entered the clubhouse.

"Miss Shepherd, how are you doing?" the assistant golf pro greeted her. All the guys in the Pro Shop knew her by name since the course had nearly become her second home.

"I'm doing fine," she answered.

"Are you looking to play?"

"No, not today. But I need some help with something."

"All right. What can I help you with?"

"Well, me and two other ladies had a seven-thirty tee-time a few weeks ago. It was on Saturday, September twenty-first," Kiwi explained. "And I'm trying to find out the name of the Marshal who was on duty that morning."

The assistant golf pro began to look through some records.

"I know most of the Marshals out here," she added. "But I'd never seen him before."

"Oh, all right then. That had to be the new guy. His name is Beckett. *Howard Beckett.*"

Blu quickly jotted down the name. "Is he around?"

The assistant golf pro scratched his head. "No, I'm afraid not. He went up to North Carolina to do some fishing with the grandkids. But he'll be back on Tuesday."

"Tuesday?"

"That's right. He's traveling back on Sunday afternoon."

Kiwi tried to hide her disappointment.

"Is there anything I might be able to help you with?" he asked, noticing her sad look of defeat.

She thought about asking him all sorts of questions but then decided that she'd wait until Mr. Beckett returned.

"It's nothing urgent," she answered. "I'll drop back by to speak with Mr. Beckett on Tuesday." Kiwi thanked him for his time.

Before leaving the Pro Shop she purchased three-dozen TITLEIST PRO V1 golf balls. She'd lost count of the number of balls that she couldn't find when they played with Yelsi some three weeks ago.

Your days are clearly numbered Yelsi Nitram, she thought to herself as she made a sharp turn into her driveway. The garage door hadn't opened. The stupid thing was acting all crazy again. As much money as she'd paid for this house she became easily annoyed by little things like this. The builder had installed the garage door openers. She hoped that he hadn't put in some cheap brand. She'd barely been living in the house for a year.

Kiwi pressed the button again on the opener, which she had affixed to the visor inside her car. The garage door grunted loudly a couple of times before it began to maneuver upwards.

Kiwi waited impatiently. She could almost imagine what the garage door would say if it could actually talk – *why don't you get your lazy behind out the car and lift me up?*

"Not when I've already paid to have a remote!" she answered to herself.

Finally, she zipped the PORSCHE inside the garage.

Seeing the shiny black Jaguar sedan already parked inside brought a glowing smile to her face. Her *man* was already home.

chapter 20

"This is Blu Addison's office," Yelsi answered. "May I say who's calling?" she asked. "One moment, please." She was about to buzz Blu's phone in her office when she noticed her coming down the corridor.

"Your door was closed so I thought you were still in your office," Yelsi said to her as she approached.

"I was on the other side of the floor. You had already gone to the break room when I left."

"Oh. Well, I have a *Mr. Anthony Merriweather* from MerLex Motors on line one."

"Thank you. Give me a sec to get at my desk and then transfer him," she instructed Yelsi. "By the way," she turned to Yelsi before closing her door. "You were right. I checked and *American Pie* was not a sixties song. It was released in nineteen seventy-two."

Yelsi smiled. "That was a really fun quiz. We'll have to

do it again soon."

"Definitely!" Blu remarked, closing her office door.

Yelsi retrieved the call that had been placed on hold. "Mr. Merriweather, Mrs. Addison will be right with you."

Seconds later the call had been transferred.

. . . .

Flavia was meeting with Kiwi in Kiwi's office. They'd been reviewing some outstanding media buys for the three clients that had chosen to leave them for MARTIN/McFINLEY.

"It looks like we'll be able to wrap up everything within the ninety-day window that we have," Flavia said, perusing the agency's media schedule.

"That's a relief," sighed Kiwi. "I thought for sure we were going to run into a situation where we had already committed the agency to a bunch of ad buys that would have been non-cancelable."

"Well, that could have easily been the case. But since I've been out of the office lately, I didn't have time to give final approval to a lot of the buys that my media planners had submitted for the first quarter of next year."

Kiwi smirked. "So, I guess you did some good after all by being away, huh?"

"Watch yourself, now," Flavia joked.

There was a knock at the door.

"Come in," Kiwi called out.

It was Blu. "Hi guys," she greeted them.

They returned the greeting.

"Where's Nathan?" Blu asked, referring to Kiwi's executive assistant.

"Oh, I sent him to the downtown branch of the library. We've been putting together a competitor analysis report on MARTIN/McFINLEY and I had Nathan going through some past issues of ADVERTISING AGE to find any articles on them."

"Don't we keep back issues here?" asked Flavia.

"Yeah, but ours only go back to January of this year," answered Kiwi.

"That sounds like a good idea," said Blu. "Make sure that I get a copy of the report when you guys have completed it."

"Will do. I figured that since they have been stealing our clients, we might as well start attacking them."

Blu shook her head. "I don't want us stooping to their level."

"Who said anything about *stooping*?" Kiwi shot back.

"You know what I'm talking about, Kiwi."

"Blu's right," added Flavia. "I have no doubt that MARTIN/McFINLEY will eventually get what's coming to them."

"Yeah, that's probably true. But I'm just going to make sure they get it in full measure," Kiwi threw in the last word.

The women discussed the possibility of reducing their

staff in the wake of the three client losses. Blu explained to them that the human resources director had put some numbers together to ascertain the impact that the eighty-five million dollars in losses would have on the agency.

"Right now, we're looking at possibly having to cut thirty people," Blu told them.

ADDISON JAMES & SHEPHERD employed a total of two hundred and twenty-seven people.

"So, about thirteen percent?" Flavia asked.

Blu nodded. "I told HR that we would wait until the absolute last minute before we did anything."

"You know this will be the first time that we've ever had a significant staff reduction since we started," Kiwi spoke solemnly.

Blu and Flavia nodded in agreement. "The most we've ever let go at once has only been *six* people," Blu stated.

"Well, I just hope we don't have to go through with it," Flavia said. "And if we do, then we need to wait until after the holidays."

They all agreed that waiting until after the Christmas holiday would be their course of action should they have to carry out the reduction in staff.

"What are you two doing for lunch?" Kiwi asked.

Blu answered, "I have an old friend that's in town who I'm meeting for lunch this afternoon."

"An *old friend*?" Kiwi asked, obviously wanting more information.

"That's all that you need to know, Kiwi."

"How old?" Flavia thought she'd ask.

"All right, you two!"

"We're just curious," Flavia remarked.

"I am a married woman, still," Blu said. And immediately after saying it she wished that she could retrieve the words.

"*Still*?" Flavia repeated.

"Well, I mean I am," Blu tried defending herself. "Listen, my point is that I have a husband, so you guys can stop with the insinuations about my old friend."

Surprisingly, Kiwi didn't press her on the subject.

"Anyway," Blu continued. "I have one more phone call to make before I get out of here, so you two have a nice lunch."

Kiwi and Flavia wished her well as she departed the office.

"So, what about you?" Kiwi asked Flavia.

"Unfortunately, I'm gonna be eating my lunch at my desk. You ought to know how much paperwork I'm buried under."

"So, y'all just leaving a sista to hang by herself?"

"Call your *man* up!" Flavia teased her. "What was his

name again?"

"Don't even try it, girlfriend! I never told you his name yet."

"It didn't hurt to try."

"Humph."

Flavia and Kiwi continued to chat for a little while longer before Flavia heard her name being paged over the intercom by the receptionist.

chapter 21

Since her two partners couldn't join her for lunch, Kiwi decided to drive out to the Golf Club at WindFair Estates to try and speak with the golf Marshal, *Howard Beckett*. When she arrived at the clubhouse she headed straight for the Pro Shop.

There was a different assistant behind the counter. A female. Kiwi hadn't seen her around the clubhouse before. The older woman greeted Kiwi. A somber look was crowding her face.

"Hi. I was wondering if Mr. Beckett is available? I was told that he'd be in today."

The woman's eyes immediately glazed over. Her head dropped slightly, her eyes shifting between Kiwi and the folder that lay on the counter. "I take it you haven't heard?"

"Heard what?"

The woman dabbed at her eyes with the back of her

hand. "Howie was killed in an automobile accident this past weekend."

"Oh my god!" Kiwi was taken aback. "Um, no I hadn't heard. What happened?"

She dried her eyes again. "Well, he was returning from a fishing trip up in North Carolina on Sunday afternoon when he apparently lost control of his pickup truck on I-Eighty-Five and veered into the northbound lanes hitting another car head-on."

"Oh no. Were there other people hurt?"

"Yes. But Howie was the only fatality."

Kiwi shook her head. While she didn't really know Howard Beckett, the loss of a life was always an unfortunate tragedy. Instinctively her hand moved to her stomach. *Life* was growing inside of her. Something so fragile, yet so precious.

"Was Howie a friend of yours?" the woman asked.

Kiwi hesitated. "Um, I'd just met him for the first time a little over three weeks ago. He seemed like a really nice man."

"Howie was great!" She then paused, as if allowing herself a moment to relish whatever memories he may have left behind. "Even though he'd only been with us for a short while, everybody around here loved him. He was funny and he was a hard worker."

"It's just so sad," said Kiwi, unsure of what else to say.

There was brief silence in the air between them.

"Um, do you know anything about the funeral arrangements?" Kiwi asked.

"Yes. The funeral will be held tomorrow in his hometown of Durham. I can give you all the information if you like? Some of the guys from here are driving up."

Kiwi shook her head. "Sure. I won't be able to attend but I'd like to send some flowers."

The woman grabbed a notepad and jotted down the information, copying it from another piece of paper. When she finished she handed the information to Kiwi.

"Thank you. And again, I am very sorry."

A caliginous cloud was cast over her mood as well as her emotions as she drove back to the office. While standing in the Pro Shop moments ago she'd debated whether to pursue her inquisition of Yelsi Nitram with the woman there, but somehow it no longer seemed a burning desire for her to find out who this girl was.

She hadn't given up. Had no intentions of giving up. And while Kiwi didn't consider herself to be religious, she knew that somewhere in the *Good Book* it talked about there being a time for everything. And right now, it was a probably a time to simply refrain and allow others to mourn.

. . . .

Flavia had just finished her lunch behind the closed doors of her office. She didn't know why she chose not to have lunch with Kiwi. The less time she spent by herself the better. Her every idle thought was being consumed by her medical condition.

As a partner within the agency, she knew that she had a responsibility as well as an obligation to let Blu and Kiwi know about her cancer. And she would tell them. Soon.

She had so many responsibilities at the agency that she did not want to leave Blu and Kiwi hanging. She gave thought to their recent client losses. That was enough motivation for her to at least try and help the agency win MerLex Motors. Besides, it was imperative that she remain busy. Flavia believed that to do otherwise would simply be a surrender to the cancer. That ominous white flag wasn't about to be waved from her hand.

Gathering up some files from her desk, Flavia left her office and headed toward the office of one of her media planners. When she arrived, the young woman's door was open. Her back was turned away from the door as she was diligently pecking keys on the computer.

"Hi," Flavia said entering the office.

She turned around. "Hi, Flavia. How are you?"

"I'm fine. I just wanted to drop these files off to you." She handed the media planner the small stack of files.

"Are these the clients we spoke about recently?" she asked, as she took files and set them on her desk.

"Yes. And all I need for you to do is simply review each of their scheduled print buys for the first quarter of next year."

"Okay," the media planner replied.

Flavia thanked her and made her way back down the corridor to her office. It dawned on her just how much she was going to miss all these people that she worked with. She'd come to consider them like family. But they, too, were oblivious to the disease eating away at her body.

None of her other friends knew either. Since finding out about her condition, Flavia had only revealed the news to her older sister living in St. Louis.

Her mom had passed several years ago and she never knew her father. And she hadn't communicated with her other two brothers in so long that she didn't know how to reach either of them.

Parker had shared the news with both his parents. He had no siblings.

Most distressing to Flavia lately, however, was how to tell her two boys. Or, whether or not to even tell them. She and Parker had discussed the matter well into the wee hours last night while lying in bed. He didn't think that it was a good idea to say anything to them just yet. But Flavia wasn't so sure that there'd ever come a *good* time to tell them.

She was trying very hard to continue each day as if it was just another day. But she could feel that she wasn't getting any better. Her total weight loss now was forty pounds from her normal one seventy-five. And for a woman of her height, she worried about appearing anorexic.

Her mind was almost made up with regards to the treatment options. She was thinking that she didn't want to undergo any of them. The side effects and difficulties that would be brought on from the treatments were not worth it. Especially since the treatment options that had been explained to her would only seek to lessen her ensuing pain, not necessarily prolong her life.

Flavia James was coming to terms with the inevitable.

. . . .

When Schuyler Conklin had arrived at Atlanta's Hartsfield International Airport, Blu gave him directions to the CIAO BELLA restaurant. She arrived at the restaurant early and obtained a table for two.

Blu stared saucer-eyed as she watched, from a cozy corner of the restaurant, the waitress escort Schuyler to the table. She would have recognized him anywhere. After twenty-something years he still looked the same in the face. His hair, a rich cocoa, no longer covering his ears, was neatly trimmed. He appeared taller and much more athletic-looking than he did back in high school. He was wearing navy trousers with a matching turtleneck and a black, two-button leather blazer.

When he arrived at the table – *finally* – Blu stood and the two of them embraced. She immediately got a whiff of the cologne he was wearing. She was all too familiar with the scent. GIVENCHY. She'd given a bottle recently to Damien for his birthday.

Their embrace seems to linger. The two of them, arms wrapped around one another, bringing back memories of their first hug together years ago just outside the doors to the gym.

Schuyler whispered into her ear how much he missed her. The breath of his voice was warm. She could feel trickles of perspiration abandoning her armpits, seeking a drier haven. Part of her thought it best to do likewise. The weaker part.

While they waited for their food to be brought to them, they took advantage of the opportunity to catch up.

Schuyler had never married, though he'd come close to taking the plunge four years ago. He had taught high school social studies for several years while coaching the high school's golf team. The last six years he'd served as the head coach of the golf team at the University of Minnesota in Minneapolis.

Blu learned that Schuyler was an excellent golfer. So

much so that he was on sabbatical from the university while he prepared to try and make the PGA Tour. He'd been accepted into the PGA's *Q-School*, which was a qualifying tournament for golfers seeking to gain entrance into the prestigious world of professional golf.

"That is absolutely wonderful, Schuyler! I never knew you even played golf!"

"Well, my father got me started when we lived in Canada. I was about twelve."

"Why didn't you play when we were in high school? I mean, I don't think you participated in any sports."

"I know. I guess I had *other* things on my mind back then," he said, smiling coquettishly.

Blu returned a knowing smile to him, her toes curling slightly inside the black leather, GUCCI stiletto-heel booties that she was wearing.

"So, how will you know if you've made the Tour?"

"Oh, I don't want to bore you with all the details," he answered sheepishly.

"Not at all! I would love to know how it all works. Not that I'm planning to sign up or anything."

"Do you play?"

"I've been playing for a few years."

"Really? What's your handicap?"

Blu became embarrassed. "I'm not that good."

"Oh, come on! I won't tell anyone," he teased.

"Fifteen."

"Not bad. And how long have you been playing?"

Blu thought for a moment. Damien had gotten her interested in golf before she started the ad agency. "I guess about seven years."

"A fifteen handicap for an amateur isn't too bad. Have you taken any professional lessons?"

"With my work schedule?"

"Okay, I'll take that as a 'no'. Well, I'd love to take a look at your swing and see if I can help."

Blu smiled. "Thanks. That would be nice." Then maybe she could give that Kiwi Shepherd some serious competition.

Schuyler decided to go ahead and give her a brief tutorial. "Okay, in terms of Q-School, basically it's one big qualifying tournament that is played in three stages of stroke play. Field sizes for the first, second and final stages are approximately *nine-hundred-fifty*, *four-sixty-eight* and *one-fifty-six*, respectively. Now, the second and final stages are made up of players advancing from the previous stage and players who meet special requirements to be exempt directly into those stages." He paused. "Following me so far?"

Blu nodded, her eyes fixed on his. Her ears soaking in every available syllable emanating from his mouth.

"The first and second stages are seventy-two hole

events which are held at different sites across the country. Each site has a field of about seventy-eight players. An equal percentage of players – I'd say about twenty – from each site advance to the next stage. The final stage consists of one-hundred-eight holes played over six days."

"Wow!"

"Yes, it's grueling. It's a test of physical and mental strength. This year the finals will be held at *PGA West* in LaQuinta, Califomia the first week in December."

Blu couldn't believe that players had to endure all that to make the PGA Tour. "So, what stage are you in?"

"Well, I'll be starting in the first stage which is scheduled for later this month."

"So, if you make it to the final stage does that mean you make the Tour?"

"Not quite. The *top thirty-five* players and any *ties* after the conclusion of the final stage will receive their PGA Tour card. And the next fifty players will have exempt status on the *Nationwide Tour*."

"Nationwide Tour?"

"Yes. It's taking over what's now the *Buy.com* tour."

"Oh." She was familiar with that tour, having watched a few Buy.com golf tournaments on *The Golf Channel*. "Do you have to pay anything to get into Q-School?"

"Most definitely. After meeting the application requirement there's about a *four thousand dollars* entry fee."

"Four grand? And what if you don't make it all the way through?"

Schuyler shrugged his shoulders. "It's a choice that every player has to make for himself. For me, it's always been a dream. So, the investment is well worth it."

Blu gave a deep sigh. "I guess it's probably the same for the LPGA too?" she asked, referring to the *Ladies Professional Golf Association.*

"Yes, it's similar. Of course, they have their own qualifying school program."

"I think I'll stick to simply playing every now and then."

They laughed.

She shared with Schuyler that she had an executive assistant who had played golf in college and now carried a zero handicap. Schuyler was impressed, saying that he'd love to meet her one day.

The waitress brought out their lunch. As they were finishing it, Blu's cell phone began to ring. She thought she had turned it off. After apologizing to Schuyler, she excused herself from the table to take the call privately.

"Is everything all right?" he asked Blu when she returned to the table. He could see the look of concern on her face.

"Unfortunately, I have to get back to the office. I'm

really sorry, Schuyler, but there's an urgent matter I have to attend to."

"No need to apologize. These things happen."

She was very disappointed. Schuyler hadn't even told her what he wanted to speak to her about.

"You're welcome to stay and finish your lunch," Blu told him. "I've already taken care of the bill."

"Why, thank you, Blu. I'll have to return the favor."

Blu was hit with a suggestion. "Schuyler, were are you staying?"

"Well, I haven't actually chosen a hotel yet. I'd planned on doing that from the airport. I was assuming that I'd have some extra time on my hands when I initially arrived, but . . ."

"Say no more. You can stay at my house."

During their catching-up period Blu had told Schuyler that she was separated from her husband.

"Oh, I wouldn't want to impose, Blu."

She fanned the air with her hand. "Nonsense! It's no imposition at all. My home has five bedrooms and I can only sleep within one of them at a time."

He chuckled slightly. "Five? And no children?"

"I guess we were thinking ahead."

"Okay. But only on one condition – "

"And what is that, *Mr. Conklin*?"

"You must allow me to prepare dinner?"

"Dinner? As in *you* cook all the food?"

"All of it."

If a black woman could blush beet red, Blu was all that and then some. "Deal."

She pulled the key to her front door from her key chain and handed the key to Schuyler. She gave him the directions to WindFair Estates. Then she phoned the security gate and gave them Schuyler's name so that he wouldn't have any problems getting in.

"I should be home around seven o'clock. So you just make yourself comfortable. The alarm system isn't on so don't worry about that."

"Are you sure you're okay with this?"

"I'm sure."

"Fine. Is there any particular bedroom I should put my things in?"

"Oh, of course. The guest bedroom is at the end of the hallway. Just turn right at the top of the stairs. The bedroom has its own bathroom and it should already be stocked with fresh towels, but if you need more the linen closet is in the hallway."

Schuyler allowed the helpful instructions to sink in. "I think I got it all down."

"All right, then. I guess I'll see you when I get home."

He winked at her.

"Don't work too hard!" he called out to her as she prepared to exit the restaurant.

As Blu drove back to the office she couldn't get over the fact of how handsome Schuyler was. And she couldn't believe how giddy she'd suddenly become.

She wasn't absolutely certain that it was a good idea to invite him to stay at her house. It felt right at the time. She realized that she hadn't seen the man in over twenty years. But after seeing him again and talking with him, it was as if no time at all had elapsed between them.

Schuyler Conklin was okay, she assured herself. He was just one of those people that you had good instincts about. She had always known him to be kind and considerate. Of course, it was during their high school days that such attributes were manifested. He was just a teenager then. But generally, people didn't change all that much over the years.

She tried to recall information from an article that she'd read which stated that a person's personality was already developed and set by the time they were *eight* years of age, or maybe it was *twelve*. She couldn't remember the exact age, but it was certainly before they were a teenager.

If Schuyler Conklin turned out to be a serial rapist or some crazy axe murderer then . . . well, she would have learned not to be so trusting of people.

chapter 22

"You are absolutely amazing!" Blu was complimenting Schuyler after devouring the last bite of the delectable dinner that he'd prepared. "This was an incredibly delicious dinner, Schuyler."

He was sitting at one end of the long mahogany dining table and she at the other. She couldn't believe that he was such an excellent cook. Who would've thought – an excellent golfer *and* an excellent cook? Even the dining table had been neatly arranged, as if *Martha Stewart* herself had paid a visit to her home.

Schuyler had adorned the table with a crisp white linen tablecloth. She didn't own one, so he must have gone out and purchased it.

In the center of the table sat a fresh bouquet of flowers, flanked by two long white candles. Her fine china plates never looked so beautiful as they framed the table.

There was a place setting at each of the eight chairs.

The man was even astute when it came to setting the table correctly. A white linen napkin was appropriately placed on the left side of each plate along side the fork. On the right lay the knife and then the spoon. There was a crystal wine glass and water glass at each place setting as well.

"I suppose it's fair to say that I've had many years of practice," he remarked, completing his last bite also. "I mean, what's a bachelor to do? One cannot eat out *every* night."

"Schuyler, with a meal like *this* I'm surprised that you are still a bachelor!"

He wiped his mouth with his napkin, folded it and returned it to his lap, and then took a long sip from his wine glass. "Mmmm. This wine is quite soothing. I hope you don't mind that I served it."

"Not at all! I told you to make yourself at home."

"Well, I didn't know if the wine rack was for decorative purposes or something."

"Oh, don't be silly, Schuyler."

Silence pervaded the room momentarily.

"You have a very beautiful home, Blu," he remarked, obviously attempting to delay having to discuss the more important conversational topic.

"Thank you. We like . . . " She cut her words short, quickly realizing that there was probably no more 'we'.

Schuyler picked up on the blunder. "Blu, if you don't mind me asking, are you and Darrell planning to reconcile?"

"It's *Damien*."

"Sorry."

She nodded, indicating her acceptance of his apology, and then continued. "Well, as I mentioned to you at lunch, our last conversation together was when I told him about the baby. I could tell that, just hearing the news was upsetting to him."

Schuyler lifted his wine glass and began to rotate it just ever so slightly, causing the red liquid to swirl around. "You know, I still can't believe that you waited so long to tell him."

She couldn't believe it either. But the fact of the matter was that she *had* waited so long. Perhaps too long. "If I had to do it all over again I would handle things differently."

Schuyler chuckled to himself. "I don't know of anyone who wouldn't relish an opportunity to go back and do something over in their life."

"That's true. But you know what, I have learned that trying to live in the past is like believing that you can walk through a fiery furnace unscathed."

"A difficult task at best."

"More than difficult – impossible."

"Yes, but don't you think that, sometimes, in order for

a person to see where they're going, they might have to go back and see where they've been?"

Blu fiddled with the spoon that lay on the table, pondering his question. "There comes a time when we all have to revisit our past. But you see, there's a big difference between *revisiting* the past and trying the *live* in the past."

He nodded. "Your point is well taken."

"Schuyler, what is it that you wanted to speak with me about?" Since he didn't seem to be broaching the subject, she decided that she would.

"I was just about to go there," he said, rising from the table. "You mind if we move into the other room. I mean, now that dinner is over I see no need for us to be so *distanced* from one another."

"Certainly. But remember, you put us at opposite ends of the table, not me."

He laughed. "Yes, I suppose I could have seated us closer."

Blu led him into the den. She sat down on the high-back over-stuffed sofa. He sat down next to her. Sitting on the edge he turned to face her. "Blu, I came here fully prepared to share what was on my mind. What I didn't expect was to learn that you and your husband had separated as a result of what happened when you were sixteen."

"How does that make any difference?"

"Well, I'm just not sure if that's an area that you want to venture into again."

"*Again*? So, I take that to mean that you came here to discuss the past?"

"Well, not so much the past, but the future. I want to find our daughter, Blu. I realize that it's been a very long time and God only knows where she is, but I figure that if we worked together . . . well, we just might get lucky."

Blu wasn't surprised at Schuyler's request. Actually, she had anticipated it after receiving his phone call last week. She'd always felt guilty about how he never had a voice in the entire adoption matter. And it was only recently that she allowed herself to try and imagine how he must have felt. His baby girl given away. Maybe he would have preferred to at least look at her when she was born. Touch her once. Allow her tiny hand to grasp his index finger, gripping it so tightly as only babies can do.

But such an opportunity was never afforded him. Perhaps if she would've had the baby in Muncie and not hundreds of miles away in Atlanta, he could have been by her side. No doubt would have been by her side.

Blu remained silent a while longer. Unsure of how to respond to Schuyler's request.

"If you're unable to help me find her or are unwilling, then I understand," he continued to speak, not wanting the absence of sound to prevail upon them. "But I have to try. I simply have to."

She cleared her throat. Her eyes scrutinizing every inch of his face, searching for and then finding the wounded look in his hazel eyes. Eyes that now were so clearly haunted by an inner pain. A pain in which she failed to see earlier when they met at the restaurant. "How long have you wanted to look for her?"

"Since *December sixteenth, nineteen eighty-one*."

"You remembered the date of her birth."

"No one forgets the birth of their child, Blu. Especially not their firstborn."

Blu looked away from him for a moment. She knew that her eyes were welling up. Silently she berated herself for being such a powder keg of emotions. "It's hard to believe that she'll be twenty-two in a couple of months."

"Yes, I know. And I hope to God that I've found her by then."

"I will do whatever I can to help find our baby. Our daughter."

His heart swelled within him. "Thank you, Blu."

"Schuyler, I am so sorry for the way things turned out. She was just as much your baby as she was mine. You should have had a say."

He took hold of her hand and placed it within his. "You

were sixteen, Blu and I was seventeen. Our parents were older and they outnumbered us."

"True. But tell me, Schuyler, can you honestly say that you were *ready*, at seventeen years of age, to be a father?"

"I don't think anyone is really ever ready. I would like to think that I would have tried my best. I mean, I knew how I felt about you and I know I wouldn't have felt any less about our baby."

Like clockwork her tears had already assembled just inside her eyelids, waiting for one blink to send them on their merry way. "I'm not sure if I can say the same thing," her voice crackled and her bottom lip curled. "I was so afraid, Schuyler."

He let go of her hand and placed his arm around her shoulder, pulling her gently closer to him. "You wouldn't have been alone, Blu. I told you that I would always be there for you."

Her tears no longer waited for permission to flow. "You are such a wonderful man, Schuyler! I didn't deserve you."

"Blu, please don't say that."

"It's true! When I came back home from Atlanta you needed me and what did I do? I broke up with you, Schuyler! I said that I didn't want to ever see you again! And you had done nothing to deserve that! Absolutely nothing!"

"Blu, listen to me. Just because you broke up with me didn't mean that I broke up with you." He paused to allow that fact to sink in. "I never dated anyone else during those final months of high school. And since high school, I've dated a grand total of *two* people – neither of them serious."

He handed her his handkerchief to dry her eyes. She accepted it. "Two people, Schuyler?"

He held up two fingers in front of her.

"That is so sad . . . wait, actually that's just pathetic."

The two of them engaged in a hearty laugh.

"I've never stopped loving you, Blu Marie Knight." His words took her by surprise. Yet the sound of them felt like an ocean tide of joy washing over her. Deep inside her heart she knew without a doubt that she'd never stopped loving him, and part of her wanted so desperately to return his timely overture. But the fact of the matter was, she was *still* a married woman.

"I don't know what to say, Schuyler."

He put his finger to her lips. "You don't have to say anything."

She asked him if wanted more to drink. He told her that another glass of red wine would be great. While she poured them both another glass, he walked over to her CD collection and began to call out some of the titles within the immense collection.

"I see you guys have a wide range of taste when it comes to music," he commented.

"Actually, those are all mine. Damien took his CDs with him when he moved out."

"I see. So, it appears that you still have a love for nostalgia."

"Meaning?"

"Well, I see a lot of stuff from the seventies. But wait, maybe I spoke to soon. Here's a current one – *Alicia Keys*. I guess maybe you are up to date."

Blu rejoined him in the den, handing the glass of wine to him. "I love all types of music," she said.

"That I can see. You have enough here to start your own radio station!"

She smiled. "What about you? Have your taste in music changed from what I remember?"

"And what do you remember?"

"Let's see . . . I recall you being a big fan of *Fleetwood Mac*, *Earth Wind and Fire*, and the *Eagles*."

"Wow. I'm duly impressed. Yes, those are all still favorites of mine. But lately, I've been listening to a lot of songs by someone who is considered more of a folk artist, although I happen to think her voice is among the best out there."

"Whom, may I ask, are we talking about?"

"None other than Miss *Eva Cassidy*."

"Are you serious?"

"Yes. Why? Uh, don't tell me you have some Eva within your mix?"

Blu set down her wine glass and began perusing her CD collection. She pulled out *four* Eva Cassidy CD cases. "Here, take your pick," she said to Schuyler, giving him all four.

Schuyler appeared dumbfounded. "You never cease to amaze me, Blu." He began to look over the CDs. "What do we have here, *Songbird*, *Imagine*, *No Boundaries* and *Time After Time*. I have each of these as well."

"I guess we're just two peas in a pod, huh?"

Schuyler grinned. "I've always known that." He chose Eva Cassidy's *Songbird* CD and placed it inside the CD player. He fast-forwarded to track number six.

"Which song did you select?" she asked, her curiosity getting the better of her.

"Just wait and listen."

As soon as the intro piped through the speakers she knew the selection.

Schuyler rejoined her on the sofa, wine glass in hand. "I thought it might be an appropriate song," he said, being careful to nestle right beside her.

"I couldn't agree more."

As Eva's incredible voice oozed forth, they remained silent and allowed themselves the freedom to reflect on the past, enjoy the present, and anticipate what the future might have in store.

Neither of them could have expressed their sentiments any more clearly than the song itself – *Time Is A Healer.*

chapter 23

By the end of the week Schuyler was still enjoying his visit to Atlanta. He explained to Blu that he wanted them to begin their search for their daughter just as soon as he was done with the PGA Tour Qualifying School. But if there was anything that she wanted to initiate before that time it was fine with him.

He stopped by their offices on Wednesday and had an opportunity to meet Yelsi, Flavia and Kiwi. Later, each of them had told Blu how nice he was and how good looking he was also. Blu pretended not to be all that interested, reiterating that Schuyler was just an old high school friend.

Schuyler was scheduled to fly from Atlanta to Orlando on Saturday to visit a cousin prior to starting Q-School. Blu did her best to shield her disappointment at the fact that he would be leaving tomorrow.

It was just after ten o'clock in the morning. Blu had

just come out of a client strategy meeting with Flavia, Kiwi and several account supervisors.

Immediately after the meeting, Kiwi left the office to go home, stating that she had begun to feel nauseated. She told Blu and Flavia that she would finish the day by working from home.

As Blu sat at her desk she was finding it a bit difficult keeping focus on the various tasks that lay before her. She was flipping through the current issue of ESSENCE magazine. An article about *'sisters making millions'* had captured her attention. She'd become so absorbed in it that she didn't hear the knock at her office door. It wasn't until the knocks grew louder that she finally realized someone was at her office door.

"Come in!"

It was Damien.

"Hey. Your assistant wasn't out there so . . ."

"Oh, she must have stepped away from her desk. Come on in."

Damien entered the office, closing the door behind him. "Do you have a moment?"

"Um, sure."

"Well, I know I probably should have called first – "

"It's all right. I was just sitting here reading my ESSENCE."

He gave a nervous smile. "I don't think you've ever missed an issue of that magazine," he remarked.

"Probably not."

Damien wasn't quite sure where to begin or how. "Uh, Blu. I came by because . . . well, I don't want to keep leaving you hanging."

Blu didn't care for the knot that was starting to form inside her stomach. "Are you trying to say that you've made a decision about us?"

He shook his head, finding it difficult to look her in the eyes. "Blu, next week I plan to . . . " He looked away from her again, choosing to stare at a distinguished African-American painting on her wall. Blu walked from behind her desk and sat in the chair across from him.

"You're filing for a *divorce*, aren't you?"

He shook his head again. "I'm sorry."

Even though she expected this action to come sooner or later, it still hit her like a piercing stab in one's gut. "Damien, is there anything that I can say to make you reconsider?"

"Believe me, Blu. I wish there was."

"But this is our marriage we're talking about. Fourteen years, Damien."

"Listen, don't make this any harder than it already is."

"Well, if it's so hard, then why are you doing this?"

He gave a sigh. "Because it has to be done."

"Has our marriage been that terrible that you can't even bring yourself to give it another chance?"

"Blu, there have been numerous chances already. The really sad thing about all this is that, I don't think you know me at all. Yeah, we've lived together for fourteen years, but do you really know me? Do you know what I'm about? What matters most to me? The things I like to do? The movies I enjoy going to see? Because I don't think that you do. Now, I think that you've assumed a lot about me over the years, but as with anybody, *assumptions* are usually ninety-nine and a half-percent *wrong.*"

"Well, if I don't know you, Damien, as you say, then will you allow me the opportunity to get to know you."

He shook his head. "It's too late now. Five or seven years ago, hearing you say that would have meant all the world to me. But I'm beyond that now, Blu."

She was fighting assiduously to remain strong. "*She* must really be something."

"What?"

"The last time we met, at your office, I asked you if there was another woman and you didn't deny that there was."

Damien gave a deep long sigh. "Blu, I hope that you'll believe me when I tell you that I never meant for things to happen the way they have."

"Is it someone from your office?"

"No."

"Someone you've just met? Recently?"

"Does that really make a difference?"

"Yes. As a matter of fact, it does make a difference. I mean, if my marriage is about to go down the tubes all because you've met someone else, then yes, I think I deserve to know who she is!"

Damien stood from his chair. "You know, you are really irritating the hell out of me when you keep trying to make it sound as if this person is why our marriage is over, because you know damn well that she isn't!"

"Would you be seeking a divorce if she were not in the picture?"

He shoved his hands into his pockets and stared out the window. "I've been at this damn divorce crossroad more than you'll ever know. And for whatever reason I just kept making a detour."

"And why is that? Because you love me?"

He returned to his chair and sat back down. "Blu, it has nothing to do with whether or not I love you! I'm not divorcing you because I *don't* love you, but because you have made it very difficult for me *to* love you!"

Blu threw up her hands. "Tell me, what is it that I've

done or keep doing that prevents you from loving me?"

"It's not that simple!"

"Well, does it have anything to do with the fact that I told you about the child I gave up?"

He stifled a laugh. "You're not thinking, Blu. Hadn't I already moved out *before* you had told me anything about what you did when you were sixteen?"

That was true. Her thoughts were becoming so scrambled that she didn't know what to think, or what to say. Her marriage was slipping through her hands and there wasn't anything that she could do to hold on to it.

"Sorry," she uttered.

"Blu, I won't deny that I wasn't hurt by your revelation. And not so much because of *what* or *why* you gave your child up for adoption, but because you didn't think enough of me to share it with me. That was in fact the final blow."

"But don't you understand why I couldn't tell you?"

He shook his head forcefully. "No! There is absolutely no reason why you had to keep something like that from your husband! None. Even if, as you say, you were worried about how I might react, that is still no excuse!"

"You're right. There is no excuse. At least not one that's going to be satisfying to you. I've said that I was sorry. What else can I do?" The question was rhetorical.

"You know, maybe it was never meant for us to be

together for the rest of our lives. Maybe fourteen years is all that we were supposed to have. Things always happen for a reason, Blu. Always. I don't believe in luck, chances or fate."

"Well, I guess we're different in that regard."

"We're different in a lot of regards."

She nodded. "So, are you going to reveal this mystery woman to me or what?"

"Actually, she's not a mystery woman. It's someone you already know."

"Someone that *I* know?" Her heart began to pound. The incessant beating was like the sounds from the drums of a marching band.

"When I tell you, I need you to let me explain how it happened, okay?"

A sickening wave of terror began to build up inside her stomach now. She refused to allow herself time to try and figure out *who* he was about to reveal. "Please, Damien. Just tell me!"

"Blu, it's Gail."

Initially, the name flew right past her. *Gail*? Gail *who*? But then, like a boomerang it flew right back to her, settling in more clearly this time. "Please tell me you're not talking about my former assistant!?"

He remained silent.

Blu literally felt sick to her stomach. Her former

executive assistant – *Gail Adams* – was the reason her husband was leaving her? Her thoughts began to jumble together. How did this come about? When? Why? She considered Gail a friend. She'd done a lot for her during the three years that she worked at the agency. She even threw the woman's baby shower.

Oh my god! *Baby*!

"Damien, how long have you two been seeing each other?" It wasn't a question that she wanted to know the answer to, but knew that it had to be asked.

"Blu, first you have to understand that neither one of us planned for any of this to happen."

"Spare me the patronizing speech, Damien! And just answer my question!"

"Okay, fine. If you really want to know, we've been seeing each other since August of last year and . . . "

"What!" she interrupted him. "Even while she worked for me and you and I were still living under the same roof!" She turned her back towards him for a moment.

Facing him again she asked, "Gail just had a baby, Damien. Is that child yours?"

He didn't answer. Didn't even have to. She saw it in his face. "How could you? How could you just make a fool out of me and then think nothing of it?"

"That's not it, Blu. I wasn't trying to make a fool of you,

you know that!"

"I *don't* know *that*, Damien! And I guess you were right about the fact that I don't know you either!"

"Will you please let me explain everything?"

"Is what you're going to explain going to change how I'm feeling right now, Damien?"

He sighed again. "Maybe not, but at least you'll have a better understanding of how things happened."

"Oh, spare me the details! I don't care to listen to how the two of you fell in love and how you just couldn't control yourselves and . . . "

"Stop it, Blu!" he yelled. "Just stop it, okay. Don't be so quick to forget the *little secret* that you kept hidden from me for the last *fourteen* years!"

Before she realized it she'd stretched forth her hand and swung it full force at him, striking him across the face, a loud smack echoing throughout the room. "How dare you compare my situation to your adulterous tryst! What I went through was a very traumatic event in my life and you have absolutely no right to sit here and try and make yourself feel better about cheating on your wife!"

"Where I come from there's not much of a difference between lying and cheating!"

"So are we supposed to be *even* now? Huh?"

"It's not about that. You can't sit here and try and

cheapen the feelings that I had toward you.You know damn well that I loved you and before last year that I had never cheated on you! What was I suppose to do, Blu? You spent more time at this damn ad agency than you did with me in our own home!"

"That's a lie!"

"The hell it is! I told you many times that I needed you and what did you do? You brushed my feelings aside!"

"Do you think that me working my butt off, twenty-four-seven, trying to make this agency succeed, was all for my benefit?"

"I didn't ask you to start this damn business, Blu! We could have made a nice living on my income alone!"

"Sure, living in a cracker box and driving around in who knows what piece of junk!"

"Yeah, yeah. It's always been about *image* to you. Worrying about what your damn friends think! Trying to out do the next person. Instead, you should have been considering your relationship with your husband, starting a family and focusing on the things that have some *substance*!"

"You may think I'm a shallow person, Damien, but I know that I'm not!"

"Yeah, right. You go right ahead and keep telling yourself that."

"What do you want from me, Damien? What one thing

is there that you just had to have that I couldn't give you?"

"It's not about what you *couldn't* give, Blu. It's what you *chose* not to give."

"Are we talking about kids again?"

"*Again*? Just listen to yourself!"

"Oh, so that is it. It always gets back to me not giving you children! And since I wouldn't have your baby you decided to find some slut who would?"

Damien leaped from his chair and towered over her. Pointing his finger, he yelled, "Don't you ever call her that again! *She* is not going to become the source of your contention!"

Blu had never seen such fire in his eyes. Brutal anger. And before she could respond, he made an abrupt turn and stormed out of her office, making certain that the door slammed hard. It did, rattling the pictures that were hanging quietly against the wall.

Having already heard the commotion from her desk, Yelsi immediately ran into Blu's office once Damien had disappeared down the corridor. "Blu, are you okay?" she asked, kneeling beside the chair Blu had slumped over in, fighting back her tears, resisting the urge to chase after him.

Blu looked up into Yelsi's face. It was littered with concern. Genuine concern. Unable to speak, she simply threw her arms around Yelsi. Yelsi put her arms around Blu as well and began consoling her as best she could, not fully understanding what had just happened.

Minutes later, Flavia, walking by Blu's office, saw the two of them. She went inside to find out the reason for their apparent sorrow. And after Blu calmed herself, she dismissed Yelsi from the room and then she broke down emotionally and shared everything with Flavia. Everything.

Flavia tried to imagine what it must have been like for Blu having to learn that she was pregnant at sixteen, and then have her parents convince her to give the baby up for adoption. And she couldn't believe it when Blu told her that Damien had just found out about it as well. She knew that Blu and Damien had been married for fourteen years. To keep something like that from your spouse . . . well, Flavia thought it was so out of character for Blu.

It didn't occur to her right away that what Blu had just shared was only the tip of the iceberg. The revelation that Gail Adams had been secretly involved with Blu's husband shocked Flavia considerably. But it was even more jolting when she learned that the baby shower that had been thrown for Gail this past June, the one that she helped to put on, had actually been for Damien's illegitimate son.

chapter 24

Their conversation had lasted almost two hours. Kiwi had just gotten off the phone with Flavia. She was just as astonished as Flavia had been when she learned of what went down between Blu and Damien.

Neither of them had any indication whatsoever that things were amiss between Blu and her husband. Blu had always spoken so lovingly of Damien. And while Flavia cherished her own marital bliss, she always believed that Blu and Damien's relationship was truly a godsend.

Kiwi nearly hit the ceiling when Flavia told her that Damien had been involved with Gail Adams since last year and that her new baby was his. Not only could she not believe that Damien would do something like that, but for Gail, someone whom they treated like a sista, to backstab Blu was just plain wrong.

Kiwi was mad as hell. She suggested to Flavia that the

two of them find the heifer and beat the devil out of her! Of course, Flavia had no intentions of entertaining Kiwi's quest for wrath on the woman.

When Kiwi didn't think the news could get any worse, Flavia told her that Blu had had a baby at sixteen and that she'd given the child up for adoption.

Still trying to digest the incredible Friday revelations, Kiwi was sitting on the floor in her den. Prior to Flavia's call, she had been thumbing through an old stack of ADVERTISING AGE magazines. Her assistant, Nathan Nichols, had been gathering articles from past issues at the library. But he'd only gotten through the last quarter of 2001. And since she had some old issues at her house from earlier in 2001, Kiwi decided to lend a hand to his research efforts.

She shook her head disapprovingly as she reached for a *February 19, 2001* issue and began flipping the pages. As her anger continued to brew, she found herself nearly ripping the pages from the magazine as she thumbed through them.

"I just can't believe that heifer!" Kiwi uttered to herself. "Flavia and Blu may not be the fighting kind, but I could just kick her behind all up and down this city!"

Then her feelings began to simmer as she thought about Blu getting pregnant at the age of sixteen and then practically being forced to give the baby up for adoption. And while she didn't agree with Blu's decision to keep her husband in the dark all these years about the adoption, it was still no excuse for Damien to act the way he did.

Kiwi began to consider the child growing inside her. Just the thought of carrying a baby inside you for nine months or more and then experiencing the joy and pain of childbirth, only to hand the baby over to a bunch of strangers, made her shudder. Blu was obviously a very brave woman. She could only image how tormenting her decision has been over the years.

It occurred to her that she could make Blu the *godmother* of her baby. Maybe that would help to ease some of the pain she'd been feeling. Blu was a good person. She had a good heart. Her baby would benefit tremendously by having Blu as a godmother.

Kiwi made a mental note to discuss it with her man sometime this weekend.

She glanced at her watch. It was nearing four o'clock. He would be leaving the office soon. She missed him. She wished that he could have spent the day with her at the house. But she knew that they both couldn't play hooky today. Although, she really hadn't felt well earlier. It was probably something she'd eaten at breakfast.

Lately, her man had been getting a little antsy keeping his identity under wraps. He told her that he felt like he was a *kept* man or something. And how tired he was getting of having to go to movie theaters way across town so that they wouldn't accidentally run into someone they knew here in Alpharetta.

She tried to explain to him how delicate the situation was. Some things just had to be handled with a little caution. She tried to assure him that she wasn't ashamed to be with him, as he had accused her. But that, their relationship, if it was going to work, needed to be handled very carefully. Especially now that the two of them were expecting a baby together.

"What the hell . . . " As she had been flipping through the magazine her eyes were drawn to a photograph that was set within an article on *fathers taking their daughters to work day*. The photo pictured a very proud-looking Leland Martin, standing in front of his agency's downtown headquarters' building. And what captured Kiwi's attention most was the person who'd been standing right beside him.

She quickly read the caption beneath the photograph and learned that the young woman was identified as Leland's twenty year-old daughter. Her name was *Paisley*.

Ripping the page from the magazine, she brought it closer to her face in order to get an even better look. It was true. Without a doubt. Unquestionably. The girl didn't look any different today than she did almost two years ago.

Her adrenaline began pumping faster than a jackhammer in the hands of a construction worker.

What a helluva day for revelations this was turning out to be. She'd finally found her answer. Confirmed what she believed to be true, but couldn't quite put her finger on it. Underscored what she'd suspected from day one.

Yelsi Nitram is Leland Martin's daughter–*Paisley Martin*.

The girl was definitely spying for her father! She never even knew that Leland Martin had a daughter–at least not one so young.

Kiwi took a moment to gather her thoughts. She had to remain calm. Handle this amazing revelation appropriately. Even though she had the mind to drive to the office right now and throw that little lying heifer out the front door.

Dammit! How was Blu going to be able to handle this development? The woman had grown mad crazy over Yelsi, or at least whom she *thought* was Yelsi.

As she continued to consider her next course of action, she wondered why the girl chose Yelsi Nitram? Although she understood why she wouldn't give her true name to them.

Then it hit her. While staring at the name beneath the photograph she figured it out. *Nitram* was simply *Martin* spelled backwards. And *Paisley* was *Yelsiap* spelled backwards. It appears that the smart girl had dropped the 'a' and the 'p'.

How clever. But not too clever for her.

She felt her heart swell with a sense of pride and satisfaction at having stuck with her instincts about the girl. Despite all the flack she had been getting from Blu, she was now glad that she didn't give up. Her gut feeling had told her that Yelsi Nitram had a hidden agenda. It was no coincidence when she just suddenly showed up at the golf course out of nowhere. She didn't really know how long the girl had been planning all this, but one thing she knew for sure – her little game plan was about to end.

And if Blu weren't already reeling from bad news, she would find it hard to resist the temptation to rub this all up in her face. Always taking that girl's side over hers. Someone she barely even knew.

Kiwi folded the entire article and stuffed it inside her attaché case. She couldn't prevent the smile from forming across her face. The girl was about to be busted – big time! And she was going to enjoy every moment of kicking her spying behind to the curb.

Paisley Martin. Kiwi allowed the name to roll slowly off her tongue. *It's time you get ready to pay the piper, girlfriend!*

There was no way that Blu could defend her once she finds out that the heifer is no more than a lying fraud! It was probably going to be one helluva shock as well. But, Kiwi recalled what her momma always said to her and her brothers while growing up: *'even though it's always best to tell it, the truth could still be a bitter pill to swallow'*.

chapter 25

After conferring with Flavia late last Friday night it was decided that they would wait until Monday to tell Blu about Yelsi. Although Kiwi had wanted the two of them to meet over at Blu's house that same evening, Flavia had argued that she didn't think Blu could handle the unsettling news right after her confrontation with Damien.

It was later that weekend that Flavia phoned Blu and told her that the three of them needed to have a meeting early Monday morning. And although Blu inquired about the reason for the meeting, Flavia only told her that it was critical for them to meet and preferably before everyone else arrived.

She told Blu that they would meet at seven o'clock. But when Monday arrived, Flavia and Kiwi had already assembled outside Blu's office by six-fifteen.

"I know this is going to be devastating for Blu," Flavia said, sipping from a cup of STARBUCKS coffee. It was a cool morning outside and the burning brew was hitting the spot with pinpoint accuracy.

Kiwi was munching on two KRISPY KREMES, washing the soft doughnuts down with some DIET COKE. "I know, girlfriend. But she's gotta know the truth. And like my momma used to say, *'the truth can be a bitter pill to swallow'*."

Flavia was thinking to herself – *if only Kiwi knew just how relevant her mother's words were to her own predicament*. Sometimes facing the truth and accepting it was an impossible feat. Especially if that truth held unbearable consequences.

Since learning of her pancreatic cancer, she'd tried to accept it. God only knows how hard she's been trying.

Flavia had found herself having to accept a lot of things throughout her forty-seven year-old life. Going without new clothes as a little girl because her mom was a single parent and could barely make ends meet for their family of four. Being ridiculed because she was the tallest person in her kindergarten class. The shameful absence of a father in her life when most of her friends had *two*. A bad first marriage.

Flavia James had learned to accept many things. Difficult as it was. They had all been like little *truth* pills. But swallowing them had been like trying to guzzle down a full bottle of vinegar.

"Well, I have no doubt that this will hit Blu pretty hard. I mean, when you called and told me that Yelsi was a perpetrator I couldn't even believe it. She is a very sweet young lady. She'd always been kind and polite to me. I didn't want to believe that she could do something like this."

"Humph. She had you two fooled. But I just knew there was something strange about her from the beginning."

Flavia's eyes narrowed at Kiwi. "Is that so?"

Kiwi shook her head 'yes'.

"Kiwi, you were mad from the beginning because the girl kicked your butt on the golf course! Now admit it."

Kiwi drained her remaining soda. "Uh-unh. That's not it at all. I could care less about her golf game. The little heifer just had those sneaky-looking eyes and that fake smile!"

Flavia chuckled. "Yeah, right! "

"You didn't see it because, just like Blu, she was able to pull the wool over your eyes."

"So, ever since that day on the golf course you've been trying to uncover her motive for wanting to work with us?"

"From day one. Think about it, Flavia. The heifer shows up at the golf course with a LOUIS VUITTON golf bag. She drives a brand new BMW Z4. Wears more designer clothes than me. Sports at least two different MOVADO watches. And she expected *me* to believe that she needed a a job – as a *secretary*?"

"Executive Assistant."

"Oh, excuse me. Let's just call it what it really is – a *glorified secretary*, okayyy?"

"You're a trip, Kiwi."

"*That* and a three weeks' vacation, okayyy? But if I wasn't, the girl would still be trying to rip us off even more than she already has!"

Flavia was reserving her judgment on Yelsi. Unlike Kiwi, she didn't believe that Yelsi was capable of helping her father steal some eighty-five million dollars in billings from their agency within the short time that they employed her. Barely a month. There had to be more to her story.

As Blu walked into her office area just before seven o'clock she was surprised to find Flavia and Kiwi sitting outside her door. "Hi guys. Am I late?"

"Oh, no. We just got here not long ago ourselves," Kiwi quickly answered.

"All right. Well, come on inside," she told them, unlocking the door to her office. "I'm anxious to find out what's going on. I mean, it's not like I haven't had enough drama over the past few days already."

Flavia and Kiwi exchanged wincing glances. Kiwi closed the door behind them. Blu dropped her attaché case onto her desk and motioned for them to have a seat on her sofa. She sat in an adjacent chair.

"All right. I'm all ears," she announced. "Let's get to the gist of this *critical* meeting."

Kiwi had her FENDI bag next to her. She reached inside and pulled out the page that she'd ripped from the magazine. "I came across this last Friday," she said, handing the folded clipping to Blu.

"What's this?" Blu asked, as she began to unfold the article.

"See for yourself," Kiwi answered.

Blu noticed the article's large bold headline–TAKE YOUR DAUGHTER TO WORK DAY A SUCCESS AT MANY AD AGENCIES ACROSS THE COUNTRY. "All right, guys. Help me out here. Is there something in this article that I should be focusing on?"

"The *photograph*, Blu." Flavia told her, reluctantly.

Blu allowed her eyes to venture downward to the middle of the page to where the photo was. She recognized Leland Martin immediately. Then her eyes became fixed on the beautiful young woman at his side. She scanned the caption–'*Pictured above and standing outside his agency's headquarters in Atlanta, is MARTIN/McFINLEY's Leland Martin along with his twenty year-old daughter, Paisley*'.

Flavia and Kiwi watched as the shock began to glaze over Blu's face. And while Flavia was regretting the moment,

Kiwi was masking a certain enjoyment at having been proven correct.

Blu looked at the top of the article's page and saw that it was dated over a year ago, *February*. Her gaze returned to the photograph. It was definitely Yelsi.

Blu stood from her chair, wavering slightly as if she'd been shot and was simply waiting to fall. "This is unbelievable," she finally spoke. "Why would she lie to us about who she is?"

"Humph. That's obvious, Blu. Her father used her as a spy against us! I told you that I didn't think our three client losses were coincidences! Leland Martin is trying to do whatever he can to knock us from this MerLex Motors review."

"But that just doesn't make any sense!" Blu shouted. "I mean, Yelsi has barely been at this agency a month! And she doesn't even have access to our client files, they're kept in *your* office Kiwi!"

Blu had wandered over and sat on the edge of her desk. Kiwi bolted from the sofa like a *Jack-in-the-Box*. "Blu, the girl has a security card! She could come in here in the middle of the night if she wanted to. And I don't always lock my office door. I mean there'd never been any reason to."

Flavia weighed in. "I hear what Blu is saying, Kiwi. It

doesn't seem logical that she could've pulled this off in less than a month."

"Well, we have three clients that have left us for her father's agency. That tells me that she pulled it off pretty damn good!"

The three of them continued to debate the issue for several more minutes. And with Blu and Flavia seemingly teamed against her, Kiwi took offense.

"So, y'all gonna just continue to defend this heifer or what?"

"Watch your mouth, Kiwi," Blu scolded her. "This is not high school, so lay off the name calling."

"No, Blu! I'm sick and tired of being made to feel like I'm the bad person here! You hired a damn snitch and you need to own up to the mistake so we can correct it!"'

Blu rose from the corner of the desk where she'd been sitting and stomped over to Kiwi, making certain that she was all up in her face. "You're loving every bit of this, aren't you? You've been against Yelsi since the day we first met her!"

Kiwi took a couple of steps backwards. "Okay, you're right. I'll admit it! Yes, I have been against her from day one. And you wanna know why? Because *my instincts* told me that she was trouble! Up to no damn good! And had *you* done the freakin' background check on her like I begged you to do, we could have cut her behind loose before she ever had a chance to wreak havoc on our agency!"

"Come on, guys," Flavia attempted to settle them. Her efforts went unheeded.

"If she wasn't even using her real name, what good would a background check have done, Kiwi?"

"Duh! It would have raised a red flag! When I found out that no records existed for anyone named Yelsi Nitram, it raised a red flag for me!"

"What are you talking about?"

Kiwi hadn't intended to let them know that she'd hired her uncle to investigate Yelsi. But the cat was now poking its damn head from the bag. "I had her checked out, okay?"

"You what!" Blu yelled, astonished by Kiwi's gumption, though not at all surprised.

"Well, *somebody* had to do it! And since I have an uncle who is a private investigator, I saw no reason why that somebody shouldn't be me!"

Blu glared at her, her emotions becoming more frigid by the second. "So you're responsible for opening this Pandora's box! You just couldn't leave well enough alone, could you Kiwi?"

Before Kiwi could respond there came a knock at the door.

"Come in!" Blu called out, her voice still an octave higher.

The door opened slowly. It was Yelsi.

"I'm sorry to interrupt, Blu. But I just wanted to see if there was anything specific that you wanted me to work on today?" She could tell by the expressions on their faces and the thick tension hovering in the air that something major was happening between them.

As Yelsi stood in the doorway, appearing as innocent as an angel. Blu found it nearly impossible to muster any ill feelings toward her. Even though she'd been lied to, betrayed, and made a fool of – *again.*

"Come inside, Yelsi," Blu instructed her. "And close the door."

Yelsi complied.

"Have a seat," Blu said to her. She sat down in one of the chairs that stood in front of Blu's desk. Blu handed the article to her. "We came across this."

Yelsi looked at the article and then the photograph. A wave of acid was suddenly taking up residence inside her stomach.

She was quite familiar with the article, having clipped it herself to save among other mementos.

Her head remained bowed. She could feel their heated gazes beaming down upon her. This wasn't how she'd intended for things to turn out. She was going to tell Blu the truth.

It was too late now. The truth had found her.

Yelsi rose from the chair. "I'll gather my things," she simply stated, heading for the door.

"Yelsi . . . or, I guess I should say, *Paisley*?" Flavia called to her.

She turned around to face them again, though she made no eye contact.

"Don't you think that we deserve some kind of an explanation?"

"You got that right!" piped Kiwi.

Blu had never seen anyone look so dejected.

"Um, I don't think that you all will believe anything that I have to say right now," she answered, moving again toward the door before turning back to them again. "But, I am very sorry for lying about who I am."

They watched in eerie silence as the young woman, whom they now knew as Paisley Martin, began gathering items from her desk. She didn't have much to retrieve so the task took less than a minute. She fished her security badge from her purse and set it on the desk. And then, with her head bowed in apparent defeat, she exited the 33 TOWER PLAZA building, saying nothing, looking at no one.

The cold wind snapped at her immediately as she stepped outside. She ignored its angry bite. Walking briskly across the parking lot she longed for the warmth of her car.

She needed a familiar place of refuge.

Breathing a sigh of relief as she sat down inside her car, her body shivered from the chill. Placing the key in the ignition she started the car. The engine moaned softly. She quickly turned on the heat. The air was initially cold as it blew forcefully from the vents. Her hair danced wildly around her face.

How she wished that her mother were still alive. She needed her now more than ever.

With the car's gear in reverse, Paisley backed out of the tight parking space. She shifted into *drive* and began a slow departure from the premises.

As she neared the end of the parking lot, she glanced back toward the building. Specifically the first floor. She saw a silhouette in the window that was Blu's office. Unsure if the person standing there, watching her drive away, was Blu or not.

Regardless, Paisley rolled down the driver's side window, and pressing her fingers to her lips, she blew a good-bye kiss into the October air, in the direction of the silhouette. "I never meant to hurt you, Blu," she mumbled to herself. "You've been like a mother to me."

chapter 26

Peering out her office window, Blu was hoping that this day was some sort of bad dream. Her eyes were still misty from watching Yelsi . . . Paisley Martin drive away from the building. She thought she saw what appeared to be a placatory gesture from her. The distance between them precluded her from being certain.

She felt a hand upon her shoulder. "Blu, are you okay?" Flavia asked, standing behind her.

Blu turned from the window and walked over to her sofa and sat down. "Actually, I'm not," she answered honestly. "But in due time I suppose I will be."

Kiwi was finding it hard to believe that Blu had grown so attached to the girl. And she began to wonder if she was going to be blamed for the apparent heartache that Blu was obviously experiencing.

"For what it's worth, Blu, I did not enjoy having to tell

you this," Kiwi offered. She was now sitting in the chair in which Paisley had vacated moments ago.

Blu shook her head in commiseration. "You know, Kiwi, I would have thought for sure that you would have had enough on your plate than to spend your time investigating my assistant."

Kiwi recognized that Blu was angry. She decided not to respond.

"But I guess I was wrong. You've had an awful lot of time on your hands. Perhaps if you were spending more time on cementing our *client relationships* rather than trying to destroy *my relationship* with my assistant, we wouldn't have lost three clients!"

Her words stung Kiwi to the core.

"That's not fair, Blu." Kiwi uttered.

"Trust me – it's fair! Because you don't know how hard I'm biting my tongue right now!"

The hell with her damn anger, Kiwi thought, unable to bite her own tongue any longer. "You know what, Blu? You're one fine piece of work! Rather than focus on what that damn heifer has done, all you can do is jump all over me because you can't seem to face reality!"

Flavia shook her head in disapproval at both of them. If they had her predicament neither one would be wasting time on this crap. Life was just too short for all this bickering.

"Oh, I'm beginning to face reality, Kiwi. And what I see is you waltzing yourself around this office like you're busier than a one-legged man in a butt-kickin' contest, when in *reality*, you got your uppity nose snooping where it doesn't belong!"

"*Uppity*? Now ain't that the damn pot calling the freakin' kettle black! I mean, from the time that the three of us became friends and started this agency we vowed to never keep secrets from one another! We said that we would always have each other's back! But I guess you didn't mean what you said, did you Blu? Maybe you've gotten so used to keeping secrets that you expect everybody else to keep 'em too!"

"That's enough, Kiwi!" Flavia yelled to her. But Kiwi ignored Flavia, continuing on with her verbal thrashing.

"You got all bent out of shape when you learned that your *other assistant* had been making a damn fool out of you! I'm sure you wished now that somebody would have opened your eyes in that situation! But then, knowing *you*, if someone had came to you and told you that your husband was messing around with your executive assistant, you probably would have turned on them too!"

Blu had to use every ounce of restraint to keep herself from leaping off the sofa and attacking Kiwi with every muscle within her body.

"You better count yourself lucky that we have an

agreement in place that prevent you from being fired! Because if there wasn't, I would take great pleasure in kicking your arrogant behind out the same door you practically shoved Yel, Paisley through!"

"Oh, I'm sure you would just love too, Blu! Because that's how you really feel, isn't it? I mean you've never respected me! Always treating me like some damn *employee* rather than a *partner* in this agency! Maybe I didn't know much about advertising when we all started, but I think I've done one helluva job proving myself since then!"

It was a rare occurrence for them to witness, but Kiwi then dissolved into tears. She tried to keep her emotions under control, but pregnancy had a way of causing moods to swing like a pendulum.

Flavia had heard enough. She moved from the sofa to a nearby chair. "Both of you ought to be ashamed. There's absolutely no reason for either of you to be attacking the other! We did not come this far with this business just to have it crumble because we choose to allow our emotions to go haywire!"

Blu and Kiwi directed their attention towards Flavia.

"Now, I am just as disappointed to learn that Yelsi has turned out to be the daughter of our archrival. But I'm willing to bet that there's more to the story than what we know. She did not want to talk to us about it today, and for obvious reasons, but I think in time she will explain her actions."

Flavia looked at Kiwi. "Did you have a right to launch an investigation into her background? No! Simply because we've never operated behind one another's back!"

"Well, I . . . " Kiwi attempted to explain.

"Just be quiet!" Flavia interrupted her. "You've said enough already. And Blu, you did not have the right to have HR omit a background and reference check on her. Why? Because we agreed that we would do that for everyone hired into this agency. And had it been done – well, maybe we wouldn't be having this conversation."

Blu simply averted her gaze from Flavia.

"Now, whether or not Paisley Martin had anything to do with our three client losses, I really can't say. But the fact of the matter is that those clients have chosen to leave. And while it's almost twenty-five percent of our annual billings, it's not the end of the world – or the end of this agency."

"You're right," Kiwi said softly.

"So, where do we go from here?" Blu asked.

"It's not a question of *where do we go?*, Blu. It's a realization of where we already are. We don't need to *go* anywhere. What we need to do is maintain our focus. Continue to do what we do best. Those client losses were not the first time we've lost clients. Of course, it had been a while since we lost a client, but you both know that's the nature of this business. It's not the first client loss and it definitely won't be the last."

"Should we confront Leland?" Kiwi asked.

"And what good would that do, Kiwi? If in fact Leland Martin has somehow wooed those clients from us, then so be it. That's his prerogative if he chooses to conduct business in that manner. But we're not going to retaliate in the same manner. Because to do so would make us no better than him. The best thing that we can do right now to pay back Leland Martin is to win the one-hundred and forty-million dollars MerLex account!"

"I know that's right!" remarked Kiwi. "But, how do we pay back his daughter?"

"We don't!" Blu interjected. "Listen, guys. One reason that I don't believe Paisley had anything to do with helping her father steal accounts from us is that she and her father have been estranged for almost a year."

"How do you know that?" asked Kiwi.

"She told me."

"Humph. She also told you that her name was *Yelsi*. And she told you that she was *twenty-five*! Well, according to that article, she was *twenty* last year, so that would mean she's no more than *twenty-one*! So, why should we believe her if she says she's estranged from her father?"

Flavia answered before Blu could. "You know, Kiwi,

Paisley is not really our concern right now. And frankly, I'm going to reserve judgment on her until we get all the facts, which I believe will happen in due time."

Blu smiled. "I appreciate you saying that Flavia. She deserves the benefit of doubt."

Kiwi rolled her eyes.

Flavia continued. "Since we're all together, I have something that I need to share with you both."

"Oh, hell! More revelations, Flavia?"

"Kiwi Shepherd, please don't make me lose my religion by having to shut that big mouth of yours!"

Kiwi threw up her hands in mock surrender. "Hey, girlfriend! Say what you gotta say!"

Flavia moved from the chair in which she'd been sitting and sat down beside Blu on the sofa. She motioned for Kiwi to come and join them. When Kiwi did it put Flavia right between the two of them.

This was going to be more difficult than she thought. She considered bailing out. Telling them that what she had intended to say wasn't really all that important.

But she realized that she'd kept them in the dark long enough. They would better be able to plan for the future if they were aware of her medical condition.

"Guys, I'm sure you're both aware of the amount of time that I've taken off lately."

Blu nodded.

"Girlfriend, don't tell us that you're leaving us for MARTIN/McFINLEY too?" Kiwi said.

"I only wish that it was as simple as that," Flavia answered.

Blu didn't like the lifeless monotone in her friend's voice. "This sounds serious. What is it, Flavia?"

Opting not to beat around the bush, she decided to come right out and tell them. "Guys, I have cancer."

Blu gave a startled gasp. "What?"

Kiwi had been stunned silent.

Flavia also found it shocking to hear the words come from her mouth again. Taking a deep breath, she relaxed and then shared the life-altering news with them.

. . . .

An hour later the three of them were still seated on the sofa. Connected physically by their hands joined together. Connected emotionally by their hearts, which held a deep love for one another.

Blu and Kiwi were both overwhelmed by the news. Nothing else or no one else seemed as important as it might have earlier. Not their agency. Not the desire to win MerLex Motors. Not Paisley Martin. Not Damien. Not Gail Adams.

Flavia James, their dear friend and business partner, was facing the crisis of her life.

"Did you get a second opinion?" Blu asked.

"I considered it. But I have no reason not to trust the doctor's findings. Maybe if the cancer was just in stage one or two, I might have gotten a second opinion. But it's in the advanced stage. I don't think that I could bear having to be told a second time by another doctor that I have pancreatic cancer."

The two of them hugged Flavia again and cried with her for the umpteenth time.

"You don't need to be *here*," Blu said as she dried her eyes.

"Blu's right," added Kiwi.

"I know. But I've already worked through all that. And for me, the more I keep myself busy, sticking to my normal routine. The better I feel about it all."

"How are Parker and the boys handling this?" asked Kiwi.

"Amazingly well," she answered. "Although, I'm not so sure that the boys really understand it. But we tried to explain it to them as best we could."

"Flavia, what can we do? I mean there must be something that we can do to help?"

"I'm trying to take it one day at a time. I didn't tell you guys sooner because I wasn't quite sure how I was going to deal with it myself. You know, whether or not to go through

through the chemo and all that."

"Are you sure that you don't want to at least try that option?"

She nodded. "I'm certain. I mean I would basically just be prolonging the inevitable. And I would be doing so at the risk of suffering even more from the treatments. So, no. I've been feeling pretty good lately and I want to continue to be able to function normally as much and as long as possible."

"I trust you have your faith?" Blu said to her.

"You better believe it! Without it I would be nothing but a basket case right now."

"Well, I know that I haven't been one for praying much, but I plan to start," said Kiwi. "If anybody can change the outcome here, I know God can."

"Thanks Kiwi. God is definitely the one who's in control right now."

"Flavia, maybe we can all get together later and determine how to lighten your work load here, all right?"

"No, Blu. That's the last thing I want to do. It would mean a lot for me to help this agency win MerLex. The review is only three months away. I plan to stay on at least until that time."

"But you don't have to do that. Take all this time with your family," Blu pleaded.

"I'm not planning to spend any less time with them. I

mean I'm only going to be working here while Parker is working and while the twins are in school. This agency will keep me from going crazy at home."

"Well, any time you want to stop, or if the work is becoming too much, then you just let us know, all right?"

"I will, Blu."

They engaged in a group hug. "Listen," Flavia began. "One of the best things that you two can do for me is to promise me that you'll stop antagonizing each other. Life is too short for all that."

Blu and Kiwi exchanged shameful glances.

"We promise," they both agreed.

chapter 27

The first week of November brought Atlanta cool temperatures and lots of drizzling rain. Just enough to make driving miserable. Fortunately, the rain had begun the day after the local elections were held. Blu, Flavia and Kiwi each took time off yesterday to cast their respective ballots for the various candidates.

The Wednesday morning ATLANTA JOURNAL-CONSTITUTION newspaper headlined all the results, including the fact that Georgia had elected its first republican governor since the *1870s*.

Two weeks had gone by since Blu had spoken to Paisley. There were several occasions where she wanted to call her, but decided not to.

So much had happened. Damien filing for divorce. Her learning that his mystery woman was her former assistant, and then finding out that her husband had had a son. Then she was forced to face the fact that her new assistant wasn't really who she'd said she was. And that was before she had heard Flavia's devastating news concerning her health, which really put all the other events into serious perspective.

It was all too much to try and digest at once. Too difficult to swallow.

She'd been moping around the office in such a funk lately as well that both Flavia and Kiwi urged her to go ahead and call Paisley Martin. Flavia even joked with her, telling her that she'd be glad to *switch* places with her. That sobered her up a bit.

But as of this Wednesday evening, Blu hadn't made the call. She'd convinced herself that she was too busy handling her laundry chores.

As she pulled a load of warm clothes from the dryer and then stuffed it into the white laundry basket, she carried it downstairs to the den and let it drop to the floor. She sat down on the sofa next to the laundry basket and began the task of folding towels, pillowcases, sheets, underwear and socks.

Her thoughts faded to the demise of her marriage. She'd been served with the official divorce papers just last week. After scanning them she simply turned them over to her attorney. She had no plans to contest the divorce. She did tell Damien that she wanted the house. He didn't put up a fight. And since they both already had separate banking accounts and separate investments, there would be no dividing of financial assets. And although her net worth was far more than his, he would get nothing from her and she would get nothing from him. Wanted nothing from him.

A few days after Damien had come to her office to reveal his *truth*, Blu had received a call from Gail Adams. The woman went on and on about how sorry she was and how she never *meant* for things to happen the way they did.

Blu never said a word in return to her. Once Gail had finished cleansing her soul of its apparent guilt, Blu simply hung up the telephone, never even uttering a *good-bye*.

She had seriously thought about making things difficult for her husband and his new fling. But it was the realization that an innocent child was in the middle that caused her to rethink her impending vengeance.

That little boy, whose name was *Denim Adams Addison* (apparently the two had already made plans to wed after the birth), did not choose the situation in which he was born. And, reflecting upon her own past, having made the mistake of giving away her baby, she had no desire to make this child suffer due to the ill-conceived actions of his parents.

Blu folded the last piece of clothing, picked up the laundry basket and retreated to her master bedroom. Some towels and linen were put away inside the bathroom closet. Then she began placing the clothes inside her dresser drawers. When everything had been put into its proper place, she collapsed onto the chaise that occupied a corner of the bedroom.

A small FEDEX package lay on the floor beside the chaise. She remembered getting it over two weeks ago and because she already knew what was in it she never bothered to open the package.

Now, she reached down and retrieved the package from the floor and ripped it open.

Pursuant to her request, her mom had sent her the other half of the *paisley blanket*. It was the only tangible thing she had left from that day–*December 16, 1981*. The other half of the blanket, she hoped, was given to the baby by the adoptive parents.

With the blanket in both hands she lifted it to her face and closed her eyes. Burying her face inside the soft material she tried to visualize what her little girl had looked like on the day she was born. Tried to gaze into her, no doubt sparkling eyes. Tried to kiss her smooth, delicate cheeks. Tried to breathe, into her nostrils, the child's newborn scent. Tried to hear her gentle cries, calling for her mommy – *hold me*, *feed me*, *love me*. Tried to grasp the small hand that was reaching out for her.

But in all her trying, she failed. The bitter truth of the matter was that such moments had already escaped her.

They would never again be recaptured. It was impossible. Like trying to seize the wind with your hands.

She folded the blanket and set it aside on a nearby table.

Her thoughts drifted to Schuyler.

His presence in her life again was as fitting as the stars hanging from a midnight sky. It had certainly made it much easier for her to absorb the loss of Damien. Even though deep within her, she realized that she'd never really given Damien her heart. Simply couldn't give it to him. How could she give away something that didn't belong to her?

Blu Addison had given her heart to Schuyler many years ago. Not just her heart, but also her mind. Her soul. Her body. And she never once doubted that he'd treasured such a precious gift. She didn't doubt it because he, likewise, had given the same to her. And together, they had created a new life.

Recently, while having lunch with Flavia and Kiwi, she'd gone ahead and told them the truth about Schuyler. They'd already known about the baby. She told them that he had been more than just an *old friend* from high school.

Kiwi shared with her that there was no time limit on true love. Regardless of how much time had passed between the two of them, if it was meant for her and Schuyler to be together, then they *should* and they would.

Flavia told her that God works everything out for His purpose. We can do all the planning in the world, but if it's not within *God's will* to happen, then it won't happen. She said that maybe God had never intended for she and Damien to have a child together. Otherwise it would have happened.

And when she told her mom that her and Schuyler had decided to look for their baby girl, Audrey Knight gave her blessing on their efforts. Her mom told her to put the whole matter into God's hands and then wait and watch His power to work wonders. Blu's mom was more religious that she was.

Blu had spoken to Schuyler a couple of days ago. She was thrilled to learn that he'd made it past the first stage at the PGA Tour Qualifying Tournament. He was equally thrilled to learn that her mom as well as her friends was in support of their efforts to find their daughter. But, he was genuinely saddened when she told him about Damien. He said that he'd been keeping his fingers crossed for her and her husband.

Unsure if she should burden him with anymore bad news, she reluctantly told him about her executive assistant turning out to be someone other than who she said she was.

And then, Blu shared with Schuyler her heartbreaking news about Flavia.

He told her that he wished that he was able to be there to provide some kind of support to her during the difficult time that she was obviously experiencing.

He encouraged her to remain strong. He asked her to give Flavia his love and to let her know that he would be praying for her.

Schuyler insisted that she talk to Paisley. He told her that if their relationship had blossomed as much as she had told him, then it was certainly *worth* trying to salvage.

It was the final push that Blu needed.

After putting away the laundry basket back upstairs into the laundry room, she grabbed the cordless telephone, plopped down on the sofa in the den and dialed Paisley's home phone number.

chapter 28

Paisley Martin didn't like having to drive late at night, and it was already after ten o'clock. But since her condo was just down the road from WindFair Estates, she was okay with it tonight. And she was not going to pass up the opportunity to meet privately with Blu.

Blu had phoned her an hour ago and asked if she could come by the house. She didn't say why. Didn't have to. Paisley was just glad that she would have a chance to explain her seemingly sinister actions.

The security guard waved her on through as she pulled up to the gate. She'd been over to Blu's house enough times now that he was obviously familiar with her. But actually, Blu had already called the gate and told the security guard that she was expecting the young woman in the urban green BMW sports car.

She was glad that the entrance to Blu's house was

different from the entrance to her father's house. There were three entrances into WindFair Estates. Blu's house was reached by going through the *east gate* and her father's house was reached by entering through the *north gate*. The security guard at the north gate knew her very well, so she would always try and avoid that route during her days as *Yelsi Nitram*.

Paisley turned onto the circle driveway in front of Blu's home. Butterflies had formed a posse inside her stomach as she walked up the steps and rang the doorbell.

"Hi," Blu spoke as she opened the door. Dressed in black NIKE sweatpants and a matching sweatshirt, Blu was trying to shield her own uneasiness.

"Hello, Blu." Paisley returned the greeting.

Blu led her back to the den. "Just make yourself comfortable," she told her. "Can I get you anything to drink?" Blu had already been nursing a glass of red wine. Her usual choice of beverage for relaxing evenings at home.

"Um, sure. I'll take a ginger ale."

Blu retrieved a raspberry ginger ale from the refrigerator and handed it to her. "You know, I stocked up on these sodas just for you. Damien used to drink them, but I never really cared for them."

"Thanks," Paisley said, accepting the soda.

Blu sat down on the sofa beside her.

"So, how have you been?" she asked her former assistant and *still* good friend.

Paisley nodded, swallowing a sip of the refreshing soda. "I've been good. A little bored, though." Since leaving the ad agency, she hadn't looked for any other work. Not that she really *needed* to.

"Well, let me start by saying that when I found out that you were not who you claimed to be . . . well, let's just say that I felt very betrayed. I mean, I had confided in you."

"And that has meant a lot to me, Blu. *You* mean a lot to me – "

"Then why?" Blu interrupted her. "Why pretend to be someone you're not?"

Paisley hesitated before answering. "Blu, I am the same person you met on the golf course that day. Yes, I lied about my name. But I never changed who I am."

"Why not just tell us your *real* name?"

"Because I didn't want it associated with my father. He'd always wanted me to work with him in his agency, but that wasn't what I wanted."

"So, are you saying that if we knew that you were Leland Martin's daughter we wouldn't have hired you?"

"Would you have?"

Blu took a sip from her wine glass. "Well, I can't say. I think our first question would have been why? I mean, even now it begs the question – what motivation do you have for wanting to work with ADDISON JAMES & SHEPHERD? As an *executive assistant* mind you, when you could obviously have a much higher role within your father's agency?"

"I guess I didn't want to be in my father's shadow. Besides, I have always admired your agency, Blu. I have a file at home of every article written about you guys that I could find. I wanted to be a part of it. And while I hadn't intended on joining your agency as an executive assistant, after meeting you, and seeing how positive and how kind you were . . . well, I guess I couldn't turn down your request."

A lot of unanswered questions were running rampant through Blu's mind. "Was the golf course a stroke of luck or did you know we would be there?"

"It was purely by coincidence. I had actually planned on calling your agency and setting up an appointment to meet with you or one of the other ladies. But when the Marshal drove me down to the tee box that morning, I recognized the three of you immediately. And I had also read that you lived in WindFair Estates, so I admit that every time I played the course I was sort of hoping that I'd run into you guys."

Flavia's words suddenly came to Blu's mind. *Everything happens for a reason. God works everything out for His own purpose.*

"What if I had done the background check and

employment reference?"

"Well, I was concerned about that. And if you had done them, I was prepared to come clean at that time."

Blu shook her head. "I just don't understand why you didn't just lay everything out on the table, Paisley. Which, by the way, I'm having a very difficult time seeing you as *Paisley* when I've gotten so used to you being *Yelsi.*"

"Sorry."

Blu continued. "I mean, even the golf tournament, which we've since dropped out of, would have exposed you. We go head to head with the women at your father's agency every year, surely they would have recognized you."

"I didn't plan to let things go that far."

"And what about your paychecks? They were paid to *Yelsi Nitram*. How were you able to cash them?"

Paisley set her can of soda on the table. She reached into her COACH bag and pulled out four envelopes. They contained her previous paychecks. "Here, I never even opened them," she said handing the envelopes to Blu.

Blu's eyes shifted between the envelopes and Paisley. She was perplexed, to say the least. "I guess you really didn't need the money."

"No. I didn't. Which is why I hope you believe me when I say that I really just wanted an opportunity to be a part of what you guys are building."

"Kiwi seems to think that you infiltrated our ranks to spy on behalf of your father."

"What!" The accusation shocked her, though it was less of a shock to learn that it originated with Kiwi.

"So, there's no truth to that?"

"Of course not! I'm not that kind of person, Blu. Not even for my father would I do something like that."

"Well, for what it's worth, I never believed you would do something so diabolical."

"Thanks."

"But, the fact remains, we have lost three clients to your father's agency over the last month."

"I know nothing about it. As I mentioned to you before, I haven't spoken to my father since Thanksgiving last year."

"You know, I recall you telling me that, and I have to tell you, Paisley, that it troubles me somewhat. I mean, you've told me that you lost your mother three years ago. That you're an only child. So, you and your father only have each other now. Why not try and mend the fences? Things can't be *that* bad between you two."

"I'm sure you're right, Blu. It's just that he hurt me so. Yes, time has healed the wounds some, but . . . I don't know," her voice trailed off.

"If you don't mind me asking, how did he hurt you?"

Paisley's eyes began to dart maniacally around the

room, picking out various objects to redirect her focus. "He started seeing another woman so soon after my mother died. It wasn't right. It wasn't respectful."

She didn't need to say anymore. Blu understood. Though Paisley Martin was a grown woman, she still needed the attention, time and assurance of her father. What little girl didn't? Him seeing someone else obviously made her feel as though he was going to replace her mother. A dreadful thought to any child.

Blu took hold of Paisley's hand. "I understand," she consoled her. "But, try and understand your father's viewpoint. I don't believe that he's looking to *replace* your mother. He's been left with a huge void in his life. Didn't you say that they were married for forty years?

She shook her head 'yes'.

"That's a very long time to be with anyone. And if it was someone you were married to . . . well, to suddenly one day have that person gone from your life, had to be a difficult thing for him to try and deal with."

Paisley had never looked at it like that. It was possible that her father had been lonely. Wanted companionship. Needed it. He could put on the biggest façade, but the man was human after all, despite his assertions to the contrary.

"What you've said makes a lot of sense, Blu."

She squeezed Paisley's hand as it lay in hers. "While

he may need a companion in his life, he still needs *you* too. You're his flesh and blood. Don't deny him your love nor your presence, or you're likely to find yourself one day regretting it."

Paisley pulled her hand away and wrapped her arms around her chest. "There's something *else* about me that I've never mentioned to you," she said solemnly.

"That you're not from this planet!" Blu joked.

The humorous remark made her smile. "No, that's not it. What I never told you is that my parents *adopted* me at birth. My mother was never able to have children, even though they had tried for several years. Then they gave up hope, until I came along. They were in their upper forties when they adopted me."

Blu's body had gone numb at the words *adopted me at birth*. A plethora of thoughts invaded her brain. Weird thoughts. Crazy thoughts. Impossible thoughts.

Paisley continued to speak, her words now resounding in Blu's ears like echoes from some dark hollow cave.

"Blu. Blu. Blu, are you listening to me?"

"Yes, Paisley. I'm listening," she answered, snapping quickly from the sudden runaway train of thoughts.

"Well, anyway, I know nothing at all about my birth parents. It was a closed adoption. My mother and father had told me once that when I turned twenty-one they would help me try and contact my birth mother. Even though it would probably be a long shot. But since my mother died three years ago, and . . . well, I haven't really been communicating with my father, so I guess nothing has ever come of it."

Blu found herself staring intently into Paisley's young, flawless, beautiful face. Silently searching for any hint of similarity. Whether relating to her or Schuyler.

Then her mind drifted away from physical features. Their personalities were undoubtedly similar. And Paisley's natural ability to play golf *could* have come from Schuyler. Was there even such a thing as *golf genes*? And if so, could they be inherited?

"Um, Paisley . . . that article from last year indicated that you were twenty years-old. Which means, the fact that you told me you were twenty-five isn't true is it?" she asked, finally finding words to speak.

"No. I lied about my age because I thought that you wouldn't take me serious if you knew I was only twenty-one. But I'll be twenty-two soon."

"When?" The question had escaped Blu's lips before she could consider the impact of the impending answer.

"Next month. December sixteenth to be exact."

Although she was sitting down, Blu nearly tumbled from the sofa, quickly regaining her balance. The wine in the glass she'd been holding wasn't so fortunate. The red spirit spilled forth from the glass, dousing the cream-colored skirt that Paisley was wearing and also spreading itself onto the carpeted den floor.

Paisley reacted by springing from the sofa.

"I am so sorry!" Blu apologized. She ran into the kitchen to get a couple of towels. After wetting one of them under the faucet, she returned to the den and handed the dry one to Paisley and then began wiping the spillage from the carpet with the other. However, the nasty stain would ultimately require professional assistance.

"I'm sorry, Paisley," she repeated.

"Don't worry about it," Paisley told her, using the towel to dry what she could from her skirt. The red spots now obvious.

"I'll replace your skirt," Blu told her.

"No, don't worry about it. It's not a big deal."

Flustered, Blu said, "I don't know what happened. I mean it was only my *second* glass of wine."

"Maybe *one* is your limit!" Paisley joked.

"You're probably right!"

Noticing on her watch that it was almost midnight, Paisley told Blu that she needed to be going. Blu thanked her for coming by. She told Paisley that she accepted her apology as well as her explanations. She also set a time for them to meet on Friday for lunch.

Paisley asked if things were good between them. Blu told her that she believed their relationship would only get better.

After Paisley had left, Blu straigthened up the den and headed to her bedroom.

She just couldn't believe it. Paisley Martin could actually be her and Schuyler's daughter! How ironic and yet incredible that would be!

She wished that she could have asked more questions of Paisley, but she knew that it was a good idea not to push things. And besides, it was rather late.

If *it* turned out to be true, however . . . no, she didn't even want to think along those lines. There were just too many implications to consider.

chapter 29

One week later Blu was scheduled to meet with Leland Martin. The appointment had been set for one o'clock on a Tuesday afternoon at his office. Her lunch last Friday with Paisley had gone very well. It was like old times for the two of them. Blu even offered Paisley her job back. She was thrilled to accept.

Adhering to Blu's advice, Paisley also met with her father over the weekend. She told him how she felt about his *behavior*, and he apologized. He assured her that he could never forget what her mother and he had shared together. Leland also told his daughter that he was available to her whenever she needed him.

Then, with some reluctance, Paisley told him about her job at ADDISON JAMES & SHEPHERD. He was visibly upset by her decision not to work with him at MARTIN/McFINLEY. He'd done his utmost best to persuade her otherwise. But she told him that it was something that she simply had to do for herself. Eventually her father relented.

Kiwi was a little less thrilled to learn that her nemesis would once again be gracing their first floor haven. But as a courtesy to Blu, she promised to cut the girl some slack. And her doctor had told her to avoid any stress as much as possible. However, because ADDISON JAMES & SHEPHERD competed with Paisley's father, Kiwi made it clear to Blu that it would not be appropriate for the girl to be privy to any sensitive information. Blu agreed and when she told it to Paisley, she didn't have a problem with the restriction either.

Kiwi had also been racking her brain lately trying to determine when to reveal her pregnancy to Blu and Flavia and *introduce* them to her new man. But since there had already been so many revelations over the past few weeks, she figured hers could wait a while.

Flavia had been away from the office for the past few days. She hadn't been feeling well. Blu spoke with over the phone this morning and she said that she should be in the office tomorrow. Blu shared with Flavia that she and Paisley had reached an understanding and that she rehired her as her executive assistant. Flavia told her that she always thought the two of them belonged together. Her sentiments touched Blu deeply.

Although, Blu made the decision not to discuss with

either Flavia or Kiwi her belief that Paisley could be her daughter. She was trying not to be presumptuous. She did, however, share her thoughts with her mother during a phone call over the weekend. And after listening to everything that Blu shared with her, Audrey Knight said that it was highly possible that Paisley was in fact her daughter. She told Blu to keep her abreast of things, but she also admonished her to handle matters carefully.

Schuyler was flying back to Atlanta this weekend. Blu spoke with him last night. She also chose not to share her thoughts with him just yet. More so because he was feeling a bit down. He did not make it past the second stage at the tour-qualifying tournament. Blu really felt bad for him. She knew how excited and enthusiastic he was about the possibility of playing on the PGA Tour. He admitted to Blu that his heart couldn't seem to get into the game. Other issues were weighing on his mind. But he assured her that he would be back trying again next year.

As Blu closed the file that she'd been going through at her desk, she looked at her watch. It was twelve-thirty. Time to head over to see Leland Martin. She hadn't told him over the phone the reason that she wanted to meet with him. He assumed that she wanted to rub into his face the fact that his daughter has chosen a rival ad agency over his own.

But the last thing Blu Addison was interested in this

afternoon was one-upmanship. Nor was she interested in discussing business.

This was a personal visit. One that could have some serious implications for him as well as for her if she got the information that she was seeking.

chapter 30

Before today, Blu had never set foot into the FIVE NINETY FIVE PEACHTREE TOWER building that was headquarters to the $2.2 billion MARTIN/McFINLEY advertising agency. The agency occupied the top ten floors of the skyscraper, which boasted a total of sixty floors.

Blu stepped from the cozy elevators onto the fifty-first floor, which is where the receptionist center was located. The office space was absolutely mind-boggling. Unusually high ceilings, measuring around fifteen feet, served as chaperones for each floor. And the eclectic use of colors on the walls as well as the furnishings seemed to generate creative energy throughout.

Within a just a few minutes of announcing herself to the polite receptionist, Blu was being escorted by one of Leland Martin's *three* executive assistants to his sixtieth-floor chambers.

As the overly polite assistant led her into Leland's gigantic suite, he immediately stood from his big fat oak desk and made his way towards her, hand outstretched.

"Blu Addison! What a pleasure it is to personally meet you!" His handshake was quite fierce. A fat cigar appeared to be barely clinging to a corner of his mouth.

"Hello, Mr. Martin."

"Aw hell, Blu! No need to be formal, just call me *Leland*!"

"All right."

She didn't know why she had become so nervous all of a sudden. As she sat in the chair that he led her to, her knees were nearly quaking. The breath in her throat was practically raw. And she could feel her hands growing clammy.

Leland made her feel somewhat at ease as he quickly launched into small talk. He went out of his way to praise their "*small but growing advertising shop*". When he was finished expending his endless supply of accolades, she thanked him.

"So, tell me Blu, what brings you to our fine agency? Uh, don't tell me you want your clients back!" He erupted into a roar of laughter at his own attempt to humor her.

"No, Leland. My visit is more of a personal nature ."

His eyebrows arched and his forehead became furrowed. "Is that so?"

"Yes. Now, I know that you're already aware that your daughter is working as my executive assistant . . . "

He removed the cigar from between his thin dry lips and blew the smoke towards the ceiling. "My daughter has always been a very independent young woman," he replied.

"Does that mean you don't have a problem with it?"

"Why should I? Paisley is quite capable of making her own decisions. Suffice it to say, I'd much rather have her here with me – perhaps working in account management as opposed to filing papers."

Blu decided to ignore his sarcasm. "Well, your support of her is to be commended."

"You make it sound as if I've done some great deed. I've always *supported* my daughter, since the day she was born."

The smoke from his cigar was beginning to irritate her.

"Would you mind putting that thing away?" she asked tersely.

"It bothers you, does it?"

"As a matter of fact it does. Not to mention that it's not good for your health."

Leland let out a staccato laugh. "At my age, Blu, there's not much of anything left that's *good* for you."

She watched as he reluctantly took the tube of tobacco leaves and grounded it into a nearby ashtray.

"Thank you."

"Let's say we cut to the chase, shall we?"

"Fine." She shifted her posture in the chair. "Paisley and I have become very close over the past several weeks. And she shared with me the fact that she's adopted."

Leland sat upright in his chair. His eyes beginning to narrow. "And?"

"Well, she also shared with me her desire to find her birth parents."

"How does my daughter's birth, or anything else personal, concern you, Blu?"

"As I said, I've grown very close to your daughter. I can appreciate what she must be going through."

"Oh, really? How so?"

"Well, you see . . ." She hesitated. "Leland, when I was a sixteen year-old girl living with my parents in Muncie, Indiana, I became pregnant. And to make a long story short, my parents sent me to Atlanta to live with my aunt and uncle until the baby was born. And my parents had decided that the baby should be given up for adoption. And . . ."

He interrupted, "Your parents decided? Are you saying that giving your baby up for adoption was done without your permission?"

"No, I'm not saying that it was without my permission. Eventually, I agreed to it. But, I was only sixteen. What choice did I have? I simply trusted my parents advice."

"Precisely what is it that you're driving at, Blu?"

She took a deep breath. "Well, during a conversation with Paisley last week at my home, I learned that she will turn twenty-two years of age on December sixteenth, correct?"

He appeared offended. "If my daughter gave you her birth date, why are you doubting it? She has no reason to lie about anything."

Blu tried to ignore her urge to tell him otherwise.

"Of course. Well, you see, Leland, I gave birth to my baby on December sixteenth, nineteen eighty-one. Almost twenty-two years ago."

"I see where you're going with this. Apparently you think that my daughter is your baby girl?"

"Well, it is possible."

"Absurd! My daughter's birth parents were an *Italian* couple. So, you must be sadly mistaken!"

Suddenly Leland appeared quite nervous. He started shuffling papers about, and making a great deal of searching for his pen.

"Where is that damn thing!" He mumbled.

Blu figured that the revelation that she could perhaps be the birth mother of his adoptive daughter was trying to settle in.

"Oh, to hell with it!" he shouted, giving up on his

impromptu search. "Listen, Blu. I'm sorry that you seemed to have wasted your time. But I can assure you that Paisley is not the baby you gave up for adoption."

"And how can you be certain?"

"Why, I just told you! You're *black*, for Pete's sake! I was told that our adoptive baby's birth parents were Italian."

"Do you know the birth parents name?"

He gave a slight hesitation. "Well, while it was a closed adoption, I was given the name of the birth mother only. But that information is privileged. I'm sure you can appreciate that."

Blu nodded. But she wasn't buying his story. The man may have been a superlative salesman, but he wasn't going to sell her this bunch of baloney! Even his behavior seemed to have changed dramatically. She knew that something rattled him. Perhaps it was the truth.

"Now, Blu," he began, standing from his chair. "If you'll excuse me, I have another appointment that I must prepare for."

"Uh, of course. I want to thank you for taking time to see me."

"The pleasure has been all mine." He quickly buzzed one of his assistants to come in and escort her downstairs.

When she had departed his office, Leland loosened his tie. "Dammit!" he yelled, banging his coiled fist against his desk. He could feel his blood pressure rising. And like a mad man he grabbed another cigar from his desk drawer, lighted it and began puffing away.

"Why was this happening *now*!" he said through gritted teeth. What business did Blu Addison have asking him all sorts of personal questions? Why was she poking her nose where it didn't belong? If in fact she had given her baby away, then that was her problem. If she really cared about the child it certainly wouldn't have taken her some twenty-two years to search for her.

Of course, he had lied to her about one thing. He knew that his daughter was *not* Italian. He knew that she *was* bi-racial.

Leland and his wife would have liked to have met Paisley's birth mother and father, but they were told that the mother wanted to remain anonymous. All they knew was that she was a black teenager and that she would be unable to care for the child.

They were likewise told little about the baby's father, other than the fact that he was *not* black.

The baby being bi-racial, however, mattered very little to Leland and his wife. They had longed for a child of their own. And once they laid eyes on the little girl they loved her right then and there.

He remembered one of the nurses bringing a beautiful

paisley blanket to him. She had explained that the birth mother wanted it to be given to the baby.

The blanket – half of it – lay inside a wall safe within his home. He'd intended to give it to his daughter when she turned eighteen, but with the passing of her mother he hadn't thought any more about it, until now.

Leland and his wife realized how difficult it must have been for the young teenage woman to give up her child. Not only did they accept the blanket, but they also decided to name the baby *Paisley.* They truly believed they had been blessed with the little girl, and out of honor and respect for what the birth mother had given to them, they chose her *first* name as their adoptive daughter's *middle* name. Perhaps it was time to share this information with his daughter.

Blu Addison may have grown close to his daughter, but it was simply preposterous for her to try and exploit Paisley's adoption for her own self-interests. He could sympathize with her for the painful ordeal she undoubtedly had to endure at such a young age. But *Paisley Marie Martin* was not her baby girl!

. . . .

Leland's assistant escorted Blu back down to the fifty-first floor where she had to sign-out. She thanked the assistant and asked her if there was a restroom on the floor that she could use. The assistant pointed down a corridor to where a set of restrooms were.

Blu made her way toward them, still admiring the opulent facilities as she walked. She had considered simply waiting until she returned to their offices, but the bottled water that she drank at lunch had begun to take its effect.

Less than five minutes later Blu exited the restroom and was heading toward the elevator when a particular visitor that she saw at the receptionist center caused her to stop dead in her tracks. It was someone she knew.

The person did not see her so she quickly did an about-face and walked slowly toward the restrooms again. But it wasn't before she had overheard the receptionist announcing to the person – *"Mr. Martin will see you now"*.

Out the corner of her eye, she watched the person get onto the elevators, *without an escort*, and make his ascension to the sixtieth floor.

Unable to believe what she'd just witnessed, Blu hastily made her way to the same elevators and frantically pushed the button for the LOBBY. When the doors opened, fifty floors later, she hurried out of the building, taking extra long strides in her stiletto heels.

Quickly unlocking the door to her MERCEDES she positioned herself behind the wheel and made a swift exit from the premises.

As she drove toward midtown she considered how long the treachery might have been going on. And all this time the finger was being pointed at Paisley. She was certainly not the guilty party.

There definitely was a *spy* inside ADDISON JAMES & SHEPHERD. And she would have never imagined it to be this person.

How true the saying was – *it's never the obvious, but the least person who you'd expect.*

But this little sneak had finally been found out. Caught red-handed. Both dirty little hands all the way inside the cookie jar. What nerve! Profiting at their expense! His own employer!

There would be no more disclosing client information. Leaking plans for upcoming ad campaigns.

Blu was determined to see to it that this person's association with their agency ended *today*. She now knew exactly who the real perpetrator was.

chapter 31

When Blu arrived back at ADDISON JAMES & SHEPHERD it was approaching two-thirty in the afternoon. After her discovery as she was leaving the offices of MARTIN/McFINLEY, she had driven faster than she ever had before on Peachtree Street. This matter needed to be dealt with immediately.

Once back inside her own office, She quickly dialed Kiwi's extension.

"Kiwi Shepherd," came the answer on the other end.

"Hey, it's me."

"What's up, Blu?"

"Is Nathan in the office?"

"Not at the moment. He left about an hour ago for a doctor's appointment. Said he should be back around three. Why?"

"I'm on my way over to your office." Blu immediately hung up the phone. She informed Paisley where she would be and then made her way over to Kiwi's office.

When she arrived, Kiwi had one of her account executives in the office with her.

"Can you excuse us for a moment, please?" Blu said to her. The young woman obliged, quickly gathering up her files and exiting the office. Blu closed the door behind her.

"I've determined who our corporate spy is," she said to Kiwi, matter-of-factly, as she sat down in one of her side chairs.

Kiwi stared at her with portentous eyes. "You have? Well, clue me in, girlfriend, so that we can fire the bastard!"

"That's exactly what I intend to do just as soon as he returns from his 'doctor's appointment'." She held up her hands using her fingers as quotation marks when she emphasized *doctor's appointment*.

"What?" she asked dubiously. "Who in the hell are you talking about, Blu?"

"Kiwi, our back-stabbing spy is none other than *your* executive assistant!"

Quickly standing from her chair, Kiwi burst into a nasty laugh, one laden with derision. "You've got to be kidding?"

Blu shook her head 'no'.

"Blu, you *are* joking, right? I mean, *Nathan Nichols*? *My* Nathan?"

"What do you mean, *'my'* Nathan?"

Somewhat flustered and surprised at the same time, Kiwi sat back down. "I was waiting for the right time to tell you guys this, but Nathan and I have been seeing each other for the past five months."

"Now you must be kidding me?"

Kiwi nodded.

"Well, you certainly did a pretty good job of keeping us in the dark. That is, if Flavia doesn't know."

"She doesn't."

Blu picked up Kiwi's phone and dialed Flavia's home number. "She needs to hear this as well."

After she answered, Flavia told them that she'd been lying down but that she was up to talking. Blu allowed Kiwi the opportunity to reveal her news to Flavia.

Likewise, Flavia too was surprised. "I guess this is the year for revelations, isn't it? I mean nobody seemed to have been able to spit out the truth from the very beginning."

"It looks like we've just proven how true, over and over, my mom's words were. The truth *is* a bitter pill to swallow," stated Kiwi.

Blu nodded in agreement. "But Kiwi, what was your point in hiding your relationship with Nathan from us?"

Flavia interjected, "I take it that the reason you didn't want us to know about the two of you is because of the fact that he's your executive assistant and your role as a partner in this agency poses an obvious conflict of interest?"

"No, that's not it," Kiwi began to defend her man. "The reason I didn't say anything was because of how you two would react."

"Meaning what?" asked Blu.

"Well, y'all were always joking about how bland he dresses, and saying that he wears too much cologne, and all that other stuff!"

"Well, lately he's been dressing quite handsomely," stated Blu. "And now we know that it isn't because *you've* been taking him to the mall." Blu went on to fill Flavia in on the fact that Nathan Nichols was discovered to be their liaison with Leland Martin.

"I'll admit that I'm somewhat surprised," Flavia told Kiwi. "I mean I never knew that Nathan was even your type."

"Why? Because he's not a thug? Because he doesn't have some prestigious position?"

"No, Kiwi. Because you're always so picky about the guys you date," answered Flavia. "But hey, be that as it may, if the man makes you happy. But, you now have to decide how you're going to handle this apparent betrayal."

Kiwi turned to Blu, "Are you sure it was Nathan?"

Blu further explained how she saw Nathan as she was leaving from her meeting with Leland Martin, which also forced her to divulge to them why she'd been meeting with their archrival in the first place. And although Kiwi still didn't want to believe that *her man* had been double-crossing them, once Blu told her that it only made perfect sense that he was the culprit, she slowly began to accept the fact.

Nathan had been with the agency almost from the beginning. He was hired soon after Kiwi had fired her female assistant after only three months into the position.

Nathan sat in on meetings with Kiwi in which client campaigns were discussed, he was involved in client conference calls, and he clearly had access to all the client files that were maintained in Kiwi's office.

The more Blu thought about it the more she was willing to bet that perhaps the only reason he began dating Kiwi was so that she'd let her guard down around him, grant him some flexibility around the office, which is exactly what Kiwi had been doing. Unfortunately, it has been at the expense of a loss of eighty-five million dollars in billings.

As Kiwi thought more about it, she began to realize that over the past three months Nathan had been requesting extended lunch breaks, taking several afternoons off, and most importantly, when the two of them were relaxing at her house he seemed to want to discuss the agency's business a lot.

Nathan had also recently purchased a brand new black JAGUAR sedan, the same style as the one Damien drove. She had questioned him as to how he could afford such an expensive vehicle when the agency only paid him thirty-seven thousand a year. After telling her that he'd always wanted a Jag and that he'd been saving his money for years, Kiwi accepted his explanation and didn't think any more of it.

Her heart, hopes and dreams all took a sudden nose dive. She had tried to proceed cautiously with Nathan. Taking things very slowly at first. But the more lunch dates and dinner dates that the two of them went on the faster things went. It was during the summer that he started spending the night at her house. And by Labor Day he'd practically moved in with her.

When she found out that she was pregnant with his child, she initially was worried. She had never given any thought to marrying the man. But after his jubilant reaction to the pregnancy, she began to look at him in a whole different light. She now wondered if that light hadn't been bright enough.

"So, what are we gonna do, guys?" Kiwi asked the difficult question.

"We have no choice but to terminate his association with this agency immediately upon his return," Blu replied. "I've already called security and told them to escort him in when he arrives at the building. He can gather up his personal belongings and then leave the building at once."

"How could he betray us like this?" asked Flavia.

"Well, my guess would be that he needed the money," Blu answered.

Uncontrollable tears began to spew from Kiwi as she reluctantly shared with them about her pregnancy. "The baby is due in May," she sobbed.

"Well, that throws a monkey wrench into everything," remarked Flavia.

Blu went over to her and placed an arm around her. "Kiwi, I don't quite know what to say."

Drying her eyes, she said, "I'll be okay. That bastard doesn't deserve me or this baby!"

"Kiwi, you don't mean that," Flavia told her.

"Like hell I don't! The more I think about it, the more I believe that he used me personally as well as this agency. He can't get away with it."

Blu tried to consider other options. "Maybe we could suspend him for a while and then reassign him to another position that doesn't involve our clients."

"Blu that would be a little difficult to do since our clients revolve around our agency. Unfortunately, I'm not comfortable with him being employed at the agency at all," remarked Flavia.

"She's right," said Kiwi. "I don't want his behind working here anymore either! I mean we could never trust him again!"

"All right then. That's the decision. We'll terminate him. I just hate to see you in this position, Kiwi," said Blu.

"Yeah, me too. But it's my own fault. I guess I was too busy watching Paisley that I couldn't see my own man stabbing me in the back. How does he even know Leland Martin anyway? I mean, did Nathan approach him or was it the other way around?"

"At this point, it really doesn't matter, Kiwi," answered Flavia.

"True," echoed Blu. "And what's even more appalling is the fact that he knew that you were accusing Paisley and he simply sat back and said nothing."

"What'd you expect him to do, Blu? Turn himself in?"

"Well, if he was willing to allow an innocent person to be blamed for his own outrageous behavior, then that says a lot about his character."

That point was already sinking deeply into Kiwi's brain.

"And I'll tell you this, Kiwi – if he wasn't the father of your unborn baby, I'd be inclined to have his behind arrested!"

Kiwi was grateful that Blu wasn't going to pursue that course of action. Although, father or not, she knew that she was going to have to do some serious rethinking about their relationship.

Just when she thought that she'd never have to

purchase another cat, the reality of having to do just that loomed before her. What would she call it?

Greedy Bastard! That's all Nathan Nichols had turned out to be. And unfortunately, that was the name she'd have to give her *fourth* cat, representing failed relationship number four.

She wondered how her other three cats would get along with their soon-to-be new sibling. Oh well, prepare yourselves, *Crazy, Lyin'* and *Cheatin'*, because mama's about to bring home a new feline.

Say hello to *Greedy Bastard*.

chapter 32

The building's security officer was waiting at the entrance to 33 TOWER PLAZA when Nathan Nichols returned to the office around four o'clock. He didn't argue when the security officer explained why he was being escorted into the offices of ADDISON JAMES & SHEPHERD.

Blu and Kiwi were waiting beside his desk when he arrived at it. A large OFFICE DEPOT cardboard box was also waiting atop his desk, waiting for him to begin stuffing it with his personal belongings.

Apparently he knew that his gig was up because as he walked into the office, he chose not to look at either Blu or Kiwi. He simply made a beeline to his desk.

Kiwi rushed up to him and began to tell him how disappointed she was with him. He didn't respond.

Blu told him to count himself lucky that he wasn't on his way to jail. He finally uttered an apology. Not only was it weak, it was also months, if not years, too late.

After placing all his personal items into the box, he handed his security badge to Kiwi. She felt like a trapdoor was opening in the floor of her stomach. And with her emotions getting the better of her, Kiwi slapped him across the face, causing him to stagger backward, nearly dropping the cardboard box he was now holding within his arms.

"I deserved that," he said.

"You damn right!" Kiwi yelled. "And this is just the beginning! I want the key to my house that I gave you and I'll follow you to your car to get my garage door opener."

"But . . ."

"*But* nothing! I'll see to it that your things are shipped to you."

"Kiwi, don't." he pleaded.

She rolled her eyes at him.

"What about the baby?"

"*My baby* and *I* will be just fine. Now get out of my sight!"

Cowering behind the cardboard box, Nathan Nichols trudged from the office, slowly inching his way down the corridor. The security officer right on his heels.

Kiwi decided to have the security officer retrieve the garage door opener from Nathan, she didn't want to be around him any more than necessary.

"I'm sorry, Kiwi." Blu said, placing a much-needed arm around her shoulder.

Kiwi dabbed her eyes with the back of her hand, unable to quiet the sniffles. "I guess I'm now *zero* for *four*."

"You'll be all right," Blu whispered. "If Flavia were here she'd tell you that maybe God is just preparing you for something bigger."

"I just thought that I had it *right* this time, you know. I really thought I had it right."

"Well, regardless of what happens between you and Nathan, you and that baby will never be alone. Flavia and I will be here to help you every step of the way."

"Thanks, Blu," she said, dabbing her eyes some more. "I'm so sorry for making things difficult between you and Paisley. I mean, thinking that she was the one betraying us."

"The important thing is that we found our leak and we plugged it."

Kiwi shook her head. "You can't begin to know how angry I am at him! I mean, if the man is willing to cheat on me as his employer, you know damn well he's gonna do it in a relationship! I don't think that I could ever trust him again!"

Changing the subject, Blu said, "Listen, Kiwi. With regards to what I told you about the possibility that Paisley could be the baby that I gave up for adoption, I need you to keep that between us, all right?"

Kiwi nodded. "Girlfriend, my lips are sealed. Besides, the way you two bonded so quickly, that girl has either got to be your daughter or your sister!"

Blu chuckled. "Well, considering that my mom never cheated on my father, nor he on her, the chances of Paisley being my sister are nil."

Kiwi gave a mocking laugh. "You never know!"

"Oh, *that* I do know!"

chapter 33

A week before the Thanksgiving holiday arrived, Paisley Martin was sitting alone in her condo on a Thursday evening. A lot had happened over the past two weeks. ADDISON JAMES & SHEPHERD had found, and properly disposed of, its corporate spy. She was surprised to learn that it had been Kiwi's executive assistant as well as her *would-have-been* fiancé.

The moment was bittersweet, however. She took no pleasure in the fact that her father had stooped to such a low level in his business dealings.

He would later apologize to her. Even tried to convince her that each of the three clients that he *allegedly* stole from them were dissatisfied with ADDISON JAMES & SHEPHERD and would have left their agency eventually.

Blu and Kiwi had grown increasingly concerned about Flavia. Over the last two weeks Flavia had only been into the office once. They were hoping that her cancer wasn't getting any worse than it already was. Especially since, for a period, Flavia had seemed so normal, full of energy and life.

Paisley had learned from Blu that the Minnesota gentleman whom she met early last month was more than an old friend. Schuyler Conklin, she was told, had been Blu's high school sweetheart.

She thought it was so sweet how giddy Blu became whenever she talked about him. And although he had to return home to Minneapolis, Blu told her that Schuyler was going to try and spend the Thanksgiving holiday with her. Paisley was holding her breath for an invitation as well, considering that her father had prior plans to go to Colorado with his *companion*.

Despite all those happenings, it was her meeting with her father last week at his house that she was still reeling from.

Leland Martin had asked his daughter over for dinner one evening. And without mincing words, he shared with her the fact that he knew the name of her birth mother. He told her that she'd been conceived out of wedlock and that the young woman, who'd given birth to her, didn't feel that she was capable of caring for a baby at such a young age. He tried his best to assure her that it had absolutely nothing to do with the birth mother not loving her.

Yet Paisley still couldn't understand how a person could just give away their child – without even looking at her.

Holding her.

Leland went on to disclose to his daughter that her birth mother was black and while he didn't know the ethnicity of the birth father, he'd been told by the adoption officials that the young man was not black.

He was quite relieved when she did not appear to be upset to learn that she was bi-racial. In fact, Paisley had told her father that she'd already assumed that much about herself. She didn't know exactly why she'd had such a presumption. But only that she knew she'd always loved people of all races and colors.

After telling her everything that he knew about the adoption, he assured Paisley that he would help do whatever she wanted him to in terms of trying to locate her birth parents, her mother in particular. Leland told her that he was secure in the fact that he knew she loved him and would always be his daughter.

Just before the evening had ended, Leland left the room and returned with a paisley blanket. He gave it to his daughter and explained to her that it was what her birth mother wanted her to have. He shared with her exactly what he'd been told by the nurse that day, that the blanket in which he was being given was one-half the entire blanket. The other half was going to remain with the birth mother.

Simple as it appeared, it had been a way for the birth mother to leave something behind with the baby.

It was that paisley blanket that she held as she sat on the sofa this evening.

Allowing her hand to caress the blanket she somehow felt a sense of connectedness now. Somewhere out there maybe her birth mother was experiencing that same connection.

Paisley began to wonder if her birth mother had ever tried to find her. Did she miss her baby girl? Twenty-one birthdays gone by. Countless bedtime stories unread. Dozens of cookies that could have been baked together. A mother-daughter confidence that should have been shared.

It had all escaped them.

Then she began to wonder if there would be any point to finding her birth mother? Wondered if the space between them had become simply too wide.

chapter 34

Blu was reviewing some files as she sat at the glass-top desk, which was the centerpiece of the office she maintained within her home. The contrasting light colors on the walls along with a dark stain on the trims lent a certain elegance to the room that she simply adored.

The spacious home office contained a mix of old as well as new furnishings, including one of her favorite pieces – a fully upholstered seventeenth century wing chair with a very high back and embellished legs.

Nestled near the rear of the house, the office space often served as a secluded retreat whenever she chose to work from home.

As she perused the files her mind drifted back and forth between the work in front of her and Schuyler.

She'd spoken to him just hours ago on the telephone. The weather in Minneapolis had turned much colder. Light snow falling. He told her that he was looking forward to coming back to the south for the holidays next week. He also hinted to Blu that maybe she could arrange a tee-time for them at the golf course. "Invite your assistant along as well," he'd also suggested, once he learned that the two of them had patched up their differences, what little there were.

She had intended to tell him about her thoughts concerning Paisley. But ever since Leland Martin was so adamant that his adoptive daughter couldn't possibly be her little girl, she began to have her own second thoughts about everything.

Even if she were to find her daughter, what would she say to her? She was certain that the young lady would perhaps inundate her with a bunch of questions that she wasn't so sure she'd be able to answer – or even *willing* to answer.

And Schuyler – well, he was so determined to find his one and only child that she just had to assist him anyway that she could. A part of her was just as eager to do so, yet a part of her was equally afraid.

As she prepared to put away the client files that she'd been going through, her doorbell rang. Blu glanced at the crystal clock sitting on her desk. It was *seven-twenty*.

While she headed towards the door she wondered who it might be. Probably someone soliciting. Despite the fact that they were in a gated community, every now and then solicitors came around knocking on doors trying to sell everything from magazine subscriptions to bug exterminating services.

'People knocking but they can't come in; people knocking but they can't come in'. Blu chuckled aloud as lyrics, from a song that she couldn't remember, popped into her head. She thought perhaps it was from a *Little Richard* tune, but she wasn't certain.

When she opened the front door she was surprised to see Paisley standing there. "Paisley!"

"Hi, Blu." Her mood appeared somewhat sullen.

"Come on in," she told her. "The security gate didn't call me, how did you get in?"

"My father, remember?"

Blu thumped her forehead with the palm of her hand. "I forgot. Your father *only* has one of the largest homes within this community. But, I guess the reason you had the gate call me in the past was because you didn't want to . . ."

"Blow my cover," Paisley answered for her.

Blu stifled a laugh. "Exactly."

Paisley was wearing a LOUIS VUITTON wool jacket, jeans and a pair of CHRISTIAN DIOR boots. Which apparently did very little to provide warmth to her, as she stood in the foyer shivering. The temperature outside was in the low thirties and steadily dropping as the evening wore on.

"Here, let me take your jacket," Blu offered, helping her to free herself from the fashionably chic raiment.

"Thanks."

"Why don't we go into the den," Blu said, leading the way. "Are you hungry? Want something to drink?"

Paisley answered 'no' to both offers. "I just wanted to talk to you for a moment, if you're not too busy."

"No, not at all. I was just going over some things from the office. But I'm pretty much done."

They sat down on the sofa.

"A week ago, my father shared some things with me about my adoption," she began.

"Really?" Blu's eyes widened, anticipation building.

"Yes. I now know that my mother was a teenage *black* woman and –"

"*Black*?" she interrupted, not intending to sound so shocked.

Paisley also wondered what caused her reaction.

"Forgive me for seeming so surprised, it's just that . . . well, I would've guessed that you were of *Italian* descent or something." Blu didn't want to reveal to her that she'd spoken with her father about her adoption.

It was Paisley's turn to show surprise. "Italian? Whatever gave you that idea?"

Blu shrugged her shoulders. "I don't know. Just a weird thought that crossed my mind."

"Well, Italian I'm not. Anyway, we don't know the racial background of the father other than the fact that he is not black."

Blu remained silent.

"But, my father did give me the name of my birth mother."

Blu could literally hear her heart thumping. It was a good thing too that she wasn't holding a glass of wine in her hands because the way her body was beginning to quaver, she would have spilled the drink all over herself.

She was holding her breath, waiting for the inevitable name to roll off Paisley's tongue. But instead of saying whom the birth mother was, Paisley reached inside her purse. And what she pulled out nearly caused Blu to double over onto the floor.

"My father gave *this* to me," she said, holding it up in front of Blu. "He told me that it was given to him by a nurse that was on duty the day that I was born."

Blu could only stare at the *paisley blanket.*

The adoptive parents had accepted it after all. Not only that, but they had kept it all these years as well.

Her weird, crazy, impossible thoughts were no longer such. Everything had just been confirmed. *Paisley Martin* was indeed her little baby girl.

"Wasn't that a lovely gesture, Blu?"

Blu could only nod, no syllables available to assist in forming words so that she could actually speak. Her eyes were welling up faster than ever before.

"My father says that the birth mother had cut the original blanket in half so that she could keep part of it. Like maybe she was trying to keep a part of *me* with her or something. And it was because of the blanket that my parents named me *Paisley*."

"Oh, my god," were the only words that Blu could finally spew out her mouth.

Paisley folded the blanket and set it upon her lap. "Blu, are you crying?"

She tried to shake her head 'no', but her face looked like a pail of water had just been thrown on it.

"Why are you crying? Am I upsetting you somehow?"

"No! Nothing like that at all," she assured her. "Just sit here for a moment," Blu told her, as she nearly sprinted from the room.

Paisley was trying to figure out what she could have said to make Blu seem upset.

Moments later, Blu returned to the room. Both hands tucked behind her back. She didn't resume her space on the sofa. Instead, she kneeled on the floor beside Paisley and slowly brought her hands forward, revealing the other half of the paisley blanket. All the while, a vast steady flow of tears gushing from her eyes.

Paisley was speechless as she stared at the blanket in Blu's hand. Her eyes drifted to the one she was holding. Her breath was escaping her body faster than she could breathe it in.

"*You* . . . you're my birth mother, Blu?"

Blu's head slowly nodded up and down.

"But? I mean, how? My birth mother's name is *Marie Knight*."

Blu attempted to clear her throat. She was unsure of how many lumps had just passed through it. "My middle name is *Marie* and my maiden name is *Knight*. It was the name that I wrote down when I entered the hospital."

Paisley didn't know whether to jump and scream with joy or simply cry her eyes out. It was most likely that she'd do both.

"What about my father?" But before Blu could answer, she seemed to have figured it out within an instant of asking the question. "It's *him*, isn't it? The man that I met, the one from Minnesota, your high school sweetheart, is he my birth father?"

"Yes, Paisley. *Schuyler Conklin* is your real father."

She began sobbing.

Blu had been bracing herself for what she expected to be a barrage of questions, some no doubt harsh. But such questions never came.

Paisley's eyes welled up with tears and before Blu could blink, she felt Paisley's arms wrap around her neck. The two of them tumbled to the floor. Both crying uncontrollably.

Blu held her daughter within her arms, continually telling her how sorry she was for giving her up for adoption.

Telling her how she didn't quite understand at the time how much the loss would impact her life.

Telling her how torn up about it Schuyler was.

Telling her how much she missed her.

Telling her how much she loved her. And then, asking her daughter if she could ever *forgive* her.

Paisley, through enormous tears and cries that made her words indecipherable at times, told Blu that there wasn't anything to forgive. After speaking with her father last week, she had a clearer understanding of why she'd been given up for adoption. She understood the difficult position that Blu was in. She understood that everyone involved did what they thought was best for the baby.

For her.

Her life had been richly blessed. And while she'd had burning questions inside her for a long time, what was most important was knowing that her birth mother *loved* her and *cared* about her, *despite* giving her up for adoption.

"I've never stopped loving you," Blu said, taking a moment from their embrace to look her daughter in the eye. "And I've never stopped thinking about you, Paisley. Not once. Not ever."

They embraced again.

Cried even longer.

chapter 35

Thanksgiving Day this year would turn out to be one of the most memorable ones for Blu and Schuyler for many years to come. Her mother had flown in from Muncie, Indiana on Sunday. Not only was she anxious to meet her first and only granddaughter, but also she was all too familiar with Blu's *challenges* when it came to cooking.

On the night that Paisley discovered that she was no longer just Blu's executive assistant, no longer just a close friend, but in fact Blu's daughter – her flesh and blood, they had called Schuyler on the phone and shared the incredible news with him. He was on a flight the very next morning to Atlanta.

Seeing Schuyler standing side by side with Paisley and it was unmistakably clear that she was his daughter. Blu couldn't believe that she hadn't seen the obvious similarities earlier – their hazel eyes, dark brown hair, and olive skin.

Audrey Knight's heart swelled with nothing but good cheer when she first laid eyes on Paisley.

The eventful news was also enough to cause Blu's brother, Lance, to put aside his recently developed grudge against his sister and come to Atlanta for the holidays as well. He had flown down on DELTA with their mother.

Paisley was overwhelmed, to say to the least, at all the fuss that was being made over her. Seemingly overnight she now had another *mother*, *father*, *grandmother* and an *uncle*.

It was Leland Martin, however, who'd put up the initial resistance to the joyful discovery. But after allowing himself to rant and rave, curse and kick over a few things at his house, he too accepted the fact he was going to have to share his daughter with her newly found birth family.

Blu had invited Paisley's father to join them for Thanksgiving dinner, but he'd already had a Colorado trip planned.

Blu wasn't so sure if old man Leland had fully absorbed the impact that *she* was actually Paisley's birth mother. But then again, perhaps he really did just wanted to see his daughter happy. And no one could doubt the joy and happiness that *Paisley Marie Martin* was exuding on this Thanksgiving Day.

During the eating of their holiday dinner together,

Schuyler and Blu, unbeknownst to themselves, were showering so many questions upon Paisley that Audrey Knight, in true grandmotherly fashion, had to intervene.

"Let my granddaughter enjoy this delicious meal that I've labored over a hot stove for hours on, before you all start asking her a bunch of questions!" Blu's mother admonished the two *proud parents*.

Blu and Schuyler acquiesced.

It had been quite a long time since this particular house, the brick and stone country estate, on *Galloping Horse Circle*, had experienced so much love, so much joy, so much laughter.

Lance was excited to share with his sister that he'd put aside his unsuccessful business ventures for a while. He'd gotten a job as a *district sales manager* with *Eli Lilly & Company*, a pharmaceutical giant based in Indianapolis.

Blu told him how thrilled she was for him. "I always knew you had it in you, big brother," she said to him.

"Well, you did kind of light a fire under my butt," he joked.

Audrey Knight told him, "You let me know when you get your first big paycheck, Lance. I want to talk to you about a little *business venture* I have planned."

Everyone enjoyed a hearty laugh. Although, only his mother and Blu were actually in on the private joke.

It was safe to assume that not a single one of them who were gathered around the large dining room table, wanted the moment to end. Nor the day, for that matter. Especially not Blu, not Schuyler, not Paisley.

But unfortunately it did end. Rather abruptly. And not because the clock had suddenly struck midnight, for it was still early evening, but because of an unexpected telephone call.

The call had come to Blu around six-thirty. The news given to her quickly brought everything to a screeching halt.

On the other end of the telephone was Parker James.

chapter 36

"I'm really sorry to have bothered you on a holiday, Blu," Parker apologized upon opening the door to their home, which was just around the corner from where Blu lived. "But we don't know if she's going to make it through the night," he added as he quickly helped Blu out of her white cashmere coat.

Blu had spent almost the entire day last Saturday with Flavia. At that time she'd seemed to be in very good spirits. Yet due to her increased fatigue, she'd been spending a lot of time in bed.

Lying in her bed, on this Thanksgiving Day evening, is where Blu would find Flavia once again.

Also gathered in the bedroom, each at different locations around the bed, were Flavia's older sister, her two brothers and the minister from Flavia's church. Her personal physician and friend, Dr. Laura Levinson, had come by yesterday before heading out of town for the holidays.

"Hey there, you," Flavia greeted Blu as she entered the crowded bedroom.

Blu forced a smile. An enormous inner aching was now flooding her body.

One of Flavia's brothers had been standing nearest to his sister. He stepped aside and motioned for Blu to assume his position. She uttered a quiet 'thank you' to him.

Once there, Blu immediately smothered Flavia with a hug and several kisses. She couldn't believe how much her friend had changed since last weekend. Her body now appeared much thinner and frail.

"Where's *Miss Thing*?" Flavia asked, referring to Kiwi.

Blu fought the tears like she was fighting to stay alive. She wanted desperately to remain strong for Flavia.

"Kiwi's on her way. She'd driven to Macon, Georgia to spend Thanksgiving with her cousin's family," Blu told her.

"I'll *wait* for her," Flavia said softly.

After hearing that, Blu had to place her hand against her mouth to stifle the wailing that nearly erupted.

Flavia's minister suggested to the others in the room that they give Blu a moment of privacy with Flavia. They complied, and one by one, each filed from the downstairs bedroom. It was the room that was ordinarily used for their guests, but since she was too weak to climb the stairs, Parker had set up this room for her.

Blu sat down on the edge of the bed. She took hold of Flavia's hand, realizing that it would take more than Georgia's *National Guard* to try and pry it away.

"I'm so, so sorry," was what Blu said, losing count of the number of times she'd said it.

The room was quiet for several minutes before Flavia spoke, her voice low and soft. "Don't you start crying on me," she began, noticing Blu's struggle to keep her tears at bay. "God just needs me more up *there* than you guys do down *here*."

Blu began wiping away the blurring moisture from her eyes.

"But if you do cry, just make sure that they're tears of joy, because there's nothing to be sorrowful about."

Blu nodded.

The two friends eventually launched into other topics of conversation. Flavia wanted to know how Blu felt about being a mother of a twenty-one year-old (Blu had shared the news with her not long after it had been confirmed). Then she asked how things were coming along between her and Schuyler. And realizing that the AAACC golf tournament had already came and passed; she wanted to know which ad agency had won the event. Blu told her that, for once, it wasn't those arrogant women from MARTIN/McFINLEY. Flavia smiled.

"So, we probably could have won this year, huh?"

"Probably." Blu answered.

Almost two hours later, Kiwi entered the room.

"This is just a minor setback, isn't it Blu?" she whispered the question in Blu's ear.

Blu's bloodshot eyes gave away the answer.

"You better get over here and hug me," Flavia called out to Kiwi.

Kiwi sat on one side of the bed and Blu on the other side. Flavia asked them to help her sit up a bit. They propped lots of pillows behind her and eased her into a sitting position.

"Now, this is more like it," Flavia said, her breathing becoming shallow.

"I wish it were *me* instead," Kiwi spoke.

Flavia shook her head in disapproval. "Don't say that. God has a plan for all of us. You can't take on mine any more than I can take on yours."

"But it's just not fair!" Kiwi sobbed. "You didn't deserve this!"

Blu had been thinking the exact same thing. Why not her or Kiwi? Why Flavia? It was just two years ago that she had committed her life to the Lord. And the change in Flavia was apparent ever since that commitment. She'd gotten her priorities in their proper place. Refusing to let work at the office dominate her life. She'd also accepted the responsibility for not having been there for her boys when they were small. For her, it had been a terrible mistake. But rather than dwell on that unchangeable part of her past, Flavia forged ahead. Becoming actively involved in just about everything that her boys wanted her to – soccer, school plays, volunteer mom – you name it.

It was hard for Blu to understand why God had chosen to take Flavia and not her or Kiwi.

Flavia would later explain to the two of them that everybody living needed to realize that God has already appointed a time for them to leave this world. And while it's always difficult accepting the loss of someone you love and care about, dying is simply a part of God's universal plan.

She explained to them that if one person dies before another, it doesn't mean that God favors one over the other. But that it was simply that person's appointed time.

Both of Flavia's twin boys, Corey and Corbin entered the bedroom. Parker had already discussed with the boys their mother's medical condition when it became apparent that she wasn't getting any better. It was the most difficult thing that he'd ever had to do in his entire life.

The boys had screamed and yelled. It had taken Parker almost an hour to get them calm. The boys were also getting some preparatory counseling from their church.

"Hi, mom!" they greeted, trotting up to the bed.

"Well hello there, you two! Did daddy feed you enough turkey?"

"I didn't have turkey, I had ham!" shouted Corbin.

"I had turkey, mom. It was good," answered Corey. Corey seemed to be handling everything a lot better than his twin brother. He'd always seemed a bit more mature.

"Well, daddy told me that you both ate all your dinner, I'm very proud of you guys!"

"That mean we get a treat?" Corbin asked.

Flavia laughed. "Of course it does. Go and tell daddy to give you each one of those lollipops from the bag in the pantry, okay?"

They bolted from the room, but within seconds Corbin had returned. He walked up to the bed. "Mommy?"

"Yes, darling?"

"Will you play with me today? Like you used to do?"

Blu and Kiwi averted their gazes elsewhere within the room, each continuing their battle against relentless tears.

Flavia reached out and took hold of her son's small hand. "Yes. Mommy will play with you. But a little later, okay?"

A wide grin spread across his tiny face, eyes beaming brighter than a lighthouse off the New England coast.

"Cool! Daddy said that today you might be going to

sleep for a real long time. So mommy, if you're sleeping when I get back, I won't wake you, okay? I'll just wait till tomorrow."

His sweet words were too much for Kiwi. She sprung from the bed and ran out of the room, crying hysterically. Blu was on the verge of trailing behind her.

Flavia pulled her son, with all the strength that she had, up onto the bed to give him a hug. "I love you so much," she told him, hugging him as tightly as she could.

"I love you too, mommy!"

She watched, with pensive eyes, as Corbin hopped from the bed and scampered from the room. Kiwi returned minutes later.

"You know, guys . . . it would be kind of ironic if my last day ended on Thanksgiving Day."

Neither Blu nor Kiwi responded. Choosing instead to listen and to cherish every word from Flavia, realizing that they would most likely be her final thoughts shared and spoken with them.

Flavia continued. "I mean I truly have so much to be thankful for."

She began to cough sporadically. Kiwi handed her the glass of water that had been sitting on a nearby nightstand. She drank it slowly. It seemed to have helped. "Thank you," she said, giving the glass back to Kiwi.

Flavia directed her attention towards Blu. "I know it

has been difficult for you going through the situation with Damien. But I want you to find it within your heart to forgive him, Blu. I'm not saying that you have to do it tomorrow, just know that you must do it. And do the same for Gail."

Blu wiped a tear from her eye, nodding her head in agreement.

"You know that I've always told you that everything happens for a reason. And I know it has to be hard walking away from a fourteen-year marriage, but just try and understand that people come into our lives at various stages and for various reasons. And most of the time, we have little, if any, control in choosing which stage and for what reasons."

She shifted her attention to Kiwi.

"You've matured a lot since I first met you. And I know how important it is for you to find that special someone whom you can share your life with."

Kiwi blinked away a tear.

"Just be patient. Be true to yourself. The worst mistake that you can make is to settle for less than what you want and desire, or settling for less than what you deserve."

Kiwi leaned over and kissed Flavia on the cheek. "I love you, girlfriend."

"And I want the both of you to make me a promise . . ."

"We'll do anything that we can for you, Flavia," Blu

said, with Kiwi nodding in agreement.

"Help take care of my boys, okay?"

"We were gonna do that anyway," Kiwi told her.

Flavia smiled. "And take care of *Marcie*, too." she added, referring to her executive assistant. "She's been such a big help to me, especially over the past couple of months."

Blu assured her that she'd be taken good care of.

"One more thing," she said to Blu. "I've heard you playing a song in your office on several occasions. Will you play it for me now?"

"Of course, which song?"

Flavia closed her eyes, trying to recall some of the words. "I'm not really sure of the name. All I know is that it's a woman's voice and throughout the song she says something about going home to see her mother, and crossing over Jordan, or something to that effect."

Blu knew exactly the song Flavia was referring to. "It's a very beautiful song by *Eva Cassidy*. It's called 'WAYFARING STRANGER'."

"Do you have it at home, or is it at the office?"

"Both," Blu chuckled.

Kiwi shook her head. "You and your music."

"I'll run over to the house and get the CD."

"Do you mind?"

"Of course not."

Less than ten minutes later, Blu returned with Eva Cassidy's *Songbird* CD.

While she'd been gone, Parker had come into the room at Flavia's request and plugged in the CD player that was retrieved from their master bedroom.

Blu placed the CD into the player and pressed the *fast forward* button until it stopped at track number *four.* As the music began, Flavia called them both closer. She took hold of Kiwi's hand with her left hand, and Blu's hand with her right. Squeezing as tightly as she could.

"I've heard you playing this song within your office several times, Blu," she said. "But I would have never realized how applicable to my life it would become."

As the CD began, the bedroom immediately filled with the beautiful, jazzy, and yet sometimes melancholy, voice of Eva Cassidy. Flavia closed her eyes, absorbing the music as well as the lyrics.

Blu and Kiwi tried to do likewise.

epilogue

Flavia James departed from her family and her friends at eleven-thirty-five on Thanksgiving Day night, November 28, 2002. Parker, Blu, Kiwi, Paisley and Flavia's sister and brothers all had been by her side at the time. Her minister had also been present. The twins were asleep in their rooms.

Her funeral was held a week later. Inside the church it had been standing room only, as hundreds of well wishers had come to pay their last respect and to say their final good-byes.

In the New Year, Parker James rehired the boys' former *Au Pair* to help care for them. They were glad to be spending time with her again. And while they were still adjusting to the loss of their mother, the twins were making good progress as each day passed.

From her own funds, Blu had set up a scholarship fund for Flavia's boys. She told Parker that it was something that she really wanted to do.

She and Kiwi took turns picking up the boys on various weekends and taking them to different activities as well as just spending time with them.

Schuyler relocated to Atlanta so that he could be closer to his daughter. He and Blu had also rekindled their once budding romance. He'd obtained a position as *Head Golf Instructor* at The Golf Club at WindFair Estates. He was still determined as ever to make the PGA Tour one day, and he'd begun to work with Paisley to get her ready for the LPGA's qualifying school.

ADDISON JAMES & SHEPHERD did not win the MerLex Motors advertising account. And as it turned out, they didn't have to. MARTIN/McFINLEY had won the account. However, ADDISON JAMES & SHEPHERD had merged with MARTIN/McFINLEY in March of the following year, after the sudden death of Leland Martin from an apparent heart attack on New Year's Eve. His controlling interest in MARTIN/McFINLEY, as well as everything else that he'd owned, had been willed to his daughter.

After grieving the death of her father, Paisley sat down with Blu and Kiwi and discussed the idea of merging the two ad agencies. She explained that she wasn't quite ready to run a billion dollar ad agency. But, she said that she knew her *mother* was very capable of such a task.

Once the merger was finalized a huge party was thrown and attending the gala along with *Mayor Shirley Franklin*, were local celebrities, industry colleagues, media personalities and several honchos from MerLex Motors.

The new agency was renamed MARTIN ADDISON JAMES & SHEPHERD. They kept Flavia's name because they knew that she would always be a part of them.

Blu was named *CEO* with Paisley serving as a Vice President and *Special Assistant to the CEO* while she learned more about the business. Kiwi retained her role as *Vice President of Client Services.* And Flavia's former assistant, Marcie, was named *Media Director.*

Most of the key management staff from MARTIN/McFINLEY was kept aboard. Although some had chosen to resign in the wake of the merger, unwilling to work under the new regime. They were mostly older white men who had been products of the *old school.*

On May eleventh of that year, Kiwi had given birth to a seven-pound baby girl, whom she appropriately named *Jacinta Flavia Shepherd.* Blu was appointed godmother, a role in which she happily accepted.

Kiwi decided not to resume her romantic relationship with Nathan Nichols. She told him that they could be friends for the sake of the baby. And while he'd promised her that he would be as good a father as he could to his daughter, she was taking anything that he said with a grain of salt.

Following Flavia's last advice to her, Kiwi had made up her mind to take things slowly within the relationship arena. She was going to trust that God would lead her to the man of her dreams soon enough.

And although it was a difficult thing for her to do, she got rid of her three cats (she never bought the *fourth* one), donating them to neighbors. However, right before doing so, she'd changed each of their names to ones that were more sensible.

Damien Addison married Gail Adams in June of the New Year, one week before their son's first birthday. When they returned from their honeymoon, he relocated his new family to his hometown of Bloomington, Illinois. His departure from Atlanta, however, had been made in peace. One month before their wedding day, Blu had met with him and Gail and offered them her best wishes for their marriage and in raising their son. It had been a difficult thing for her to do, but she was determined to keep her promise to Flavia that she would forgive them both.

JUST THINKING TO MYSELF

By Cornell Graham

Are one's eyes as nervous as one's heart
When for the first time your souls meet
To unwrap those emotions once set apart
Saved for a rainy day like jasmine so sweet
I'm just thinking to myself

Admittedly it can be hard to ignore the butterflies
That courageously gathers and seems to only linger
Weakening your efforts by such tempting cries
Resisting her smile or the simple touch of her finger
I'm just thinking to myself

The feeling is so unreal, much like that of a dream
In which you never really want to awake
Or like the gathering of flowers near a river's stream
That flows quietly and gently into a serene lake
I'm just thinking to myself

Who can she be, is there a clue to her lovely name
The questions might confound you each day and night
Until you can no longer play her guessing game
For which you surrender all, without so much a fight
I'm just thinking to myself